6

***Jack curled his warm hand
around hers and with a powerful
tug, hauled her to her feet.***

Megan steadied herself with a hand on his shoulder, while Jack held her close.

Rather than helping her find her equilibrium, Jack's touch, his proximity and his spicy scent made the room tilt. A dizzying rush of blood pounded in Megan's ears. For a few dazed moments, she didn't move, couldn't think. She tipped her head back to peer up at him, and his lips twitched into a grin.

Jack's eyes darkened, and his gaze drifted to her mouth. When she nervously moistened her bottom lip, his pupils grew with desire. He slid his hand from her waist to her back, anchoring her in his arms.

Slowly he dipped his head. Closer. Closer.

Megan's breath snagged in her throat. Her lips tingled in anticipation. Waiting…

Dear Reader,

Danger at Her Door was a difficult story to write.
Yet something about Megan's story pulled at me
and wouldn't let me quit writing. Seeds of this story
started forming when I heard about numerous cases of
criminals preying on women by posing as policemen.
That manipulation of a woman's trust struck a raw
chord in me.

In order to write the heroine, Megan, a survivor of rape,
I tried to place myself inside her head as best I could.
My hope was to portray her anguish, her fears and her
anger as fairly and accurately as possible. The process
was emotionally exhausting.

But I also wanted to convey with this story a sense of
hope. The healing found through love is a powerful
thing. Megan learns that she is surrounded by love. The
love of a trusted friend, the love of an innocent child
and even the love of her faithful dog. Oh…and the love
of a good man, of course! *Danger at Her Door* is about
more than Megan finding her soul mate. Megan also
learns to reclaim her soul—her story is a celebration
of the triumph of love over adversity and the power of
believing in yourself. Enjoy!

Beth Cornelison

Beth Cornelison

DANGER AT HER DOOR

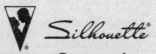

Romantic

SUSPENSE

 SILHOUETTE BOOKS

ISBN-13: 978-0-373-27548-9
ISBN-10:   0-373-27548-X

DANGER AT HER DOOR

Copyright © 2007 by Beth Cornelison

All rights reserved. Except for use in any review, the reproduction
or utilization of this work in whole or in part in any form by any
electronic, mechanical or other means, now known or hereafter
invented, including xerography, photocopying and recording, or in
any information storage or retrieval system, is forbidden without
the written permission of the editorial office, Silhouette Books,
233 Broadway, New York, NY 10279 U.S.A.

This is a work of fiction. Names, characters, places and incidents are
either the product of the author's imagination or are used fictitiously, and
any resemblance to actual persons, living or dead, business establishments,
events or locales is entirely coincidental.

This edition published by arrangement with Harlequin Books S.A.

® and TM are trademarks of Harlequin Books S.A., used under license.
Trademarks indicated with ® are registered in the United States Patent
and Trademark Office, the Canadian Trade Marks Office and in other
countries.

Visit Silhouette Books at www.eHarlequin.com

Printed in U.S.A.

Books by Beth Cornelison

Silhouette Romantic Suspense

To Love, Honor and Defend #1362
In Protective Custody #1422
Danger at Her Door #1478

BETH CORNELISON

started writing stories as a child when she penned a tale about the adventures of her cat, Ajax. A Georgia native, she received her bachelor's degree in public relations from the University of Georgia. After working in public relations for a little more than a year, she moved with her husband to Louisiana, where she decided to pursue her love of writing fiction.

Since that first time, Beth has written many more stories of adventure and romantic suspense and has won numerous honors for her work, including the coveted Golden Heart Award in romantic suspense from Romance Writers of America. She is active on the board of directors for the North Louisiana Storytellers and Authors of Romance (NOLA STARS) and loves reading, traveling, *Peanuts*'s Snoopy and spending downtime with her family.

She writes from her home in Louisiana, where she lives with her husband, one son and two cats who think they are people. Beth loves to hear from her readers. You can write to her at P.O. Box 52505, Shreveport, LA 71135-2505 or visit her Web site at www.bethcornelison.com.

To Paul, my husband and best friend!

Chapter 1

"Megan Hoffman, you're under arrest."

Raising her gaze from the latest you're-over-the-hill-at-thirty birthday card from her colleagues, Megan met the unyielding stare of the police officer standing beside her chair in a private room of an upscale coffee shop. Her fellow teachers had convinced her to join them for lattes and birthday cake on their way home from school, and, though tired, Megan had accepted the thoughtful offer.

But the policeman staring down at her quickly put a damper on any fun she'd been having. "E-excuse me?"

The sight of the uniform prodded a memory that lurked daily at the corners of her thoughts, and a shiver crept down her spine. Shock rendered her mind blank and her jaw slack.

"I have a warrant here for your arrest, Miss Megan," he said, arching a black eyebrow.

"What on earth for?" She realized too late how loud and

panicked her voice sounded. Casting a nervous glance around the table at the other teachers, she found all eyes on her. Even Principal Wilkins witnessed the unfolding drama with a peculiar, amused expression on his face.

Clearing her throat, Megan repeated the question more calmly.

A smile touched the corner of the officer's lips, and that hint of a grin, along with his informal use of "Miss Megan," rang warning bells in her head.

The young police officer unfolded a sheet of paper and gave it a once-over. "According to this, you turned thirty today."

Megan blinked, confused. "Yes, but—"

The officer reached behind his back and whipped out his handcuffs.

The loud whoosh of rushing blood filled her ears and drowned out his reply. Numbly, she watched the bright flash of silver swim before her eyes. He tugged her arm up and snapped the cold metal shackle to her wrist. She froze in shock as he quickly threaded the cuffs under the armrest then shackled her other wrist as well. Her panicked yelp rang mutely in her ears, as if from under water. She fought the imprisoning cuffs, jerking her hands back to free them. No use. The cuffs fettered her to the chair. *No! Not again! Please, God, not again!*

The blare of music, reverberating from the white plaster walls, snatched her from her dazed struggle. Galled by the turn of events, she searched the faces of her fellow teachers and sought an ally.

The usually stoic third-grade teacher smiled and sipped her Coca-Cola. Propped next to the creams and sugars on the condiment counter, the physical education instructor laughed. At the end of the table, the principal's secretary bit her lip to cover a giggle. "It'd been so long since you had a date, we figured you could use a man for your birthday!"

The secretary's comment brought a murmur of chuckles from the rest of the table, but the swirl of panic spinning through Megan's brain muddled her thoughts and made it difficult to comprehend what was happening.

The police officer turned her chair and stepped into her line of vision, his broad chest obscuring her view of her colleagues. The pounding beat of music echoed her heart's frantic rhythm. An all-too-familiar sense of terror washed through her, paralyzing her limbs. Megan fought for a calming breath.

On some level, she realized this was a birthday prank. But the raw memories of other handcuffs, another fake policeman, and a desperate battle for her life erased any humor in her colleagues' ploy.

Squeezing her eyes shut, she tried to shake off the haunting images that flickered through her mind. Just as she drew a reinforcing breath and peeked up at the faux officer, he ripped his shirt open and leaned dangerously close to her.

Her attacker pinned her wrists with one hand while he tore at her shirt with the other. Her scream tangled with the sound of ripping fabric.

Megan flinched and kept her eyes shut. Her anxiety snowballed, choking the air from her lungs. A fresh surge of the anguish she'd spent the past five years subduing swept through her, immobilizing her.

"Stop!" The desperate, strangled quality of her voice surprised even Megan. Past and present twined around each other.

An insistent voice in her head impelled her to move her frozen arms. She fought the hard shackles binding her until her wrists stung.

"Come on, Megan. Be a sport! It's all in fun!" the science teacher called over the thumping music.

Drawn back from the memories that taunted her, Megan heard the giggles around her fade to curious whispers.

"Please stop! Just let me go!" She knew her behavior, her pleas, would raise questions—questions she wasn't ready to answer. If she'd thought she'd outrun the past, she'd been wrong. A bitter brew of emotions swirled in her gut, biting, clawing. But one ever-present emotion reigned over them all.

Fear.

For five years, fear had been her constant companion. She'd battled it, bargained with it and analyzed it. Yet no matter how she hated it and prayed to be free of it, fear ruled her life.

The stripper grabbed the buckle on his pants, and she wailed, "No! *Stop!*"

Tears streamed down her cheeks and dripped from the tip of her nose. With her hands cuffed to the chair, she couldn't even wipe the drops of moisture, the visible evidence of her agony.

"All right, hotshot. That's enough. Joke's over. She's obviously not amused."

Megan recognized Principal Wilkins's voice but kept her head down until the music stopped and the shadow of the stripper moved away from her. How did she face the other teachers? How could she explain her reaction to their prank? She couldn't. Wouldn't. Not after the response she got to the truth last time.

Sucking in a deep breath, she searched for the strength to fight down the demons again. Somehow she had to find a way to put the horror of that night, five years before, behind her. So much of her life had been put on hold because of that tragic night—her master's degree, her impending marriage, children.

How could she think of a future until *he* was locked up for good? For her own sake, for every woman in Lagniappe Parish, Louisiana, she wouldn't rest easy until *he* was permanently behind bars. Maybe then she could rebuild her life and rid herself of the debilitating fear.

"Megan? Are you okay?" Principal Wilkins asked. When he laid a soothing hand on her shoulder, Megan flinched away.

"Chill out, lady. It was all in fun. Geez!" The stripper crouched beside her and unlocked the handcuffs.

Rubbing her sore wrists, she glared at the nearly naked man. "You have a warped idea of fun."

She glanced at Mr. Wilkins. "If it's all the same to you… I'd like to go h-home now."

He nodded and put a hand under her elbow. "I'm sorry, Megan. When the ladies approached me with the idea, I had misgivings. I only agreed to this gag because it was off campus and after school hours, I—"

"I'll be all right. Really." Despite her noble attempt to stand alone, Megan wobbled as she rose. Remnant adrenaline left her body trembling as she stumbled across the coffee shop for the door. She avoided eye contact with her coworkers, but she felt the weight of their confused and concerned stares following her.

The heels of her navy pumps pounded a resonating cadence as she hurried down the sidewalk to her car. Her resentment for the man who'd ruined her life flared, and latte and cake soured in her stomach.

The drive home, past fields of cotton and Spanish moss-draped cypress trees rising from muddy bayous, calmed her. The serene beauty of north Louisiana always soothed her after a difficult day, but she craved a serenity that could last longer than her twenty-minute drive home. More than anything, she needed a peace that could permeate her heart and soul and push the ugliness of her attack out once and for all. She was tired of being a prisoner of her fear, ready to put the past behind her and move on. But how?

When she pulled onto the quiet, residential street where she lived, she sighed in relief. Soon this horrible day would be over. No more birthday cards from well-meaning friends, teasing her about being "over the hill." No more reminders that, at thirty, she was still alone and her childbearing years were disappearing. And no more policeman strippers.

Megan shuddered.

Huffing her frustration, she climbed out of her Honda Civic and headed to the back door of her small, brick house. As soon as she pushed through the door, dumping her stack of files and papers on the kitchen counter, Sam, her German shepherd, greeted her with his usual enthusiasm. As she relocked the door, he jumped on her with a slobbery lick and a wildly wagging tail. Good ol' Sam.

Her loyal friend. Her canine garbage disposal. Her lethally trained protector.

"Hey, Sam. Give me a minute to change clothes, and we'll go for our walk, okay?" Sam responded with a bark that could only be interpreted as *Yes!*

After throwing on a pair of shorts and a T-shirt, Megan took Sam's leash from the hook beside the back door. Sam pranced and circled her with unrestrained exuberance.

"Hold still! I can't hook your leash with you wiggling around like that."

Sam woofed, and if she hadn't known better, she'd have sworn the dog grinned at her. The corner of her mouth lifted in bittersweet response, and a fresh lump of emotion clogged her throat. "You crazy dog. What would I do without you?"

Wiggling loose and scratching at the door, Sam seemed to say, *Yeah, yeah. Enough of that. Let's cruise!*

With a deep cleansing breath, Megan shoved down her

maudlin thoughts and unlocked the door for Sam. The late-August heat and inescapable Louisiana humidity hung in the air like a suffocating blanket. By the time she'd walked one block with Sam, sweat beaded on Megan's forehead and dampened her back. Despite the hot weather, she picked up the pace, hoping a little exercise might help clear her mind and exorcize the day's demons. Sam loped along beside her, his tongue hanging out of the side of his mouth and his eyes bright with excitement.

They jogged past the old homes of the Lagniappe Garden District, many of them recently remodeled by new tenants, and Megan waved at neighbors who worked in their yards or rested in rocking chairs on their front porches.

As she neared her house after circling the block, Megan watched a young girl, with dark ponytails flying, dart into the street. The child ran to intercept her and Sam.

"Hi! Can I pat your dog?" the girl asked, even as she wrapped her arms around Sam and ruffled the fur behind his ears. Sam licked the girl's face, and she giggled.

"Um, sure, sweetie." Megan glanced across the street to the empty yard where the girl had been playing. The house had recently been bought by a new owner, and Megan had been meaning for days to introduce herself to the new resident. Most of her neighbors knew her and Sam well because of their daily walks and because she made a point of meeting and greeting them. For security reasons, if nothing else, it paid to know who lived around you. The older residents, who stayed home all day, kept an especially close watch on the comings and goings in the area, which pleased Megan immensely. She'd learned the hard way one could never be too careful.

Finding no sign of a parent or older sibling watching the little girl, Megan twisted her lips in a scowl. "Honey, does your mommy know you're playing outside?"

The girl, whose age Megan estimated at around four years, peeked up at her with a puzzled look. "My mommy? Nuh-uh. My mommy went away."

Burying her face in Sam's fur again, the girl continued scratching Sam behind the ears. Sam sat down, his tail thumping the sidewalk, and tipped his head to accommodate his new friend's loving hands. Clearly, Sam had found canine nirvana.

"Well," Megan said in her best teacher's voice, "you didn't look before you crossed the street. Your mommy would be real sad if you got hurt by a car."

The child peered up at her again, wrinkling her freckled nose. "I told you my mommy went away. How would she even know if I gotted hurt?"

"Well, she…uh." Megan paused and chewed her lower lip. "Can you tell me where your mommy went? To the store? To work? Do you have a babysitter?"

"Nuh-uh. Just my daddy. Daddy hasn't got me a new sitter yet."

Squatting down to eye level with the girl, Megan studied the child's freckled face. As a teacher, she'd been trained to look for signs of abuse, but this child showed none of the telltale marks. Her pink sundress was wrinkled but clean, and the child appeared healthy and happy.

So where was her guardian?

"Is your daddy home? Does he know you're outside playing?"

Her mood was already grim thanks to the stripper prank and gag card reminders that her prime childbearing years were passing her by. But her concern for this child's poor supervision started a slow gnawing in the pit of her stomach.

The dark-haired girl shrugged her shoulders. "He locked me out."

"Locked you out?"

When Sam licked her face, the child grinned. "He kissed me!"

"Your father locked you out of your house?" Megan asked patiently, determined to find out why the girl lacked a chaperone.

Bobbing her head in affirmation, the little girl asked, "What's your name?"

Realizing she wasn't likely to get a satisfactory explanation to her own questions, Megan followed the girl's lead.

"I'm Megan, and this is Sam. We live down the street in the red brick house." Megan pointed toward her house, but the girl ignored the gesture, her attention absorbed by Sam. "What's your name, sweetie?"

"Caitlyn. I wish I had a dog, but Daddy won't let me. He says dogs is too much trouble, and the last thing he needs now is more trouble."

Megan mulled over the child's remark about her father not wanting more trouble and factored in the vague comment that her mother had gone away someplace. Other people might consider Caitlyn's home life none of their business and bid the girl goodbye as they walked away.

But not Megan.

As a teacher, she was duty-bound by law to investigate and report neglect. To her, those who looked the other way were as guilty as negligent parents.

"Come on, Caitlyn, let's go see your daddy." She took the child's hand and led her across the street, making a point of reminding the girl to look both ways before they crossed.

Sam trotted along beside them contentedly, his ears perked and alert. He seemed intrigued by the change of course, and his nose searched the air for new smells.

"You know what?" Caitlyn skipped as they crossed her yard.

"What?"

"This mornin' when Daddy was making breakfast, our toast caught on fire!" Caitlyn giggled and covered her mouth with her hand.

"Oh, my!" Megan clapped a hand to her cheek, adding the sort of animated and enthusiastic look of surprise her first graders loved. "What did he do?"

Caitlyn's eyes twinkled with a mischievous gleam. "He threw the toast in the sink like this. Oo, ah, ow!" The little girl imitated her father juggling the burnt toast from hand to hand. "Then he said a bad word! Wanna hear it?"

Surveying the girl's impish expression, Megan lifted an eyebrow. "No, thank you. I feel sure it's a word you shouldn't be repeating."

Caitlyn shrugged. "Yeah. That's what Daddy said, too. He said it was a grown-up word, and it slipped out on accident."

Megan figured she had to give the girl's father credit for at least *trying* to cover his gaffe. But he still had a bit of explaining to do for his inattention to his daughter's whereabouts at the moment.

They tramped up the brick steps to the front porch together—woman, child and dog—and Caitlyn wiggled the doorknob. "See? Locked out!"

Megan pounded on the front door. When no one answered after a few moments, she pounded again.

"Are you mad at me?" a tiny voice squeaked.

Glancing down at the girl, Megan met a wide, dark-eyed gaze that melted her heart. Tears puddled in Caitlyn's eyes, and Megan caught her breath. "Oh, no, darling. I'm not mad at you. Really." She knelt beside the girl and tugged on her ponytail. "I just want to be sure you are safe and that your daddy knows where you are. Okay?"

She flashed Caitlyn an encouraging smile, winning a

bright grin in return. Finally the doorknob rattled, and as the front door swung open, Caitlyn sidled behind Megan.

Turning her gaze toward the portal, Megan encountered bare feet and a pair of long masculine legs. Her gaze drifted upward, past a damp blue towel wrapped low on lean hips, to a broad, bare chest. Tiny rivers of water trickled down the firm, flat stomach to disappear beneath the towel.

Megan's mouth went dry. Images of the stripper's gyrating hips flickered in her memory. Yet where the stripper had evoked terrifying memories, this wet, masculine body stirred a more innate female response, something physical and wholly unexpected. Unsettling in a way that had nothing to do with fear.

"Can I help you?"

The question jerked her attention back. She gasped and rose to her feet. The man at the door dwarfed her by several inches. As Megan gaped, an awkward flip-flopping in her gut, water dripped from his hair and puddles collected at his bare feet.

"You…w-were in the shower." Megan grimaced and gave herself a mental thump on the head for stating the obvious.

"Uh…yeah." A lopsided grin, much like Caitlyn's, tugged the corner of his mouth.

"Sorry, I didn't realize. I—"

He shrugged a muscular shoulder dismissively. "Whatever. Lately, finishing much of anything without interruption is a rarity." His smile turned wry, exasperated. "So—" He raised a palm. "Was there something you needed or can I go back to my shower?"

Just like that, the reality that she was standing there conversing with this nearly naked man slammed home.

Megan swallowed hard, and the bravado she'd mustered to challenge his parental negligence slipped.

If his dishabille bothered him, he didn't let on. He had the presence of a man who knew how to wield control of a situation.

But Megan hadn't felt truly in control of her life in years. She slid a hand into Sam's thick fur to draw strength and comfort from her canine protector's presence. Squaring her shoulders, she mustered the presence of mind to meet the man's hazel eyes.

"I presume you're Caitlyn's father?" Megan reached behind her and guided the girl into view.

His brow furrowed, and his gaze flew to the little girl. "Caitlyn, what have you done now?"

"Nothing!" Caitlyn whined.

"Did you know she was outside…by herself?" Megan placed meaningful emphasis on the last words. "Locked out?"

He looked baffled for a moment. "No. How—? She was supposed to be locked *in!* Caitlyn, how did you get outside?"

Caitlyn ducked her head and picked at a scab on her arm. "The window."

"What window?" her dad asked, frustration rife in his tone.

The child aimed a finger at a sill where the screen had been popped out, cockeyed.

The man's eyes rounded. "Caitlyn! How'd—"

He stopped and drew a slow breath before raising his gaze to Megan's again. "Thank you for bringing her home."

Warmth and appreciation filled his mossy brown eyes, and Megan's body answered with a tug of feminine interest she hadn't felt in so long she almost didn't recognize it. But she couldn't deny the gut-level attraction to her new neighbor that zipped through her veins, steamrolled by a dose of adrenaline. Her reaction to this man was unexpected, overwhelming. *Tantalizing.*

And what are you going to do about it? a voice in her head asked.

The man tugged lightly on Caitlyn's ponytail, deep affection lighting his eyes along with exasperation. "And, no, I didn't know she was outside. I locked the doors to keep her *inside* while I was in the shower." He sighed tiredly, tiny creases beside his eyes adding to his roguish appeal. "I thought she was watching the video I put on for her."

Megan nodded mutely while her thoughts raced and her stomach performed another forward roll.

It's still too soon. How can you even think of starting something with a man until you get your head straight? Until you've put the attack behind you in every way?

Caitlyn's father tightened the towel on his hips then held his hand out. "I don't usually meet new neighbors in my birthday suit, but under the circumstances…I'm Jack Calhoun."

His birthday suit. Oh, heavens!

Her pulse increased its tempo, and a tiny quiver shook her knees. She raised an unsteady hand and gave his a quick shake. "Megan Hoffman. I'm at one twenty-two. The red brick across the street."

Jack leaned out the front door far enough to glance toward her house. "So now I know where to go to borrow sugar. Or— more likely—tranquilizers." Jack cut a side glance to her. "Kidding. Sort of."

Megan caught a whiff of his spicy deodorant soap, and a sensuous tingle slid over her skin. She rubbed goose bumps from her arms, despite the muggy day. Her response to Jack rattled her, caught her off guard.

And *off guard* was a position she'd promised herself to never be trapped in again.

The past five years had been all about finding stability and control over her life.

"Well, I'm sorry if Caitlyn bothered you. Clearly I need to further explore all potential egresses from the new house before my next shower." He flashed another heart-tripping grin that he divided between Megan and his daughter, and he reached down to take Caitlyn by the arm. "Back inside, young lady. Pronto."

"Awww, Daddy." The girl pouted and pulled against her father's restraining hand.

"Cait, I'm not going to argue with you. You're in big trouble already, missy." Clutching at his towel with one hand, Jack pulled firmly on Caitlyn's arm to lead her in the door.

"Noooo!" Caitlyn whined.

A low, deep growl drew Megan's attention away from the protesting girl. Jack, too, turned a startled look to Sam, whose teeth were bared. The fur on Sam's neck bristled. Megan blinked in surprise then recognized why Jack's parental force with his daughter and Caitlyn's cries had triggered Sam's training. "Sam, no. Down!"

Sam quieted but kept a vigilant stare on Caitlyn's father.

Jack lifted a wary gaze to Megan. "Is your dog always so…uh, easily riled? I know how Caitlyn is with dogs, and if your dog has a problem with kids, I'll make sure to keep her away from…*Cujo* there."

Megan lifted her chin. "Sam would never hurt a child."

Jack shot her a skeptical look and shrugged. "Just the same, Caitlyn doesn't always know where to draw the line with dogs. I'd feel better if you didn't let her play with your dog without supervision."

Megan huffed a short laugh of disbelief. Who was he to warn her about leaving Caitlyn unwatched?

"It wasn't my dog who crawled out a window to play outside, Mr. Calhoun." Megan tugged Sam's leash and turned to leave.

"Touché." The rich baritone melody of Jack's low laugh followed her down the steps.

"Good luck sealing all the exits and keeping Miss Adventure under surveillance," she called over her shoulder.

"Oh, wait…"

Megan paused and pivoted back to face Jack. Sam strained against his leash, eager to get home for supper.

"You wouldn't know any good babysitters with combat training, would you? Being new in town, I'm having a hard time finding anyone I trust to keep an eye on Miss Adventure."

"Hmm…" Megan bit her lip as she thought. "Nobody comes to mind at the moment…but I'll keep my ears open."

"Thanks. Someone with a lot of patience and eyes in the back of their head would be best." Jack gave her a wave and backed inside. "Nice to meet you."

Megan returned his wave, and as she crossed the street toward her own yard, she found herself wearing a sappy smile. Even if she wasn't ready to jump back into the dating game— *yet*—she liked Jack. His sense of humor and easygoing nature made him approachable. And though it-seemed he had his hands full with Caitlyn, he clearly loved his daughter.

Entering her house, Megan was greeted by the insistent ring of her phone. She took the time to relock her door then nudged Sam out of the way as she hurried to answer the call.

"There you are! I was getting worried when you didn't answer and the machine didn't pick up."

"Hi, Ginny."

Ginny West had been Megan's counselor and best friend since they met at the women's center just after Megan's attack. They'd spent hours talking, bonding, working through Megan's recovery efforts, and later bemoaning Ginny's own issues with her well-meaning but meddlesome family.

Megan unhooked Sam's leash. "Maybe I was just ignoring you after that cruel birthday card you sent! When you turn thirty, look out! I'm not pulling any punches."

"Are you watching the news?" Ginny interrupted. Her best friend's voice sounded uncharacteristically agitated.

"No. Why?"

"Turn it on. They made an arrest. It's all over the news."

Megan didn't need to ask what the arrest was for. The man who had attacked her and several other local women in a string of home invasion rapes had been the focus of enough conversations between Megan and Ginny to make such inquiry unneeded.

Megan grabbed her remote and aimed it at her TV. When the local news filled the screen, Megan watched as a man in handcuffs was shoved into the back of a police cruiser.

"The five-year-old Gentleman Rapist case had gone cold until the arrest today," the reporter's voice-over said. "The similarities between the attacks Smith is charged with and the unsolved attacks in the Gentleman Rapist case prompted police to investigate Smith for the older assaults as well."

"Is it him? Can you tell?" Ginny said.

Absorbed by the pictures on her TV, Megan had almost forgotten she had Ginny on the phone until her friend spoke.

"I can't see him. The cop's in the way." Megan's palms sweated, and her stomach roiled. Heat crept through her limbs and stung her cheeks as buried anger clawed its way to the surface. The idea that *this man* on her TV screen could be the man responsible for her suffering prodded the dormant rage and frustration she'd had to tame years ago in order to function, to preserve her sanity.

But seeing a flesh-and-blood target for her anger after so many years fueled the simmering tempest in her blood. This could be the man responsible for stealing years of her life, for the humiliation of the exam when the E.R. collected the rape kit evidence, and the invasion of her home as the forensic team picked through her possessions. The isolation as her impatient fiancé and friends drifted away. The frustration of dealing with well-meaning coworkers and neighbors who labeled her a victim and treated her with kid gloves, when all she wanted to do was forget what had happened. Megan swallowed the rising bile in her throat as the images on her TV reopened the Pandora's box of emotions and memories.

"The results of DNA tests on samples taken from Smith won't be known until late next week, officials said," the reporter's voice-over continued. "Based on discrepancies in the evidence collected during the five-year-old Gentlemen Rapist investigation, authorities believe a copycat rapist could have been responsible for several of the attacks. Police wouldn't say if Smith is believed to be responsible for the initial series of attacks or if he's thought to be the copycat assailant."

Megan walked slowly toward her living room, squeezing her phone in one hand and jabbing up the volume with the remote in her other hand.

"The serial rapist was dubbed the Gentleman Rapist by police," the monotone voice of the reporter continued, "because the assailant tricked his victims using gallant politeness and offers of assistance. His victims admitted him into their homes or cars when he pretended to be a Good Samaritan helping with their flat tire or an off-duty policeman conducting security checks of area homes in light of the rising crime rate."

Megan's heart kicked and self-disgust knotted in her chest. She fell into the latter category. She'd let a strange man into her house because she'd blindly trusted his police uniform and friendly assurances.

"You know what this means, right?" Ginny asked calmly, pulling Megan from her self-flagellating thoughts.

"What it means?"

"They're gonna call you to come down and identify him. View a lineup."

Megan's legs gave out, and she collapsed on her couch with a gasp. "I—I can't."

"Megan, he can't hurt you anymore. If this is the right guy, he's in police custody, and he won't be going anywhere near you again. No judge in his right mind would grant him bail. It's just a lineup. I'll go with you if you want."

Megan nodded, her mouth dry, then realized Ginny couldn't see her answer. "Yes…please."

The news report cut to the mug shot of the man named Smith who'd been arrested. Megan studied the picture, and her heart sank. Acid pooled in her gut.

She squeezed a throw pillow to her chest and blinked back tears. Despite the optimism of the reporters that the police finally had a break in the unsolved case, the nightmare wasn't over for her. No matter what else the man on the television had done to get himself arrested, he wasn't *her* attacker.

The man who'd sent her life into a tailspin five years ago was still out there.

Chapter 2

After drying off and dressing in a T-shirt and jeans, Jack walked into the living room where his daughter sprawled on the floor watching her favorite cartoon video. He took a moment to collect himself, deciding how to address Caitlyn's disobedience. Again. Nothing he said to Caitlyn seemed to get through to her.

"Caitlyn, we need to talk."

Thank goodness his neighbor—Megan, she'd said her name was—had returned his wayward daughter in one piece.

He grinned as he remembered the stunned expression that had washed over Megan's face when she'd seen him wearing only a towel. He'd caught the spark of interest that flickered in Megan's eyes, too. Discerning, jade eyes. Yeah, he'd done a little looking of his own. His new neighbor was a beautiful woman. The fact that she cared enough about Caitlyn's interests to bring her home scored points for her, as well.

He just hoped his inability to control his rambunctious daughter's wanderings hadn't colored her against him. Jack was definitely interested in getting to know Megan better. *Much* better.

But when? That was the problem.

Sighing, Jack dismissed thoughts of dinner and dancing with Megan. As it was, he barely kept his head above water. What little free time he had belonged to Caitlyn—time to read her books and listen to her talk about preschool. Maybe if he could carve out more quality time with her, Caitlyn wouldn't feel compelled to crawl out windows or finger paint the kitchen with peanut butter and jelly when his back was turned.

But his job at the newspaper didn't allow him more time with his daughter. If only he could figure out how other single parents balanced work and kids. If only Lauren hadn't walked out on them…

Jack pinched the bridge of his nose and shoved the "if onlys" out of his mind. The fact remained that Lauren *had* walked out on their five-year marriage, and no amount of regret or wishing would change that. He had to figure out how to be a single dad before his failings as a parent resulted in bigger problems than Caitlyn crawling out a window while he was in the shower.

Dragging a hand down his face, he strode over to the TV and jabbed the power button. Cinderella's mice friends faded to black.

When Caitlyn faced him, her lower lip poked out in a pout. "But Cinderella's my favorite."

"I know that, munchkin, but you've already watched it twice today." Jack sat on the edge of his worn-out plaid sofa and struggled for the right words to discipline his daughter.

"Caitlyn, haven't I told you that when I'm working or in

the shower or on the phone, you have to stay inside? I can't be two places at once, and you can't go in the yard without someone to watch you."

"But there weren't any cars in the street!" Caitlyn whined, her protest giving Jack new insight to her disobedience.

He knitted his brow in a frown. "You're also supposed to stay away from the street."

"I had to pat the doggie!" Caitlyn spread her hands and gave him a look that said she felt her excuse exempted her from punishment.

Sitting straighter, Jack patted his leg and wiggled his fingers to motion Caitlyn closer. She gave him her I-know-I'm-in-trouble-but-aren't-I-cute look to counter his fatherly scowl.

"Honey, you can't go in the street. *Ever.* Not without an adult holding your hand. And I've told you before not to pat strange dogs. Not all dogs are nice."

"Sam was nice, and so was Megan." Caitlyn scratched a mosquito bite on her arm and shrugged.

Jack quirked an eyebrow. He didn't bother to argue the fact that Sam didn't seem so nice to him.

"I think Megan looks like Cinderella." Caitlyn grinned and pranced over to him, twirling like a ballerina. "Did you think she was pretty, Daddy?"

What he thought about Megan was too racy for a four-year-old. Megan's petite body had enticing feminine curves, and although she hadn't worn much makeup, her cheeks had been flushed pink from the summer heat. Jack felt his own brow warm as he thought of other ways Megan could get flushed and out of breath. With him.

"Daddy?"

Caitlyn's summons snapped him out of his sultry day-dreams. "Yeah, I thought she was pretty."

For crying out loud, he didn't even know if Megan was

married. He had no business fantasizing about her. Even if he was in the midst of months-long sex depravation.

Caitlyn clambered onto his lap, her bony knees and elbows jabbing him awkwardly. "Can I go to her house sometime and play with Sam?"

"I don't know, Cait. Sam's not the sort of dog I want you playing with. He was pretty big and—" *Mean.*

She slapped her arms across her chest and poked out her lip. His little drama queen.

Cut to the chase. You've got an article to write.

"You could get hurt if you don't obey the rules. The rules are: don't go outside alone, don't go in the street and don't pat strange dogs. Okay?"

"But I didn't get hurt!"

"Caitlyn, the point is—"

The loud jangling of the telephone interrupted the point.

"Don't move. I'll be right back," he told Caitlyn and shoved off the sofa.

Snatching up the phone, he balanced the receiver on his shoulder while he rummaged through the freezer for a frozen dinner he could zap in the microwave for Caitlyn's supper. "H'lo?"

"Jack? Burt, here."

As soon as his boss said his name, Jack winced. With all the interruptions this afternoon, he hadn't finished his article for tomorrow morning's edition. Without looking at the clock, he knew he'd missed his deadline.

"Burt, I know. I'm late. I'm sorry."

Aggravation knotted Jack's stomach. He'd never get the big story assignments and lead headlines if he couldn't even get the fluff articles on Burt's desk by deadline. Generally, Burt Harwood, the news editor, cut him a lot of slack. He knew Jack's situation as a single father in a new town. He made allowances for Jack missing a deadline here and there.

But Jack didn't want allowances. He wanted better assignments, bigger pieces to write, more credit for his journalistic talent. He wanted to prove to his boss he could handle his job *and* his family.

He could do it. He *would* do it. Lauren had given him no choice.

"Listen, Burt, I'll have the piece on the sheriff candidates' rally finished tonight." He expelled a whoosh of air in frustration. "Give me until nine. Caitlyn goes to bed by eight, and I'll e-mail you the article as soon as it's done. I swear. Things have been crazy around—"

"Listen, forget the candidates rally for now. We've got something breaking down at the police station."

Jack perked up. He smelled a big story. This could be his break. Finally.

"They've arrested a guy—some white-collar banker type—turned in by his girlfriend. They think he could be connected to an old serial rape case they never solved. One the cops dubbed 'The Gentleman Rapist' because the guy gained entry to the women's houses by posing as a cop doing courtesy security checks. The Good Samaritan ploy."

Good Samaritan... Jack's thoughts flickered briefly to Megan. Her shy smile. Her flushed cheeks and clingy, sweat-dampened T-shirt.

With a shake of his head, Jack refocused his thoughts. "Burt, I want this story. Give me this one, and you won't be sorry."

"Can you get down to the police department tonight and get the particulars for the morning edition?"

Jack grimaced as he slid Caitlyn's dinner in the microwave. "Not tonight. I don't have a babysitter."

"Then I'm sending Parker."

Jack's stomach clenched in irritation. "Look, Caitlyn has preschool in the morning. I'll be free to talk to the cops then. I'll talk to the guy's neighbors. I'll call his first-grade teacher if I have to, but I'll get you the story. You know I can write a better story than Parker. I'll find a fresh angle, something that the TV guys and the *Lagniappe Herald* missed."

Jack raked his fingers through his hair, searching for the tidbit that would tip the scales in his favor. He hoped that mentioning the *Herald*, the other newspaper in town, would appeal to Burt's competitive nature.

"I'm sending Parker." Burt hesitated and sighed. "But you can pick up the story in the morning. After I see what you and Parker each bring to the story, I'll make my final assignment. Don't let me down on this, Jack. This is the biggest story to break in this town for months."

"I hear you, Burt. And I won't let you down."

The next morning, Megan stared at the men lined up behind the one-way glass and fought the urge to throw up. Anxiety, anger and frustration twisted inside her until she thought she might shatter under the pressure.

But not now. Right now she had to pull herself together. She had a job to do. The sooner she did her job, the sooner she could get out of the small room where the walls seemed to close in on her. The stale odor of cigarettes and the noxious fumes of floor cleaner hung in the air, contributing to her queasiness.

More unsettling were all the uniforms gathered around her, the men with guns on their hips and badges on their chests.

Policemen are our friends, she'd taught her class on career day. *They protect us and help us during emergencies.*

But the man who had attacked her had exploited her trust in a police uniform, used that trust to get inside her home. And the sea of blue uniforms was a too-vivid reminder of the army of officers who'd replied to her 911 call and tramped through her home gathering evidence. They'd asked endless questions when all she wanted to do was block out the horrid images and escape the sounds replaying in her head.

Beside her, Ginny hovered quietly, her hand on Megan's shoulder in a silent show of support.

"Do you recognize anything about any of them?" The police detective in the dark room with them asked his questions in low, modulated tones. Ginny and the detective had taken pains to make Megan's task as easy on her as possible. Still, the notion that one of the men in the next room, lined up for her inspection, could be the man who'd haunted her for five years sent a chill slithering down her spine.

When she tried to answer, no sound left her mouth. After clearing her throat, Megan tried again. "I recognize number three. He's the man I saw on the news last night."

The detective shifted his weight and scribbled in the small notebook in his hand.

"But—" Her gaze remained locked on the glowering faces behind the window.

In the periphery of her vision, the detective stopped writing and raised his head. "But what?"

Drawing a slow, shaky breath, she shoved down her discouragement. "I can't say with any conviction that he, or any of the others, is the man who—" When Megan faltered, Ginny reached for her hand and squeezed it. "The man who raped me."

Facing the detective, Megan sighed. "God knows I wish I could. But the man who attacked me had a lightning bolt tattoo on his forearm. And…he was balding and—"

A shudder race through her, remembering the face that

she'd worked five years to erase from her nightmares. "He's not any of those men."

"You're sure?"

She heard frustration in the detective's voice. With a nod, she glanced back at the lineup of men, and the knots in her stomach tightened. The man she recognized from the television stared straight ahead. His light gray eyes stabbed her like shards of flint.

As cold and frightening as his pale glare was, the menacing eyes she recalled so vividly from the night of her attack had been dark brown, almost black. The man in the lineup had no decoration on his arm, nor any scar indicating the removal of a lightning bolt tattoo. Though she wanted to believe her assailant had been caught, the inconsistencies led her to the only conclusion that made sense.

Her rapist still walked the street.

"I'm sure," she whispered. "Wanting him to be the right one doesn't make him so."

The detective nodded and shoved away from the wall where he'd propped during her viewing. "All right. Thank you for coming down, Miss Hoffman. The officer at the desk will have some papers for you to sign. That's all."

Megan raised her head as the officer opened the door and held it for her and Ginny. "I'm sorry."

Ginny frowned at her and tucked a wisp of her pale blond hair behind her ear. "You have nothing to apologize for." Lifting Megan's purse from the floor, Ginny handed her the bag and met Megan's gaze with unwavering certainty in her blue eyes. "You're not to blame for anything that's happened since the day that bastard hurt you. This guy doesn't fit the description of your assailant, and you've done nothing wrong by saying so."

Megan slid her purse strap over her shoulder and flashed her blond friend a weak smile. "Right, right. I know that. I do."

"I know you *know* it. I want you to *believe* it."

"I'm working on that part." Before her friend could respond, Megan hurried through the open door and into the corridor, eager to escape the confines of the dark, stuffy room. She spotted the ladies' room down the hall and made a beeline for it.

She barely got the stall door closed before her stomach pitched and heaved.

"Megan? Are you all right?" Ginny called to her.

Wiping her mouth with a wad of toilet paper, she sagged against the side of the stall. "Just dandy."

"Can I do anything for you?"

Bless Ginny's heart. How could she have survived any of this horror without Ginny's levelheaded reassurance and unflappable friendship? Opening the door, Megan staggered out of the stall and to the sink to rinse out her mouth. "Do you have a breath mint or a piece of gum?"

Ginny rummaged through her purse and extracted a roll of peppermint Life Savers. "How about one of these?"

Megan splashed water on her face then nodded. "Perfect."

"All in the line of duty." The blonde rubbed Megan's arm. "Feel better now or would you like to sit down somewhere?"

"No, I'll be fine. I just want to sign those papers and get out of here." Megan popped one of the mints in her mouth and glanced in the mirror as she reached for a paper towel to dry her face. Her complexion seemed waxy and pale, and puffy bags under her eyes testified to her sleepless night. Her liberal use of water to cool her cheeks left her mascara smudged and damp tendrils of her hair plastered against her neck. In short, she looked a wreck.

Wadding the paper towel in a ball, she jammed it in the trash by the restroom door and followed Ginny out to the front desk. The officer at the desk handed her several forms to sign. She scratched her name in sprawling script in the designated blanks, eager to shake the dust of this morning's task from her sandals and go home.

"Megan?"

She lifted her gaze to find a familiar pair of hazel eyes studying her, and her pulse went haywire.

Jack Calhoun.

Chapter 3

"Jack," Megan whispered, drawing a shaky breath.

Just yesterday this man's nearly naked body and warm smile had awakened long-dormant desires deep inside her. Today, his coffee-brown hair brushed the collar of a wrinkled, white button-down shirt, and he wore a pair of loose-fitting khaki pants. But Megan could still see his wide, chiseled torso and muscular legs in her mind's eye, and the mental image snagged the breath in her lungs.

He stuck out his hand for her to shake. "Hey, neighbor. I thought that was you."

A rakish grin lit his face, and like a summer breeze, a pleasant warmth skimmed through her.

"Hi," she rasped. Painfully aware of how ragged she looked, Megan took his hand. His long fingers curled firmly around hers.

Warm. Confident. Secure.

She mustered a smile, despite her jumpy nerves, but when she tried to pull her hand back, Jack held tight, giving her fingers another squeeze. The strength of his grip sent wings of ill-ease fluttering through her.

Her attacker pinned her wrists above her head, immobilizing her.

Megan gasped as the full-color memory flashed in her mind. She yanked her hand free from Jack's and clasped it over her galloping heart.

"Ginny West." Quickly Ginny sidled in front of Megan and grabbed Jack's hand, giving Megan the moment she needed to catch her breath.

Good ol' Gin. So often, she seemed to be one step ahead of Megan, anticipating every emotional swing, every need.

Jack greeted the blonde politely then turned his gaze back to Megan. Shoving his hands in his pockets, he cocked his head and tugged his mouth in a crooked but disarming grin. "What are you doing at the police station? No trouble, I hope."

Megan swallowed hard, fumbling for an answer. He couldn't know the truth. If her neighbor found out, how long would it be before the whole street knew her past? She'd worked so hard to protect her secret and rebuild her life.

When she met his inquisitive expression, a sinking sensation swamped her. She'd struggled for five years to conquer her past, to regain control. But in the hazel warmth of Jack Calhoun's incisive gaze, Megan felt exposed, lost.

And vulnerable.

The intelligence and concern in his green-brown gaze seemed to cut through pretenses and see straight to her soul.

"She came with me to pay my parking ticket," Ginny said smoothly.

Megan didn't deny her friend's white lie, but she didn't like starting her relationship with Jack with a deception.

"Pesky things, parking tickets. Huh?" When Jack grinned, a dimple pocked his cheek, and Megan's stomach did a little flip-flop.

Steeling herself, she raised her chin and pulled in a cleansing breath. "Yeah. Pesky's a good word for them." She adjusted the strap of her purse on her shoulder. "Speaking of pesky, I'm, um…sorry if I came off as nosy or bossy yesterday. It's just seeing Caitlyn alone like that, running across the street…well, it scared me. For her. I'm a first-grade teacher, see, and I guess I'm a bit sensitive about kids—"

Jack placed a warm hand on her arm to halt her argument. "No apology needed."

Startled by his touch, Megan darted her gaze up to his. Just as it had yesterday, the heat in his mossy brown eyes burrowed to her core, nudging a purely feminine response… and a quiver of reciprocal apprehension.

"In fact," Jack said, "I should be thanking you again. My daughter has boundless energy which she uses for getting in to rather…creative mischief. I appreciate your interest in her."

Megan nodded. "I know her creative mischief is a challenge now, but it also shows her natural intelligence and curiosity. She seems like a very bright little girl."

"Thanks." Jack's grin spoke for his fatherly love and pride.

"Well, I need to run. I'm already late for work." Mustering another smile for her neighbor, she sidestepped toward the door, only to bump in to Ginny.

"Yeah, I'm running a little late myself." He inclined his head toward the back halls of the police department.

Megan's breath stilled. "You're a cop?"

"No," he replied, chuckling. "I'm a reporter for the *Lagniappe Daily Journal*. I'm following up on a story."

A reporter. Not a cop. But almost as bad.

No doubt he was a pro at asking questions, digging up information. A reporter was *not* the kind of person she needed to spend much time around if she wanted to keep certain aspects of her past a secret.

Megan felt the blood drain from her cheeks, and she swayed woozily.

Jack's brow furrowed. "Megan, you okay? You look sort of pale."

"Yeah. I, uh—"

Again Ginny rose to the occasion. "Well, it was nice meeting you. Tell Caitlyn 'hi' for us."

She took Megan's arm and pulled her toward the front door.

Jack's puzzled gaze followed them.

As Megan stepped outside, the Louisiana humidity slammed into her as if she'd walked into a wall. The heat sapped what little energy she had left after rehashing painful details of her assault for the police then losing her breakfast in the ladies' room.

Ginny gave her curious sidelong glances as they made their way to Ginny's Jeep Cherokee.

"My, my, my." Ginny shook her head and clucked her tongue like a mother scolding an errant child.

"What?" Megan drilled her friend with an exasperated glare.

"You've been holding out on me." Ginny colored her tone with an exaggerated note of disappointment.

"Come again?"

"If you want to give that gorgeous hunk of man the cold shoulder, that's your business. But I thought we were friends. Couldn't you have sent him in my direction if you didn't want him? Is that too much to ask?" Ginny gave her a teasing grin and pulled out into the flow of downtown Lagniappe traffic. "How long have you been hiding Mr. Tall, Dark and Dimpled from me?"

Megan gaped at Ginny in disbelief before sighing. Ginny's teasing normally lifted her spirits. She realized that must have been Ginny's aim, but the attempt at levity chafed at the moment.

Troubling thoughts about the man sitting behind bars at the police station made joking about anything else difficult. "I'm not hiding him or anyone else from you, Gin. He's my new neighbor, and I only met him last night."

"Your neighbor, eh? How convenient." Ginny's eyes lit with humor. "So are you blind or did you notice that he's as attractive as sin?"

Not wanting to encourage her friend on this track, she shrugged. "Yeah, maybe."

"He sure was checking you out." Ginny cut her glance from the road to give Megan a calculating grin. "I didn't see a ring. I think you should—"

"Not interested."

"Megan, he's gorgeous. And employed! That's more than I can say for the last bum I dated."

Huffing her impatience with the direction of the conversation, Megan turned toward the passenger-side window and tried to forget the pathetic impression she must have made on Jack Calhoun this morning. If her bleak appearance wasn't bad enough, she'd stuttered and jumped at his touch like an idiot.

She studied the buildings as they passed, remnants of a once-thriving downtown. The empty shells of restaurants and banks lined the narrow streets, harkening to a pre-mall era.

On some level, Megan empathized with those dilapidated buildings. Before her attack, she had flourished. But the self-assured graduate student, engaged to her boyfriend of four years and ready to take on the world, crumbled that horrible night.

The trauma left her a ghost of her former self. Graduate

school took more effort than she could give while nursing her broken spirit, and she'd dropped out. Like the shoppers who fled downtown for the suburban mall, her fiancé had abandoned her, unable to cope with her withdrawal and impatient with her lengthy recovery. The outgoing, undaunted young woman she'd been now lived behind locked doors and slept with a dog who'd been trained to attack on command.

"May I ask why not?" Ginny's question intruded on her thoughts, and Megan turned back toward her friend.

"Why not what?"

"Why aren't you interested in a charming, gorgeous, employed, *interested* man? Are you planning on living like a hermit the rest of your life?"

Though delivered in Ginny's typical get-off-your-butt-and-stop-feeling-sorry-for-yourself manner, Megan understood the loving concern behind the sarcastic question.

"I'm not opposed to dating someone. I do want to get some semblance of a normal life back, but…" She paused and chewed her lower lip. An image of Jack Calhoun as he'd looked yesterday, wearing only a towel, filtered through her mind.

Square jaw. Hard chest. Broad shoulders.

Testosterone personified. A tremor raced through her.

"But?"

"But not him." Megan wrapped her arms around her middle to calm the uneasy quiver.

Ginny frowned and shook her head. "Why not him? He seemed pretty nice, and he's totally gorgeous. What's the problem?"

While she tried to verbalize her reluctance, Megan stared down at her shoes. "He's too…male."

"Meaning?"

The car bounced over a set of defunct railroad tracks, and

she grabbed the armrest for balance. If only she had something comparable to an armrest in her life, something she could cling to for balance and security. From the day she'd met Ginny down at the women's counseling center, her mentor and friend had told her that "something" had to come from inside her. Things, even other people, made nice security blankets, but real, lasting peace-of-mind and self-assurance came from deep within oneself. Though she'd made significant progress in reclaiming her life, Megan hadn't yet rediscovered the spring of pure self-confidence she'd lost. But she kept hoping, kept searching.

"What do you mean, 'he's too male'?"

With a sigh, and knowing how pitifully weak and irrational her reason made her sound, she expounded. "When I met him yesterday, he was wearing a towel. *Only* a towel."

Ginny arched a well-manicured eyebrow. "Oh, yeah? And?"

"And he's…all muscled and toned and…male!"

"Sounds good to me."

Her friend's glib response belied the woman's insight into what bothered Megan, she knew. Ginny was prodding her, trying to make her vocalize her fears. The first step to conquering the demons was naming them, bringing them into the light for scrutiny. Only then could she begin tearing those little devils apart, piece by piece.

"Look, you know I'm not afraid of men," Megan argued. "It's not as bad as that!"

"Then how did you feel when you met him?"

Shutting her eyes, Megan pictured Jack Calhoun in her mind again. "Vulnerable."

"Why?"

"Because he…could overpower me." She scowled. That excuse fell short, and she knew it as well as Ginny did.

"So could most men, but you aren't afraid of other men. Not even Billy. And he bench-presses two hundred and fifty pounds." Ginny sent her a skeptical glance.

"Billy's different. He's your brother. He's in high school. He—"

"Doesn't get you hot and bothered like Mr. Neighbor does?"

Megan jerked her gaze to Ginny's smug expression. "What?"

"That's it, isn't it?" Ginny stopped for a red light and turned to face her passenger. Her knowing eyes, honed like razors, cut through Megan's defenses and denials. "You're attracted to him, and it scares you. Because attraction could lead to a date, and a date to a relationship and a relationship to intimacy."

The light changed, but Ginny didn't move, not even when the car behind them blasted its horn. The piercing intensity in her eyes softened when Megan's silence confirmed her assertions.

"I'm not ready." Megan whispered her admission, yet it seemed to reverberate in the quiet car. Swallowing past the knot forming in her throat, she allowed the rest of her fears to float to the surface. She had to face them in order to move past them. "What happens if I get involved with someone, someone I really like, and when the time comes to…be intimate, I freeze."

"If he's got any kind of decency at all, he'll understand and be patient with you, support you and—"

"Greg didn't." The icy memory of her fiancé's desertion due to her inability to make love to him stabbed her heart.

Ginny huffed and shook her head. "Greg was a self-centered ass. We've been over this before. There are men out there who can be gentle and understanding and supportive. The ones who aren't simply aren't worth your time."

Megan looked away, unable to stand Ginny's unrelenting stare any longer. That gaze saw too much. As much as she loved Ginny's insightfulness and friendship, she hated those qualities, too. Sometimes she wished Ginny would leave her alone, let her hide behind her locked doors and lick her wounds. Instead, Ginny pushed her, probed her, gave her little leeway for excuses. She demanded so much from Megan because she cared that much, too.

"The light's green," she told Ginny, hoping her nonresponse would make the point that she hadn't the energy for any more questions.

She knew Ginny didn't consider the topic of Jack Calhoun closed. What's more, since Jack was her neighbor, she knew she'd have to face the reporter—and her disturbing attraction to him—again.

And again.

Somehow she'd have to come to terms with her confusing feelings for Jack Calhoun.

Chapter 4

One evening later that week, Megan sat at her computer reviewing the lesson plan she'd drawn up for the upcoming week, but Sam's restless barking filtered in from the backyard, making it difficult to concentrate. Grumbling over the interruption, she walked to the window and opened it.

"Sam!" she called through the screen, "Pipe down, would ya? I'm trying to work."

Sam's barks softened to a whimper at the sound of his master's voice.

"Thank you!" Leaving the window open, she strolled back to her computer, stretching the kinks from her shoulders. No doubt her well-trained guard dog was protecting her house from a vicious squirrel again.

Although Sam had been through training similar to a police dog's, he was first and foremost a dog. A dog who hated squirrels. But for Megan, Sam's foibles made him that much more lovable.

She'd never regretted the decision to get Sam for protection. His gentle disposition and loyalty made him a trusted companion, as well as her guardian. His presence in the house at night, and most often sharing her double bed, gave her a reassurance she needed. Experience had taught her that danger could find you even in the sanctity of your home.

Ginny called Sam a crutch, but even if Megan didn't rely on the German shepherd for added protection, she'd keep him for the unconditional affection and companionship he offered. Her self-imposed isolation over the last five years made for a lonely existence.

Returning to her lesson plan, she scanned the calendar for a day when one of the girls in her class could bring her puppy for show and tell. Megan decided to tie in the puppy's visit to a lesson on responsibilities to pets or similarities between animals or—

Sam's barking intruded on her thoughts again. But now the timbre of Sam's bark had become dark and ominous. His snarling and growling sent a chill creeping over her skin. Apprehension accelerated her pulse. Surely a squirrel wouldn't set Sam off like this. Did she have a prowler?

Megan froze…until the wail of a child's terrified scream rent the air.

As she flew to her window, Megan realized Sam's barking had now stopped. From the open window, she searched her fenced backyard for him.

But Sam was gone.

Icy horror washed over her. Where was Sam?

Another chilling scream shattered the quiet neighborhood, coming from the street in front of her house. Moving stiffly, her limbs wooden with dread, Megan made her way to her living room and peered out the front window. Her heartbeat slammed against her ribs as she spotted Sam across the street and two houses down. In Jack Calhoun's front yard.

Sam stood over the crumpled figure of a dark-haired little girl.

"No!" Denial rattled from her dry throat.

Jack burst through the front door of his house at that moment, leaping down his porch steps in a single bound. "Caitlyn!"

Megan heard the fright, the horrible anguish in the father's voice, and bile rose in her throat. She'd believed herself familiar with every form of fear that existed.

She'd fooled herself.

The panic that coiled around her heart sprang from the tenderest place in her soul…her love for children. The idea that she could be even remotely responsible, through Sam, for any harm to a child filled her with unimaginable grief. Adrenaline, born from her horror, propelled her to the door. Her sandal-shod feet pounded the pavement as she raced down the street to Sam.

And Caitlyn.

Oh, God! Poor Caitlyn! Please let her be all right! But the nearer she got to the child, the more evident it became that she wouldn't get the answer she hoped for with her prayer. The girl lay deathly still. Bright red tears on her fragile arm seeped blood into the grass.

Jack snatched up a plastic baseball bat littering his yard amongst other lawn toys and tried to ward off the dog. "Get away from her, you vicious beast!"

Sam snarled and snapped at the bat, but he remained poised over the girl's body. Jack tried to move in closer to reach his daughter, only to be chased back by Sam's angry bark.

Sam's fur bristled, and he squared off with Jack, a low, menacing growl rumbling from his chest.

"Sam!" A sob wrenched from Megan's throat. She gulped for air as she stumbled up to the grassy lawn. Her stomach knotted when she saw the child's mauled arm and scratched neck and face. "Oh, no!"

"Do you see what that animal of yours did?" Jack screamed at her, his face dark with rage. "So he'd never hurt a child, huh?"

Her chest squeezed painfully as she heard her assertion tossed back at her in a scathing tone, and she stared at the proof of her apparent misjudgment.

"I—I'm sorry. I never imagined—" Hot tears streamed down her cheeks, and without waiting for a reply, she raced up the steps of Jack's porch and into his house.

She found his cordless phone on the kitchen counter and punched in 911. Even before the emergency operator came on the line, she grabbed a kitchen towel and was rushing back outside.

"Get your devil dog away from my daughter!" Jack shouted when he saw her return to the yard.

Megan's throat closed when she tried to call Sam off. Gripping Jack's phone with a trembling hand, she stepped closer to the dog and child, sucked in a deep breath. "S-Sam, n-no! Down!"

While Megan hurriedly gave the operator Jack's address and asked for an ambulance, Jack nudged the bat toward the German shepherd again. Sam barked and snapped at the bat.

"Stop poking him! He thinks you're the enemy!"

"Damn right, I'm his enemy! I could kill the monster for this!" Jack's face contorted with anguish, and Megan's heart thundered.

"Please, put down the bat and step back! I have to calm him down!"

He hesitated and cast her a wary, angry glance.

Tears stung her eyes, and his image blurred. "Please."

Stepping back with a venomous glare riveted on Sam, Jack set the bat on the ground. "There. Now get rid of him!"

Megan shoved the phone into Jack's hand. A muscle in his jaw ticked, and his hard stare shifted to drill into her. Any trace of warmth she'd seen earlier in the week at the police station had disappeared. Anger radiated from him like the waves of heat rising from the pavement. Pressing the phone to his ear, he said, "No, we haven't moved her."

Inching closer to Sam, Megan clucked her tongue. "Easy, boy. It's okay now. He's a friend." She saw Jack's brow furrow in disagreement with her last statement. Wetting her lips, she focused her attention on the task at hand. "Down, Sam. Come here, boy. Come here."

Sam turned his head to look at her and wagged his tail. With a whimper, he licked Caitlyn's face then trotted over to Megan's side.

Immediately, Jack flew to Caitlyn, falling to his knees. "Caitlyn? Sweetie, it's Daddy." His voice broke, and the love and concern in his tone twisted Megan's heart.

"Down! Stay!" she told Sam fiercely. The dog settled on his stomach and laid his chin on his outstretched paws. The black eyes that peered up at her reflected the same sweet eagerness to please that characterized the Sam she knew and loved. The Sam that could attack a little girl puzzled and horrified her.

Megan hurried back across the yard, crouching beside Jack as he stroked the hair back from Caitlyn's face. She used the towel still clutched in her hand to staunch the bleeding on Caitlyn's arm. "Caitlyn, sweetie. Can you hear me?" she crooned.

"Four years old. Almost five," Jack said into the phone then glanced around at Megan. "A dog attacked her. No, she's unconscious."

When Jack fell silent, Megan met his worried gaze. "Let me drive you two to the hospital. I want to do something to help."

"An ambulance is on its way." A muscle twitched in his jaw, and he hitched his head toward Sam. "Just get that damn animal out of my yard."

Though his anger and distrust of Sam were justified, his brusqueness still chafed. Surely he didn't think she'd let this happen? That she would ever knowingly let any harm come to a child?

Megan gnawed her lip while acid churned in her gut. No matter how it looked, she couldn't believe Sam had hurt Caitlyn. He was trained to protect, to defend.

Frowning, she stood and took a step back. The distant wail of a siren heralded the approach of the ambulance.

Jack said something to the operator, then with a glance down the street, he disconnected the call.

He sent Megan and Sam another accusing glare as he pushed to his feet. "As soon as I know Caitlyn's all right, I'm going to call animal control. That dog is dangerous and should be locked away."

Megan's eyes widened in shock and dismay, and her chest tightened. "Locked away? But—"

Jack stalked past Megan toward the street to flag down the ambulance, ignoring her protest.

She stayed back, her heart in her throat, as the EMTs assessed Caitlyn's condition and loaded her into the ambulance. She watched numbly as Jack hopped into his Tacoma to follow the emergency vehicle to the hospital, leaving her standing in his front yard, shaking.

She whispered a prayer for Caitlyn's recovery then blinked back tears as she stared at Sam. Jack couldn't take Sam from her. He just couldn't! She needed Sam's friendship, cherished his loyalty and depended on his protection.

Her crutch. When Ginny's assessment rang in her ears, a hollow sensation tugged at her chest. Maybe Sam was a crutch. But weren't crutches made to help patients healing from an injury?

She *was* healing, too. Slowly. She'd just had a minor setback this week because of the renewed activity around the Gentleman Rapist case. The revived memories.

And the unsettling reminder, in the form of a handsome new neighbor with sexy hazel eyes, of all she was missing while she licked her wounds.

She had to rejoin the dating world and let a man into her life someday if she was going to have the family and future she wanted. Jack Calhoun brought home in vivid color the rut she'd allowed herself to get into in the name of protecting herself. And now, if he had his way, he would send another piece of her protective wall crashing down.

Because losing Sam, even for just a little while, would mean losing her sense of security.

Leaning over the railing of the hospital bed, Jack gently wrapped his hand around his daughter's and rested his forehead on his arm. Guilt gnawed at him. He blamed himself for Caitlyn's injury, for the sorry state of his life. For the way he'd lashed out at Megan.

When Caitlyn mumbled something, he opened his eyes to check on her, but she slept on. She'd drifted in and out of sleep for the past half hour, since the E.R. doctor had admitted her to a private room overnight for observation. Even though the doctor had assured him that Caitlyn would make a full recovery and that Jack had time to grab a bite of dinner before her sedative wore off, Jack had stayed put. He refused to leave Caitlyn and risk having her wake up in her hospital room alone.

His daughter seemed so tiny, so frail lying in that big hospital bed. When he thought about how much worse Caitlyn's injuries could have been, that he could have lost her, icy fingers closed around his heart. If he hadn't been so absorbed in the article he'd been writing about the history of the Gentleman Rapist case, maybe he'd have realized Caitlyn had snuck outside again.

Of course, the real culprit in all of this was that monster... that canine terror. Megan's dog.

Yet he'd seen the alarm and sorrow in Megan's eyes when she arrived on the scene and as they loaded Caity in the ambulance. An overwhelming protective urge had swamped him, and he'd wanted to draw Megan into his arms and comfort her. Despite the distraction of the devil dog and his deep concern for Caitlyn, he'd still had the gut-level yearning to soothe the troubled look in his neighbor's eyes. Those big, expressive green eyes.

Jack sighed. He'd been far too harsh with her, allowing his fear for Caity to morph into an ugly, undeserved lambasting of his neighbor. Megan's anguish tangled inside him even now. He longed to hold her close, calm her trembling, whisper his apologies against her smooth skin. How would she feel, nestled in his arms?

Squeezing his eyes shut, Jack shook his head to dispel the image. What in the world was he doing daydreaming about a beautiful woman when Caitlyn lay injured in a hospital bed?

Caitlyn whimpered, and her head rolled to one side on her flat, hospital pillow.

"Caitlyn, honey? Daddy's here. Can you hear me, baby?"

"I'm not a baby," Caitlyn grumbled in a sleepy voice. "My arm hurts." Her bottom lip poked out in a familiar pout.

"I know, munchkin. I'm sorry."

Stroking her hand with his thumb, he thought how small and fragile her little hand looked, and his chest constricted. She was so tiny, so dependent on him. He had no room to mess up. He had to do a better job taking care of Caitlyn because she had no one else.

Jack picked up the cup beside the bed. "You want a sip of water?"

She shook her head, her eyes heavy-lidded. "Daddy, do they give awards to doggies if they're heroes?"

Knitting his brow, he fumbled to answer her out-of-left-field question. He'd become accustomed to her fastball questions catching him off guard, and he'd learned to anticipate, with some success, where the questions might lead.

"I suppose if a doggie did something very brave, they might give him some kind of award."

Caitlyn nodded and closed her eyes for a moment.

"I think you should sleep now. The doctor wants you to stay in bed until you feel strong again." Jack brushed a kiss on her forehead.

Caitlyn's eyes fluttered open again. "I want to watch *Cinderella*."

"It's at home, munchkin. We'll see it later."

"Daddy?"

Jack yawned, his own fatigue catching up with him. "Yeah, munchkin?"

"Can we give Sam an award?"

Jack's chest clenched. "Sam?"

"Miss Megan's doggie."

Jack heard a gasp. Raising his head, he found Megan standing by the door, a small teddy bear in one hand and her other hand pressed to her mouth in surprise. Her pale face showed her strain and worry, and those emerald eyes flashed with apprehension. "Megan, what are you—?"

"I was worried about Caitlyn. I needed to know she was all right." Her tongue darted out to wet her lips, and his eyes locked on the moistness left on her full, bowed mouth. Desire kicked him in the gut.

"She has a broken arm and a load of stitches." He gritted his teeth and felt his nostrils flare as he huffed his frustration with the whole situation. "She'll probably have scars for the rest of her life."

"Oh, Jack." Megan pressed a hand to her mouth, and tears welled in her eyes.

Jack turned away, a fresh dose of self-censure for his abrasiveness twisting in his stomach.

"I'm so sorry this happened. Sam's usually protective and gentle with children. I just can't understand what…why…" Megan tugged nervously at the pearl earring in her lobe. Her brows knitted with concern. "Can I do anything…anything at all for you or Caitlyn? I know I can't make this up to either of you, but—"

"Megan?"

Jack's and Megan's gazes both flew to the bed where Caitlyn stirred.

Caitlyn rolled her head to the side and peered over at Megan. "Sam…" She hiccuped a sob then swiped at her eyes with her good hand. "Sam's my h-hero."

Jack blinked. Held his breath. Wrinkled his brow. "Why's that, Caity?"

Megan hesitated only a moment before stepping to the other side of the bed. She placed a hand on Caitlyn's knee and tucked the stuffed bear by Caitlyn's shoulder. "What happened with Sam, honey?"

A fat tear spilled from Caitlyn's eyelashes, and she turned her wide dark eyes toward Jack. "I wanted to pat the big doggie. I thought he'd be nice like Sam. But he wasn't."

Jack could feel his heartbeat slow. *Another dog?*

"What big doggie, munchkin? Sam?"

"Not Sam. The other one. The white one. H-he bit me and growled and—" Caitlyn's voice broke, and she sniffed as she cried. "Sam saved me. He chased the other dog away."

Jack raised his gaze to meet Megan's. "A white dog? You know the neighbors better than I do. Can you think of a white dog in the area?"

Megan drew her brows together as she frowned. "No. It must've been a stray."

"Which means that dog could be anywhere now." He sighed his frustration. "Great."

Despite her clear concern over the idea of a mean stray in the neighborhood, the tension surrounding Megan visibly eased. Her dog had been exonerated.

The hope, relief and dawning of understanding reflected in Megan's eyes were the mirror opposite of the feelings spreading through his chest. Remorse for his false accusation, dread that another vicious dog was loose somewhere in the neighborhood and compunction for the grief he'd caused Megan by jumping to conclusions about her dog gnawed at him.

Megan's eyes filled with tears, and she drew her bottom lip between her teeth.

Jack expected to see gloating or accusation in his neighbor's expression. But he didn't. As her gaze clung to his, something passed between them, something beyond apologies or vindication. Something a lot like expectation.

Now that Sam's innocence had been established, where did that leave them? The attraction he felt for Megan had to be as plain as the wrinkles in his shirt.

"Megan, I…" He fumbled for a place to start. "I'm sorry for the way I—"

The harsh trill of the phone beside Caitlyn's bed interrupted him, breaking the spell that had held her gaze on his for the past few electric moments.

He expelled a disappointed breath through pursed lips as he snatched up the receiver. "Hello?"

"Jack? It's me." Caitlyn's mother sounded distracted, hurried. "Why is Caitlyn in the hospital?"

Jack wanted to believe the inflection in his ex-wife's voice reflected concern for her daughter, but all he could honestly identify was surprise, inconvenience. He absorbed Lauren's tepid reception of the news about Caitlyn like a prize fighter's punch in the gut. He rubbed the back of his stiff neck and wondered how he could have so totally misjudged the woman he'd once married.

Had he missed the signs of her fickleness? Had he ignored clues that she could selfishly cast her child and marriage aside, claiming she needed her freedom?

"Jack? Jack, are you there?"

He sighed and pushed his troubling thoughts out of his mind for another time. "Yeah, I'm here."

"So what happened?" Lauren asked in a tone that she might have used to discuss the weather.

What happened? Not "how is she?" Not "can I come?" But *what happened?* Jack squeezed the receiver tighter. He wanted to throw the question back. *What happened, Lauren? What happened to us?*

"She was bitten by a dog." He glanced up at Megan, who was clearly trying to give him at least the impression of privacy for his call. Her attention was now focused on Caitlyn as his daughter drifted back to sleep.

"Is that all? You called me about some little dog bite?" Lauren's impatient tone called his attention back to the phone.

Flexing his fingers then balling his hand in a fist, Jack

counted to ten before he answered. "She has twenty-seven stitches and a broken arm."

"So why is she in the hospital, for heaven's sake? I've never heard of hospitalizing someone for a broken arm."

"Because she lost a lot of blood and went into shock. She's better now and resting, but I thought you should know about it…in case you wanted to come—"

He heard Lauren sigh. "Jack, I'm leaving for London in the morning. I can't just drop everything whenever Caitlyn skins her knee."

Because he was already edgy from the afternoon's events, Lauren's dismissal of her daughter lit Jack's temper. "This is a little more serious than a skinned knee, Lauren! You're her mother, for God sake. Doesn't that mean anything to you?" His tone could have frozen the phone lines all the way to Lauren's apartment in Texas.

He should have known this conversation would go sour, should have waited until Megan wasn't around to overhear.

"Of course it means something, Jack! But like I've told you for months, I wasn't cut out to be Betty Homemaker. It's not me. I'm not mother material and don't want to try."

"You should have thought of that before we had a daughter, Lauren."

He should have known better than to get into this argument with his ex again, but her blasé dismissal of her child grated, especially now.

"If Caitlyn is too much for you to handle then my parents—"

Jack bristled. "Never. I love my daughter, and I will do whatever it takes to care for her. Alone. Tell your parents I will not give them custody of Caity. Ever. Sorry to have bothered you with your daughter's trauma. I won't make that mistake again." He wished he could slam down the receiver to make his point. Instead, the disconnect button gave an un-satisfactory blip when he jabbed it.

His pulse throbbed at his temple, and he clenched his teeth until his jaw hurt. He stared at the floor, seething, until a gentle voice reminded him he wasn't alone.

"Maybe I should leave."

He jerked his head up and met a sympathetic green gaze. He pinched the bridge of his nose and released a harsh breath of frustration. "I'm sorry you had to hear that."

"She's not coming, is she?" The sad, perplexed tone of Megan's voice stood in such stark contrast to Lauren's indif-ference that it caught Jack off guard for a moment. Made him ache all over for his motherless daughter. He needed to scream, to punch something. Instead, he cracked his knuckles and held Megan's compassionate gaze.

"No."

She licked her lips again and turned her eyes toward Caitlyn. A profound grief and disbelief filled their depths. Lifting her chin, she faced him once more. "I want to help, Jack. Please."

He pushed to his feet and paced restlessly across the room. "Thanks, but no. I'll manage."

"You don't have to just manage. Let me help. I can bring you some dinner or sit with Caitlyn. Do you have something you need to do for work?"

"Nothing as important as my daughter. It'll have to keep." Jack slid his hand over his face, thinking of the unfinished article still glowing on his laptop screen at his house.

His laptop.

"Unless…" He pivoted to face Megan, who was straight-ening Caitlyn's covers.

Megan glanced up. "Yeah?"

"Would you bring me my laptop? It's on my kitchen table.

I was working on an article when I heard Caity scream and…"

"Oh, uh…sure." Megan's face brightened, clearly glad to be able to do something to help.

He dug in his pocket for his house keys. "Thank you. I appreciate this more than you can know."

She waved him off. "Forget it. Glad I can help."

"You'll need to save the file before you close it and bring the extra battery from the black case beside the chair."

She nodded and smiled. "Right. Back in a jiffy."

"Megan?"

She stopped at the door and looked over her shoulder.

"I'm sorry. I was an ass this afternoon, screaming at you about your dog. Accusing him of…"

When he let his sentence trail off, she lifted a corner of her mouth. "Apology accepted. I admit the evidence was pretty damning. But I know Sam. I know his nature and his training. He'd never hurt Caitlyn. I swear."

"So it seems." Jack shoved his hands in his pockets and jangled the coins there. "I also apparently owe you a debt of gratitude. If he, in fact, chased some other dog away…"

He hesitated. *Care for some salt on your crow?*

Megan's smile brightened a bit. "I'll pass your thanks on to Sam. He definitely gets an extra Snausage tonight."

Jack gave her a lopsided grin and stroked a hand along his chin. "Tell him he's got a whole box of dog treats coming from Caitlyn's dad."

She nodded and ducked her chin, glancing shyly to her feet. "I'm just glad Caitlyn will be okay. I was so scared for her…."

Megan sighed and looked over at his daughter, who was resting peacefully in the bed. The tender expression Megan wore as she watched Caitlyn sleep twisted inside Jack. In the past week, this woman had shown more loving concern for his daughter than Lauren had in the past year. That alone was enough to get Jack's attention, even before he factored in his neighbor's kindness and sense of humor or her sexy lips and heavenly curves.

"So…" He paused and cleared his throat. "Are we… okay?"

Megan shifted her gaze to him. Her lips parted as if to speak, but she hesitated.

"Give me a second chance, Megan. I'm really not such a belligerent oaf…usually."

She fidgeted with her earring again and gave him a forced smile. "Yeah. We're fine. I, um…I'll be right back with your computer and files."

Quickly Megan slipped out the door, out of sight, and Jack kicked himself. Her hesitation and lukewarm reception of his apology said what Megan was too polite to say.

He'd screwed up. Big-time. He'd freaked when he'd seen Caitlyn bleeding, seen Megan's dog hovering over his daughter. His daughter's injury was more his fault, because of his inattention, than anyone else's. And he'd taken his fear, his guilt and his frustration out on the one person who least deserved his wrath.

As soon as Caity was released to go home, he would find some way to make amends with Megan. She deserved no less.

Megan drove home, lost in thought. She was still mulling over Caitlyn's claim that Sam had saved her from another dog, when she turned onto her street and spotted two vehicles parked in front of her house. The sedan had a light bar on top and an insignia on the door. The truck had something like a cage in the back and black letters printed on the side.

A-N-I-M-A-L C-O-N-T-R-O-L.

Chapter 5

A prickling sensation chased down Megan's neck as Jack's promise to have Sam taken away echoed in her brain. "No!"

She wheeled her car into her driveway and leaped out. "Wait!" she cried to the sheriff deputy who watched as another man took Sam with a stiff lead to the waiting truck. "That's my dog! You can't do this!"

The deputy turned to her as she raced across the yard.

Panic rose in her throat, choking her. She'd be lost without Sam. He was the only reason she could sleep at night. His presence and protective instincts gave her the peace-of-mind she needed to live alone while her rapist walked the streets.

And she loved Sam. They'd been best friends from the day he'd come home with her from his trainer's house. At a time when so many other friends had drifted away from her, Sam had been her anchor, her unconditionally devoted companion.

"Are you Megan Hoffman?" The sheriff's deputy pulled a folded sheet from his pocket.

She swallowed hard, fighting down her learned fear of the uniform before her. She stood several feet away from the man, and when he stepped toward her, she backed up warily.

"Yes, I'm Megan. I-I know what Mr. Calhoun must have told you earlier. But Sam didn't attack his daughter! I just left the hospital, and Caitlyn told us there was *another* dog."

The deputy took a deep, tired breath, and for an instant, Megan sympathized with his unpleasant duty of overseeing the removal of a woman's pet.

"Ma'am, all I have to go on is the report filed from the hospital. According to the information taken in the emergency room tonight, your dog attacked a little girl."

Megan shook her head vigorously. "I just came from seeing Caitlyn. She cleared Sam. There was another dog—"

"Just the same, I'm required by law to follow through on this complaint. Your dog has to be quarantined for ten days at the animal shelt—"

"But Caitlyn cleared Sam! He didn't do it! You can't take him without proof—"

"The law says I can." The apologetic tone he used didn't buffer the impact of his statement.

Bile burned in her throat, and she turned in time to see Sam cooperatively hop onto the back of the animal control truck.

"You don't understand," she said hoarsely. "I—I need Sam for protection." Megan wrapped her arms around her middle and struggled to draw a breath.

"This is just for ten days, ma'am. If we see no evidence that the animal poses a threat, you can claim him at the shelter at that time."

Ten days. Even ten days was too long.

"Another dog hurt Caitlyn. Sam's innocent."

"Don't worry. He'll be taken care of. Please sign at the *X*."

Megan lifted her chin a notch. "And if I don't?"

He sighed. "Don't make this harder than it has to be, ma'am."

Defeat knotted in her chest. Hands shaking, she signed the paper and passed the clipboard back to the officer. As the officer strode away, Megan staggered to the end of the truck where Sam sat, imprisoned behind crisscrossed bars.

"Oh, Sam," she whispered, a hot tear dripping from her eyelashes to dampen her cheek. She poked her fingers through the cage, and with a wag of his tail, Sam licked her. The lapping of his warm tongue wrenched her heart. "I'll get you out, Sam. I promise."

When the truck driver cranked the engine, Megan stepped back onto the curb and watched helplessly as the truck pulled away, taking her friend and guardian from her. Stealing the anchor that gave her peace-of-mind.

As she watched the taillights of the truck fade in the distance, the dark menacing eyes of her attacker flickered in her mind. Megan's mouth grew arid. The chilling prospect of ten dark, sleepless nights, alone with her memories, sent a tremor spiraling through her.

Megan slid Jack's key in the knob of his front door, only to find the knob turned without being unlocked. Megan blinked then remembered Jack's hasty retreat, so concerned for Caitlyn that he'd dashed off to the hospital without locking his house.

Her pulse tripped at the idea of entering Jack's home after it sat unsecured for the past few hours. Anyone could have gotten inside.

If she'd had Sam with her, she might have brushed Jack's oversight aside and gone in.

But Sam was gone. Her chest ached at the thought, and she swallowed the emotion that tightened her throat.

Turning, she marched down Jack's steps and crossed his yard to the house next door. She knocked on her neighbors' door, and when the recently-retired auto salesman who lived there answered her summons, she mustered a smile. "Hi, Mr. Hollins. I need to get something out of the house next door for Mr. Calhoun, and I was wondering if you'd go inside with me."

She explained about Caitlyn's injury, about the door being left unlocked, about the laptop she'd promised to retrieve for Jack.

Mr. Hollins gave her a flirtatious wink. "Sure thing, hon. Just let me tell the missus where I'm off to."

With Mr. Hollins beside her, Megan trooped back to Jack's house, answering the older man's questions about Caitlyn's condition and the vicious dog that had been loose in the neighborhood.

Yet even with her neighbor accompanying her, Megan's stomach swirled anxiously as she stepped inside Jack's house. She groped in the darkness for a light switch and searched the shadowed foyer before making her way to the next room. Holding her breath, Megan swept her gaze around Jack's cluttered living room. The stacks of boxes waiting to be unpacked gave prowlers numerous places to hide, and the target of her search, Jack's laptop, filled the adjoining kitchen with an eerie bluish glow.

Mr. Hollins clicked on a lamp and picked up a framed photo from the end table. "Is this the little girl? Cutie pie, isn't she? I think I've seen her playing in the yard."

Megan glanced at the photo and nodded. "That's Caitlyn. She's four."

Her neighbor grinned and set the frame down. "What was it you came to get?"

Megan pressed a hand to her jumpy stomach, eager to be out of Jack's house. "His computer. I'll be right back."

She hurried to the kitchen, flipped on the lights and spotted the laptop in the middle of jumbled files and notebooks. Megan stroked her finger over the keyboard mouse to bring the laptop out of sleep mode, and a document blinked to life on the screen.

Again she rolled the cursor across the screen with the mouse to begin shutting down the computer.

With a beep, the message "Save file *Exposing the Gentleman Rapist?*" popped onto the screen.

Megan's breath snagged in her throat. She cast a frantic glance around the scattered files, and acid pooled in her stomach.

On Jack's notepad, he'd scratched out *Find a unique angle.* The label on a manilla file read *Victims' Profiles.* A yellowed newspaper article headline screamed *Serial Rapist Strikes Again: Police Suspect Copycat.* Jack was researching the history behind the town's biggest news story.

Megan's knees buckled, and she sank onto one of the kitchen table's ladder-backed chairs.

How deep would Jack have to dig before he realized she was one of the Gentleman Rapist's victims? Her name shouldn't be in the files the police released. Louisiana's rape shield laws forbid the release of rape victims' names to the press. But despite the shield laws, her identity had leaked out years ago. The police had apologized profusely for the so-called administrative error that had left her name in released documents, and the TV station that reported her identity had been highly criticized by women's groups. Yet the damage had been done.

Megan rubbed her temple wearily, recalling people's reaction to learning what she'd endured. She hadn't even been able to go to the grocery store without the cashier recognizing the name on her check and giving her pitying looks. At the school where she'd taught, faculty and parents, well-meaning though they were, treated her with excessive deference and saccharine kindness. She'd felt like a pariah, some sort of pitiable freak that people whispered about behind their hands. She was "the one who had been *raped*." The poor girl whose fiancé left her because she couldn't cope with her trauma. Even if she'd wanted to move past the experience, her coworkers, neighbors and acquaintances wouldn't let her.

Having her darkest, most degrading horror as common knowledge at the school was bad enough, but people's awkwardness around her and kid-glove treatment drove her crazy, keeping the trauma fresh in her mind. She hated having others define her by the rape.

She'd had no choice but to leave the school in order to have peace and privacy. She'd sworn never to tell anyone again. When Megan had finally changed jobs and moved out of her old neighborhood, she'd decided to use her middle name. Going by Megan distanced her from the Sara who'd been attacked, and it gave her a little breathing space, a fresh start. Now Megan wondered if the administrative error that had caused her problems the first time had been corrected. She prayed that if Jack did come across her name in his files that he wouldn't draw any connection between Sara Hoffman and Megan Hoffman.

And what other identifying information might be in the police files Jack had? Could Jack piece together the truth from any other statistics the police released to the media?

Megan paged through the top file, and, sure enough, there was a newspaper clipping, a five-year-old editorial, discussing the TV station's poor judgment. It wouldn't be hard for Jack to find footage of the news broadcast mentioned if he became curious. The transcript was public record. Megan groaned and slapped the file shut.

Jack, not just a reporter but her *neighbor*, was getting too close to her past. She faced the prospect of living through that notoriety, the awkwardness and pitying looks again. She had no doubt that if he learned the truth, he'd pump her for information, dig up her painful past. After all, exposing the truth was his job.

Talk about a *unique angle*. His own neighbor was one of the madman's first victims. The last thing she needed was for Jack to write about her rape, telling the world her darkest, most agonizing secret.

She swallowed the bitterness rising in her throat as nausea knotted her stomach. Even if she refused to talk to Jack about what happened, her secret would be compromised. What if he called her school asking about her history? What if he let it slip to their neighbors?

Megan's heart thumped a nervous rhythm as she gathered Jack's files and closed the laptop. For now, the best way to protect the truth of her past was to keep her distance from Jack.

But if keeping her secret were what she wanted, why did the prospect of avoiding Jack feel so bleak?

"Jack?"

A warm hand gently shook his arm, rousing Jack from a catnap. At least he'd intended it to be a catnap. He mashed the button that lit his watch and blinked the display into focus. 8:09 p.m. He'd slept for more than an hour. Scrubbing a hand over his face, he dropped his feet to the floor from the end of Caitlyn's bed and sat up. In the dimly lit room, his gaze sought Caitlyn, and he found her still snoozing.

A soft fruity scent taunted him, telling him who'd wakened him even before he turned in the chair to face Megan. His pulse gave a little kick at the sight of her, her honey-colored hair swept over one shoulder and the gold glow of the nightlight by the bed making her skin look like sculpted ivory.

"Hi," he said, his voice craggy with sleep. *With desire.* Megan looked good enough to eat.

"I brought your laptop." She held his computer and satchel of files out to him.

"Oh, right. Thanks." He took the items from her with a smile of appreciation.

"How's Caitlyn?" Megan asked, stepping closer to his daughter's bedside and smoothing the covers.

"Well, she's still asleep. That has to be good."

Megan hummed her agreement and nodded stiffly. "Sorry to wake you. I'll let you get back to your nap."

Jack set his laptop aside and stood, stretching the kinks from his back. "No. I mean, I don't need to be napping. I've got work to do."

"Then I'll let you get to work," she said with a nervous smile. Megan stiffened slightly and backed another step toward the door.

Jack frowned. "You don't have to go. Caitlyn would love to see you when she wakes up. Her sedative is bound to be wearing off soon."

Megan shook her head, twisted her purse strap. "No. It's getting late, and…I have work tomorrow."

"Oh…right." Jack didn't consider eight o'clock late. Megan's fidgeting told him something else was at play, making his neighbor jumpy. "Thanks again for bringing the laptop. I owe you one." He watched her edge closer to the door and added, "Maybe we can get dinner sometime?"

Hell, it was worth a shot.

Megan stopped, snapping her gaze up to his. "What?"

"Dinner. You and me. A date." He scratched his cheek and flashed a lopsided grin. "That is if I can find someone trained for combat to watch Miss Adventure."

Megan shook her head again. "I don't think that'd be a good idea."

"After Caity's feeling better, I mean."

Megan fumbled with her pearl earring. "No. Jack, I…can't. I, uh…"

Angling his head, he narrowed a concerned gaze on her. "Megan, what's wrong? Is it because of the way I acted about your dog? I'm really sorry—"

She drew a sharp breath and turned toward the door, bracing a hand on the frame.

"Megan?" Closing the distance between them, he grasped her arm and guided her around to face him again. He saw the glimmer of tears pooling in her eyes and felt a catch in his chest. "What is it?"

"They took Sam." Her voice cracked, and the ache in his chest wrenched tighter.

"They?"

She raised her chin. "The police. Animal control. They were already at my house when I went back for your computer. They took Sam for quarantine."

Hurt shadowed her eyes.

"You think I called them." He took a step back, stung by her assumption, until he recalled having shouted threats of just such a thing as he raced off to the hospital.

He lifted a hand in his defense. "I didn't call them, Megan. I swear. I was too worried about Caitlyn and making sure she was all right to deal with anything else. And you were here when Caitlyn cleared Sam. I had no reason to call the authorities on your dog after that."

"Well, *somebody* called the authorities, because he's gone. Locked up in quarantine." Wrapping her arms around her chest, Megan ducked her chin. She sniffed, and a tear spilled onto her cheek.

That tear landed a sucker punch to Jack's gut. "Geez, Megan, I'm sorry. The hospital probably called. I…did mention Sam when I explained to the E.R. staff what happened to Caitlyn. I think it's the law that they have to report animal bites." Again he closed the space between them. Wanting to soothe her, he stroked a hand over her shoulder.

She flinched away and jerked her head up, her eyes wide and startled. Sidling back another step, she swiped at her eyes. "I guess it doesn't matter who called. Sam's still gone. Quarantined for something he didn't do."

Jack drew a slow breath and speared his fingers through his hair. "Would it help if I called animal control in the morning and tried to sort this out?"

She narrowed her eyes warily. "You'd do that?"

He grinned. "Sure. Remember, I'm only a surly ass part of the time. I'm usually a pretty nice guy."

He spread his arms, inviting her to accept his comforting hug. When she only eyed him with a hesitant but hopeful expression, he moved closer, pulling her into his arms. Megan held herself stiff, refusing to relax into his embrace.

Still the sweet peach scent of her hair, the soft curve of her body and the warmth of her cheek against his were heavenly. Jack's body responded with a low and urgent thrum.

"Belligerent oaf," she whispered hoarsely.

Frowning, Jack leaned back to meet her eyes.

"That's what you called yourself this afternoon. A belligerent oaf. Not a surly ass."

"Oh." He quirked a grin. "Right. Either way, I'm sorry. So…are we okay? You think we can we have dinner sometime?"

Her face grew shuttered again, and she wiggled free of his grip. "Will you still help me get Sam released if I say *no?*"

He winced teasingly. "Really? We're still at *no?*"

She gave me an apologetic smile and fiddled with her earring again. "It's just…I don't date much, and…I'm pretty busy with the new school year."

"Oh." Jack nodded and shoved his hands in his pockets.

"Okay." He understood *no*, even couched with thin excuses, and wouldn't push her on the subject.

But something in her expression gave him pause. She stared at him with a wistfulness, a poignant vulnerability and skittishness that plucked at him. The mixed emotions he read in her eyes told him her excuses were just that. Excuses. She was telling him *no* for some other reason, a reason that had her feeling lost, scared.

"I'll still see what I can do to spring your dog from the hoosegow tomorrow. It's the least I can do if he really did save Caitlyn from another dog."

"Thanks, Jack." Megan grew teary again, and her chin quivered. Her sadness had him itching to pull her back into his arms, hold her and quiet the turbulence swirling behind her jade eyes.

But her touchiness when he'd tried to comfort her earlier warned him not to try again. Instead he sent her an encouraging smile and shrugged. "No problem."

She blinked her tears away and sucked in a deep breath, visibly gathering her composure. "Well, good night. I'd better go now."

"'Night."

To Jack, it seemed putting on a good face and soldiering on took all the energy Megan could muster. Determination appeared to be the glue holding her together.

What burden was she carrying that had worn her down, put such raw emotion in her eyes? He wanted answers to so many questions concerning Megan.

But not as a journalist. As a man. A man who felt an inexorable internal tug that drew him to this beautiful woman.

She might have turned him down for dinner, but he wouldn't give up on her. He could wait, and eventually he'd figure out what made Megan Hoffman tick.

Chapter 6

The silence that met Megan when she got home from school the next day should have been a welcome respite from the noise and activity of her energetic first-grade class. Instead it felt suffocating. Oppressive. Lonely.

She missed Sam's exuberant greeting and wagging tail. His slobbery licks.

The lonely quiet surrounding her as she kicked off her shoes became a hollow ache inside her, an ache she knew was rooted in more than just Sam's absence. As she dropped her purse on the kitchen counter and headed back to her bedroom to change clothes, she let herself imagine what it would be like to come home to a house where she had more than just an enthusiastic dog to welcome her home.

Her birthday, her students, her empty house all served as painful reminders of the family she dreamed of having. A dream she'd put on ice because of her attack.

And lately, when she thought about the children she wanted playing in her backyard, she pictured a little girl with dark ponytails. Daydreams of a husband who'd welcome her home with a warm kiss starred a man with hazel eyes and a sexy grin.

Jack's grin.

Megan sank down on the edge of her bed and sighed. She couldn't deny how many of her thoughts today had centered around her handsome neighbor and how much she'd wanted to accept his invitation for dinner. But turning Jack down had been the smart move, hadn't it? Time spent with Jack meant time for him to pick up on subtle clues to her past and her connection to the story he was writing on the Gentleman Rapist.

Already she felt transparent around him, as if he could see straight through to her soul and all her hidden fears and desires. Last night when she'd told him about Sam's quarantine, her emotions had been dangerously close to the surface. She'd wanted nothing more than to cry on Jack's wide shoulder and accept the soothing strokes of his warm hands.

But beneath his offer of comfort, she'd sensed his keen journalistic instincts had been on full alert, dissecting her every move, searching her eyes for a glimpse of some hidden truth.

Or maybe she'd imagined it. Maybe the stress of the week was making her conjure threats to her privacy and peace-of-mind where there were none.

Her mind spinning, Megan stripped off her skirt and blouse and pulled a pair of shorts and a T-shirt from her dresser. She might not have Sam to walk, but she needed a jog to clear her head.

After locking her house, Megan headed out, making sure not to go the same route she'd used earlier in the week. Her personal safety trainer had ingrained in her the importance of varying her routine. Regular habits made it easy for someone to stalk her.

Setting a brisk pace, she kept a sharp eye on her surroundings as she jogged the familiar streets of her neighborhood. Mrs. Rochelle called a greeting to her, and she waved back. Mr. Hollins gave her another of his flirtatious winks as she passed him at his driveway.

She'd just reached Jack's house when a pickup truck pulled alongside her and honked.

"Hey, good-looking, got a minute?" Jack called from the open driver's window.

Even as Megan slowed to talk to Jack, her pulse tripped faster. Stepping off the curb toward his truck, she acknowledged the reason for the light tingly sensation scampering through her. She was happy to see Jack. Maybe not school-girl giddy, but surprisingly pleased nonetheless. She drank in the sight of his stubble-darkened jaw and devilish half grin, and a sweet vibration started low in her belly.

"Hi yourself." Realizing Caitlyn was in the backseat, Megan ducked her head and sent the little girl a bright smile. "Look who's home from the hospital! How are you feeling, sweetie?"

Caitlyn's face lit with excitement when she spotted Megan. "Hey, guess what! Daddy says when we get Sam tomorrow, I can get a cat!"

Megan's brain snagged on the mention of Sam. She hesitated a beat, and sent Jack a querying glance before answering Caitlyn with an enthusiastic smile. "A cat? That's great! How exciting."

She heard Jack's soft groan and turned her attention back to him with a puckered brow and wry grin. "I hardly know where to start. Amazing how one statement from a child can raise so many questions."

Wearing a look of chagrin, he jerked his head toward his driveway. "Let me park and get her inside, and I'll explain everything."

Megan stood back as Jack pulled into his driveway. She helped Caitlyn unbuckle her car seat while Jack gathered his laptop and files from the front seat. Even with her arm in a cast and sling, Jack's daughter sprang from the backseat of the extended cab with a gleeful leap and hopped around Megan on the balls of her feet. "Can you come with us when we get my cat, Miss Megan? Please?"

"I, uh…don't know. We'll see." She tugged gently on Caitlyn's ponytail. "How's that arm?"

The girl's brown eyes widened, her expression dismayed. "It's bwoken! But don't worry," she said waving her good hand in a placating manner. "This cast will make it all better. I just gotta be re-e-eally careful for a while. So it can get fixed."

Megan matched Caitlyn's adultly serious expression and nodded. "That's good to hear. I'm sure your arm will be good as new in no time."

"Run on inside, munchkin. I want to talk to Megan for a minute."

As Caitlyn skipped off toward the front porch, Jack's mouth slanted in frustration. "The cat is a compromise. She spent the whole morning at the hospital begging for a 'dog like Sam'. I still can't see us getting a mutt at this point. So we settled on a cat." He paused and lifted one eyebrow. "They're low maintenance, right?"

"Not as low maintenance as a goldfish."

"Doh!" He smacked his forehead. "A goldfish! Why didn't I think of that?"

Megan grinned and tucked her sweat-dampened hair behind her ear. Why was it Jack always seemed to catch her looking her frazzled worst?

She slid her gaze over her neighbor, who managed to make wrinkled clothes, rumpled hair and a roguish shadow of stubble on his chin look temptingly sexy. As if he'd just rolled out of bed after a long night of passion. The vibration deep inside her kicked up a notch.

He still wore the same clothes from yesterday, further testifying to the fact he hadn't left Caitlyn's side in nearly twenty-four hours. Jack's dedication to his daughter stirred a warmth in Megan's chest that spread throughout her body as she met the spark of humor in his hazel gaze. Why did Jack have to be so deliciously tempting?

And if he weren't a reporter, would she have had the courage to accept his dinner invitation? If anyone could entice her back into the dating scene, it would be Jack. The man had some potent pheromones at work. He positively exuded charm and sex appeal.

Shoving down the heady butterfly sensation rippling inside her, Megan cocked her head. "Then again, I'm not sure a goldfish would have satisfied Caitlyn. I think she's in the market for something furry. You can't hug a goldfish or cuddle with it in your bed at night."

In a heartbeat, Jack's expression changed. His grin grew more sultry, and his eyes darkened, heated. When his gaze flickered down to her lips, Megan realized what she'd said. She knew the direction his thoughts had gone, because hers weren't far behind.

"Yeah," he said, a husky edge to his voice, "a bed can get lonely without someone to cuddle with."

The summer air, already thick with humidity, crackled with energy. Like heat lightning, a sizzling charge arced between them.

Megan couldn't stop the image that sprang to mind. Jack. Naked in a bed. A sheet riding low on his hips. She remembered every detail of his bare chest and legs from her encounter with him in a towel just over a week ago. Taut and muscular. Lean and large. Oh, so sexy.

Her breath stilled in her lungs. Her face tingled as her cheeks flushed.

Realizing her gaze had locked with his, she jerked her chin down and sucked in oxygen, mortified.

How much of what she'd been thinking could he read in her eyes?

She cleared her suddenly dry throat, redirecting the conversation to the question that had begged an answer too long already. "Um…Caitlyn said something about getting Sam tomorrow." She tilted her head up enough to see Jack nod. "And…?"

"And…I made several calls today. To the Lagniappe P.D. Animal control. Took a while to cut the red tape, but everything's cleared up. When the animal shelter opens tomorrow, we can go claim Sam."

Joy leaped in Megan's chest and a wide smile spread on her face. Elated, she threw her arms around Jack's neck in a jubilant and grateful hug. "Oh, thank you! Thank you, Jack! You have no idea what this means to me!"

"Oh, I have an idea." His arms curled around her, warm and strong. "You were pretty upset last night. It wasn't hard to guess how important Sam is to you."

Megan closed her eyes and sighed. *You don't know the half of it.*

When Jack stroked a hand down her spine and back to her nape, a delicious shiver raced over her skin. She allowed herself another moment to sink into the solid strength and comfort of his arms. The tension in her muscles unwound a notch, and she savored the reassurance and balm of his embrace.

She hadn't realized how much she missed having someone to hold, to hug, to lean on. Sure, her mother and Ginny gave her hugs, and her students often gave her affectionate squeezes. But Jack's arms enveloped her with a feeling of security and protection she hadn't known in a long time.

In her head, Megan heard herself telling Ginny that Jack was "too male" because of his *GQ*-worthy physique and good looks.

And just like that, Jack's hug morphed from soothing to scintillating. She became acutely aware of her body pressed to his, the play of sinewy muscles beneath her fingers, the spicy scent of him. Her head swam, until a nagging voice in her brain whispered, *He's researching the Gentleman Rapist.*

Instantly, her muscles tensed.

Breathless, she wrenched out of his arms. Her heart tap-danced against her ribs as she stepped back, avoiding his gaze.

Why couldn't Jack be a plumber? A pilot? Anyone but a reporter whose latest story threatened to expose secrets she'd worked years to put behind her.

"Dad-dy!" Caitlyn called from the porch. "The door is locked. I can't get in, and I gotta pee!"

Jack chuckled. "Way to announce it to the neighborhood, munchkin," he said under his breath. He caught Megan's hand and started backing toward the door. "Follow me. I have to let someone in before she has an accident, but I want to make plans for us to get Sam in the morning."

Megan let him pull her along a few steps before she jerked her hand away. Her skin felt scorched, branded by the heat of his fingers. "Us? I can go alone to get Sam. You don't need—"

"Ah, but we're getting a cat. Remember?" His lips twisted in a wry grin. "Might as well ride together. As I understand it, the animal shelter is several miles south of town near the old airport."

"Daddy, let me in!" Caitlyn hollered, doing an impatient jig on the porch.

Jack jogged backward, sending Megan an apologetic grin. He hitched a thumb over his shoulder toward his daughter. "Sorry, I gotta go before she does—all over the porch. The shelter opens at eight, so wanna say seven-thirty? I'll drive."

Jack had reached the porch steps, and his expectant expression sought a quick confirmation.

Megan fumbled, opening and closing her mouth without answering.

Her mind screamed, *No!* The last thing she needed was to spend more time getting chummy with this tantalizing man. He was the right kind of temptation at the wrong time. And a reporter to boot.

No, getting involved with Jack would be crazy. He was dangerous to her privacy and peace-of-mind.

When she continued to gape at him without answering, Jack gave a smile and a wave as if the matter of the morning outing were settled. He spun on his heel and jogged up the porch steps, key in hand, to let Caitlyn inside.

He disappeared through the front door, leaving Megan standing in his front yard, feeling as though she'd been too long on a carnival ride. Her head spun, and her limbs shook. Her mind was a little numb.

Yet a thread of excitement wove through her veins, and tiny grin tugged the corner of her mouth. Sam was coming home. Through his efforts today on Sam's behalf, Jack had helped restore a tiny piece of the security she craved and counted on. She owed him for that.

But the voice of caution told her she had to draw a line in their relationship, put the brakes on the attraction flaring between them. She refused to burden a man with her fears and doubts. She had only to think of the restless and tormented hours she'd spent last night without Sam to know she was a long way from ready to open her life to a man.

The specter of her attack still haunted her, still imprisoned her. Right now all her energy had to be focused on freeing herself from that prison.

"Want to tell me what's got you so distracted today or should I guess?" Ginny asked later that night. She stuffed a French fry in her mouth and lifted one pale blond eyebrow, inviting Megan's reply.

When Ginny had called and asked Megan to meet her for dinner, Megan had accepted happily. Anything to get her out of her too quiet house. Plus the outing gave her the opportunity to bounce her circular thoughts off Ginny's sounding board.

"I thought you wanted to talk, but you've been quiet and frowning ever since I got here." *Here* being the mom-and-pop restaurant perched along the bank of the river that flowed through Lagniappe. They sat on the deck overlooking the water and enjoyed the shade and the zydeco music playing over the speakers.

"I told you about my neighbor's daughter, right? How she went to the hospital last night?" Megan poked at her blackened catfish, seasoned with Cajun spices as hot as the Louisiana summer.

"Yeah. Poor thing. How is she?"

"She'll be fine. Jack was just bringing her home when I left for my run this afternoon."

"That's wonderful. So why so grim?" Ginny asked and sipped her iced tea.

Deep in thought, Megan pushed bites of fish around her plate. Something more than Sam's quarantine had her edgy, but she wasn't sure she understood her bad mood herself.

Caitlyn was doing well. Jack had straightened things out with animal control. Sam was coming home in the morning. Good news all around.

But a nagging despondency still clouded her mood.

Sighing, she set her fork aside and met Ginny's blue gaze. "Jack asked me out."

Ginny's face lit, and she grasped Megan's hand. "Yes! I knew he was interested. He couldn't take his eyes off you at the police station the other day. So where are you gonna go?"

"No place. I told him *no*."

Blinking, Ginny cocked her head. "You're kidding! *Why?*"

Megan caught her hair up in her hand, lifting the thick tresses off her neck as a breeze stirred the muggy air. She gazed across the water toward the buildings of downtown Lagniappe. "Because he's a reporter, Gin. And if that weren't bad enough, he's covering the Gentleman Rapist case."

Ginny flopped back in her chair, and puffed the bangs out of her eyes. "Geez."

"Yeah, *geez*. I plan to stay away from him and pray he never links me with the Sara Hoffman whose name was leaked." Hand shaking, Megan lifted her iced tea and sipped. "Or…"

Megan peered over the rim of her glass at Ginny, not liking the speculative gleam in her friend's eyes.

"*No*. Whatever you're concocting in that brain of yours, the answer is *no!*"

"You *could* go out with him—"

Megan scoffed and shook her head. "Ginny—"

"And just see if there are any sparks…"

Sparks? Megan's pulse leaped remembering the heat in Jack's eyes that afternoon and the jolt that rocked her body when he'd stroked her back, held her close as they hugged. The intensity of her response to him was why she'd back away.

"Chemistry's not the problem, Gin. We've got plenty of that flying around."

"So does your refusal have to do with this idea you have that you're going to freeze up when you want to be intimate?" Without waiting for an answer, Ginny grabbed Megan's hand again and squeezed. "Maybe with all this chemistry you two have cooking, he's the one to help you past your fears, to remind you how good sex can be with the right man."

Megan sputtered and pulled her hand away, uneasy with the direction of the conversation. "He just asked me to dinner! I'm not about to jump in his bed!"

"Yet. But dinner could lead to something more. And that's the problem, yes?" Ginny was nothing if not blunt.

"Well, it's part of it, sure. But—"

"You can't stay celibate forever."

Megan flipped her hair over her shoulder, a gesture far more nonchalant than the roiling emotions inside her. "Sure I can. Why not?"

"Someday you *have* to have sex in order to make those babies you want."

Megan's gut clenched as if absorbing a physical blow. Leave it to Ginny to cut straight to the heart, pull no punches.

"Can we talk about something else please?"

"You brought him up."

"I'm not ready to start dating."

"I think you are. It's been *five years*. You've made tons of progress. It's time you got out there and made a real life for yourself."

"Maybe. But not with Jack. He's a reporter!"

Ginny raised her hands and made a mock frightened face, playfully dismissing the notion that Jack's occupation should be a deterrent.

Megan scowled. "Gin, he's investigating the Gentleman Rapist! I saw his work last night when I took his laptop to him at the hospital."

"So you said. Why is that such a problem for you?"

Megan gaped at her friend. "Hello? If we start dating while he's reporting on the Gentleman Rapist, and he finds out that I was one of the women attacked…"

"So tell him before he finds out some other way."

Megan firmly shook her head. "No way. I can't tell him."

"Because…?"

Megan slapped her hands down on the arms of her chair and frowned. "Don't you remember what happened when my name leaked out before? The way people treated me? I can't go through that again."

"And you think Jack's knowing the truth would make that happen?" Ginny kept a calm, professional tone. Her friend's laserlike blue eyes speared into her, pried open Megan's soul. "You're not giving him much credit. If he cares about you, if he has any kind of professionalism and decency as a journalist, he'll find a way to report the story and still protect your identity. And that's assuming the rape survivors' stories are even the angle he's pursuing."

Megan sighed and used her straw to idly stir her tea. "I just want to be careful. Be certain. Protect my privacy. I already left one job because everyone treated me like a time bomb that could detonate any second. Having your neighbors know you were violated in your own home because of your own stupidity is bad enough without dealing with it every day at work, too. It was horrible and awkward, and I won't go back to living like that."

"You didn't ask to be attacked, Megan." Ginny leaned forward, her tone urgent. "Trusting a policeman is not stupid. You made a mistake by not verifying his credentials before you let him in your house. But that doesn't make the rape your fault."

Megan closed her eyes. "I know. We've gone over this a thousand times. You're missing my point."

"And you are still using terms like 'stupidity' to make your point. You *say* you know it wasn't your fault, but I don't think you *believe* it. And I think that's why you're still scared. You don't trust yourself, your judgment, your ability to prevent the same thing from happening again. Am I right?"

Megan shifted in her resin lawn chair and sucked in a deep, unsteady breath. The spicy scent of Cajun cooking, usually an enticing smell to her, turned her already sour stomach.

She didn't know how to answer Ginny. Maybe her friend and counselor was right. Seeds of truth certainly poked at Megan's conscience and took root.

After all she'd done in the past five years to protect herself, how could she still feel unsafe? She'd gotten Sam, a dog trained to protect her. She'd taken self-defense classes and learned to use the handgun she kept in her bedside drawer. She changed her door locks regularly, and her phone number was unlisted. All these steps gave her a measure of reassurance and comfort. So why did she still feel so vulnerable?

"Maybe rather than keeping your rape a secret any longer, the time has come to dust off your memories and confront them. For the last few years, you've held the memories at bay, locked them away where they couldn't hurt you. You've changed your name, moved to a new house, found a new job and isolated yourself from all but your closest family and friends." Ginny's eyes were soft and understanding despite the harsh assessment she offered. "You've been trying to escape the pain of what happened by pushing it down and denying it, by running from what happened."

Megan stared at Ginny, stunned. "That's not true! There's not a day that goes by that I don't think about what happened! It's always there! And believe me, I feel the pain."

Even now the agony, the fear and the resentment that were the legacy of her rape clawed her throat and strangled her breath.

"That's my point, hon. You need closure. You need to come to terms with what happened and get your head to a place where you can tell people about your rape and not care how they react. When you've looked your fears in the eye and truly faced them down, those ghosts won't have the power to haunt you every day. Maybe telling Jack is the first step toward taking a stand and fighting to regain control of your life."

Megan's heart rose to her throat. "Learn how to swim by jumping into a pool of sharks?"

Ginny's mouth curved in a gentle smile. "Jack is not a shark, hon. He's not out to hurt you."

Closing her eyes, Megan sighed. "I can't. I—"

"Okay, so don't jump in the pool. Stick your toe in. Go out with him and just test the waters. Take baby steps for now, but move forward."

"Baby steps?" Megan twisted her earring and considered Ginny's advice. "He did ask me to go with him to the animal shelter in the morning. A combined trip to get Sam out of lockup and pick out a cat for his daughter."

Ginny's grin brightened. "There you go. That's a first step." Leaning forward in her chair, Ginny lowered her voice. "I know it's hard. I know it's scary. But you are stronger than you think. Braver than you give yourself credit for. You are ready for this, my friend. And I'll be right behind you every baby step of the way."

Tears pricked Megan's eyes, and she nodded. "You'd

better be. No shoving me off the diving board then leaving me in the pool to drown."

"Hey, I've got to stick around to hear all the juicy details about your hunky neighbor. Remember, I'm living vicariously through you right now. This dry patch of mine has got to end soon, or I'm just gonna shrivel up and die!"

Wiping her eyes, Megan laughed. "You are desperate if you think my love life is gonna help you out, vicariously or otherwise."

Ginny checked her watch and groaned. "Listen, hon, I gotta run. Billy's truck is in the shop, and I have to pick him up from work."

Nodding, Megan pushed back from their table and rose to give Ginny a quick hug as she left. "Tell him I said 'hi'."

"I will. Call me if you want to talk more later, 'kay? And promise me you'll reconsider going out with Jack. A sexy man is a terrible thing to waste." Ginny flashed an impish grin as she snatched the check from the table and hurried inside the restaurant.

Megan took her iced tea over to the deck railing and watched a pair of mallards swim aimlessly in the slow-moving current of the river. Like the deceptive surface calm of the water, beneath her still contemplation of the ducks, her emotions swirled and eddied.

Her thoughts drifted to Jack. His dazzling smile. The electricity that hummed between them when he was close.

Just a friendly hug from him had sent shock waves pulsing through her body.

But how did she reconcile her intense attraction to him with the risk of having Jack learn the truth about her attack? Could she tell Jack who she was, what happened five years ago, and not have the fragile balance in her life crash down around her?

Just thinking about how *that* conversation would go had her pulse jumping and her stomach in knots. Megan curled her fingers into her palms and dragged in a calming breath.

Stick your toe in. Just test the waters.

Maybe she could do it. She owed it to herself to try. She'd deal with Jack's article and the awkward position it left them in if and when she had to. For now, she had to get her life back.

One baby step at a time.

Chapter 7

When Megan arrived at Jack's early Saturday, she handed him his newspaper and greeted him with a sunny smile. "Good morning."

"Morning yourself," he returned, longing to bask in the warmth of her grin for…oh, a few years maybe? The sadness and vulnerability he'd seen in her eyes two nights ago had faded, replaced by a green sparkle. Spots of healthy color tinted her cheeks, and her face simply glowed. He'd always thought Megan was attractive, but this morning, her chipper mood made her breathtaking.

He stepped back to let her in. "I'm afraid we're not quite ready to go."

The tantalizing scent of peaches accompanied her as she entered his foyer. "Sorry, I know I'm early. I guess I'm a little eager to have Sam back."

Last night when he'd told her they could pick Sam up, her

enthusiastic hug had said much the same. Not that he was complaining. Brief though it was, her hug had confirmed everything he'd suspected. Beneath Megan's wary and reluctant exterior beat the heart of a warm and passionate woman. A woman who felt just as good in his arms as he'd imagined. Better, in fact.

For a moment last night, he'd sensed a connection with her, seen an answering heat in her eyes, felt her body relax against his and quaver with desire…before she'd again tensed and retreated behind her protective walls.

This morning, though, she seemed to have left her defensive shields at home. Maybe they'd finally moved past the awkward stiffness and distance he'd sensed in her earlier.

Well, a guy could hope.

Jack yawned. "Caitlyn was up at five this morning, asking when we could leave to get her cat. You'd think it was Christmas."

"For her, it sort of is. Getting a new pet is a big deal." Megan held his gaze for a change rather than nervously shifting her attention away. More progress. Jack's own spirits lifted a little.

"Megan!" Caitlyn squealed and bolted from the kitchen to fling herself against Megan's legs. "You wanna eat breakfast with us? I'm havin' a Pop-Tart."

Grinning broadly, his temptress neighbor squatted in front of Caitlyn to give her a hug then dusted jellied crumbs from the corner of his daughter's mouth. "So I see. Got another Pop-Tart for me?"

"Sure. Come on!" Caity grabbed her hand, and Megan stumbled to her feet as his gung-ho four-year-old towed her toward the kitchen.

Jack followed them into the kitchen, listening to Caitlyn chatter excitedly about their trip to the store the night before to buy supplies for her new cat. Megan answered with genuine interest and encouragement. The rapport she had with his daughter was heartening, and yet…an uneasy niggling started in his brain. He'd been so preoccupied with mending fences and advancing his own relationship with Megan, he hadn't considered all the ramifications of his daughter's attachment to Megan.

Caity had latched onto their pretty neighbor with both hands. Megan's kindness and instincts with children were bound to fill a void in Caitlyn's life. Little girls needed mother figures. But could Jack afford to let his daughter grow attached to a woman who had flatly refused any relationship with him?

I think it would be a bad idea.

And while she seemed more open and receptive this morning, Megan was inconsistent toward him at best, clearly uncertain at times of how to respond to him. He sensed a struggle inside her, and he couldn't be sure, when all was said and done, that he and Caity would come out on the winning end.

As a father, his first job was to protect Caitlyn. His daughter's heart had been broken once. She'd lost one mother already. How could he stand aside and watch Megan create false illusions for his little girl?

Caitlyn deserved better than a sometimes mommy, a part-time substitute.

Yet standing in the doorway, watching Megan retie the ribbon on Caitlyn's ponytail, Jack's heart did a slow tuck and roll in his chest. They looked so natural together. So right.

So where was the mistake Megan saw in something that felt so good, so right to him? Jack frowned. If and when he gave his heart to another woman, he had to be sure the woman was as committed to making things work as he was.

So far, Megan didn't fit that picture.

Caity ushered Megan to the pantry and showed her the box of strawberry Pop-Tarts, and Jack shoved away from the doorframe with a grunt. "I think we can do better than fruit pastries for our guest, munchkin." He took the box from his daughter and slid the Pop-Tarts back on the shelf. Lifting his gaze to Megan's, he motioned toward a chair at the oak table. "I can cook eggs, and we have waffles in the freezer."

Rather than take a seat, she reached around him to take the box of pastries back off the shelf. Her movement brought her body tauntingly close to his own, teasing his senses with her sweet fruit scent and the outdoor warmth still shimmering from her body. The soft swell of her breast nudged his arm as she leaned toward the shelf, and desire puddled in his gut like warm syrup.

"Pop-Tarts are fine, thanks. No need to go to any trouble."

Trouble. Only trouble he had was keeping his hands at his sides and not plowing his fingers through her glossy hair and hauling her close for a good morning kiss.

Given their four-year-old chaperone and his vivid memory of her rejection of previous overtures from him, he tamped his lusty urges and put a safer distance between himself and the intoxicating aroma of her shampoo.

The ringing of his phone provided Jack the distraction he needed to regain control of his rampaging libido. Jack dragged a hand down his jaw and checked the caller ID before lifting the receiver. Burt's home number.

"It'll be on your desk by this afternoon, Burt."

"I'm sure that will make Burt happy. He's such a stickler for deadlines." A woman's chuckle followed.

Caught off guard, Jack stood straighter and cleared his throat. "Um, I'm sorry. I—"

"Thought I was the boss checking up on you?" Another

warm laugh. "Not this time. It's Abigail, Burt's wife. Don't tell him I called, or he'll get suspicious. We're organizing a surprise party for his fiftieth birthday, and we want you and your wife to come if you can. No gifts, please. Just bring your smiling faces and help us celebrate Burt's half century."

Rocking back on his heels, Jack scrubbed a hand over his mussed hair and grinned. "I'd love to come, but…I'm not married."

Jack sensed Megan's curious gaze lift to him. He glanced toward the table where Caitlyn was showing Megan her artwork from preschool.

"Oh," Abigail said, "Burt had mentioned your daughter and I assumed…well, you could bring a date then. The more the merrier. Our daughter is flying in, and Burt's brother and his wife will be coming from Dallas. In fact… Ah! I have someone I'd just love for you to meet!"

Jack's gut clenched. God, no! Don't let his boss's wife make it her mission to set him up with a blind date. Talk about *awkward*.

His face must have reflected his panic, because Megan's brow furrowed and concern darkened her eyes.

"My friend's daughter is divorced, and I could call Edith and—"

"Actually, I'm seeing someone." Jack winced as he blurted the lie in self-defense. "We're pretty serious, and I'm sure… Megan—" He winced again as Megan's eyebrows shot up and her jaw dropped. "—will come with me. Thanks anyway though."

He met Megan's you-have-some-explaining-to-do scowl with a grimace and chagrined half smile.

He rubbed the sudden pounding in his temple while he listened to Burt's wife give him the date, time and directions to her house.

"I'm looking forward to meeting you, Jack. Burt tells me you're his star reporter, with all the earmarks of taking over as editor when he retires."

Jack arched an eyebrow. Star reporter? Editor? That tidbit stroked his ego but made his fib about Megan chafe all the more.

When he finished the call with Abigail, Jack continued staring at the phone, the dial tone buzzing, while he mentally regrouped. "Caitlyn, go brush your teeth so we can go. Okay?"

"Yea!" his daughter squealed as she sped off toward the bathroom.

"Jack…what just happened?" Megan's voice wobbled. "Did you just tell that person we were seriously involved?"

He raised both palms to stall Megan's protest as he strode over to the table. He turned a chair around and straddled it backward as he met Megan's wide-eyed disbelief head on.

"That was my boss's wife. Burt is turning fifty, and she's throwing a surprise party next Saturday. I…need a date." He read the reluctance on her face and rushed on. "I know you said you thought our dating was a bad idea, so maybe you could think of it as…a favor to me."

Megan shook her head. "Knowing how I felt, knowing that I'd already turned you down once—"

"Twice…actually." He screwed his mouth sideways in a wry half grin.

"Then why'd you tell her we were dating? That we were serious?"

He saw shades of withdrawal and distance creeping back into Megan's expression, and fingers of regret and compunction gripped his heart. Just last night he'd sworn not to push her. She stared at him with a tight jaw and questions swirling in her jade eyes. She looked as skittish as a fawn, ready to bolt if he so much as said *Boo*.

He met her gaze evenly, flattened his hands on the table. "The thing is…she was trying to fix me up with a friend, and…hell, I panicked. Visions of nightmare blind dates flashed before me. And you were sitting there, right in front of me while I was scrambling for an out, and…I just blurted the whole girlfriend-named-Megan thing. I—" Jack plowed his fingers into his hair and pressed the heel of his hand into his eyes. "I'm sorry. It was rash and stupid. I'll…call her back and tell her I'm coming alone."

"No."

The one word was so quiet he almost missed it as he berated himself for putting Megan on the spot. He raised his head from his hands. When he met her gaze, the soft glow in her eyes, the hesitant smile that tugged at her lush lips made his heart somersault. "What?"

"Don't call her back." Megan drew a slow deep breath and released it. "I'll go."

Jack sat straighter. "You will?"

She nodded, and her smile brightened. "I guess the third time's the charm."

He laughed. "Guess so." Sobering, he reached for Megan's hand, stroked her wrist with his thumb. "You're really okay with this. I don't want to impose."

"Yeah, I'm fine with it. It sounds like fun."

Another thought occurred to Jack, and he groaned. "I told her we were serious. Think you can pretend we're a happy couple to stave off any more of Abigail's matchmaking?"

He felt the flutter of her pulse beneath his fingers, and her free hand flew to her earring, fidgeting. "What are you proposing?"

"Nothing you're uncomfortable with. Just enough casual touching and pet names to make her believe we've been together for a while." He cocked his head. "You game?"

Megan studied the table for a few taut seconds, chewing her bottom lip. The nervous habit both plucked at him and made sensual heat lick his veins. If he played his cards right, maybe soon he'd get the chance to nibble that plump lip for himself and taste Megan's kiss.

She peeked up. Caught him staring.

Heat flashed in her eyes, and she nodded. "Yeah, I'm game."

Megan rode with Jack and Caitlyn to the animal shelter, relieved to find he'd had the foresight to bring a travel carrier for the cat they picked out. The trip home with an energetic German shepherd squeezed into the cab of his truck would be interesting enough without adding a loose cat to the mix.

She pointed out the upcoming turn to Jack and glanced in the back seat with a smile for Caitlyn. "Almost there."

Rather than the excitement she expected from the little girl, Caitlyn knitted her brow. "Miss Megan, how come you're not married?"

Jack sent Megan an apologetic grin then met his daughter's eyes in the rearview mirror. "Caity, that's a rude question."

"No, it's all right." Megan turned in her seat to face Caitlyn. "I almost got married once. But it turned out the man I was going to marry…" She hesitated, and Jack cut a side glance at her that clearly said he was waiting for her answer as well.

"Well, he just didn't love me enough to get through some bad stuff that happened. So we broke up." Determined not to let thoughts of Greg's desertion spoil her upbeat mood, she mustered another smile for Caitlyn as Jack parked. "Last one inside is a rotten egg!"

Caitlyn squealed her excitement as she jumped out of the truck after Jack and scampered toward the animal shelter door.

The attendant jangled a set of keys and led them to the kennel area. Megan's heart thudded an eager cadence as she waited for the man to bring Sam out. Caitlyn seemed edgy, her eyes wide and darting about, her thumb sneaking in to her mouth. She sidled closer to Jack's legs, and when the worker opened the door to the kennel area, the cacophony of barking dogs sent Caity scrambling to be picked up. "Daddy!"

"Easy, Caity," he said, hoisting her into his arms. "Those dogs can't get you."

The play of muscles under Jack's snug T-shirt distracted Megan from watching the paunchy guard stroll down the line of cages. Jack tucked a wisp of Caitlyn's hair behind her ear and whispered something soothing. Megan imagined the feel of Jack's warm breath caressing her own ear, and a delicious shiver scurried over her skin.

Her gaze lingered on the father and daughter as she ruminated on the plans she'd agreed to for next Saturday. Her heart pattered when she thought about pretending to be romantically involved with Jack.

Nothing you're uncomfortable with.

His promise was reassuring, and yet…

A sharp bark and the frantic scratch of dog claws on the concrete floor was her only warning before Sam bounded through the kennel door and leaped up on her. The force of her ninety-pound canine's greeting knocked Megan off balance. With a startled gasp, she landed with an unceremonious thud on her behind.

Jack chuckled as Megan struggled to right herself amid Sam's excited cavorting.

"Why are you laughing?" Caity asked, peeking up at her dad.

"Miss Megan's dog is real happy to see her. Look." He turned so Caitlyn could have a better view.

She smiled and wiggled to get down. "Sam!"

Jack let his daughter slide to the floor.

Sam's ears pricked up, and he tramped over to meet the little girl with a wildly wagging tail.

"Be careful with your hurt arm, sweetie," Megan said, grabbing for Sam's collar so that he couldn't knock Caitlyn down as well.

When Sam licked Caitlyn's face, she squealed her delight.

Jack strolled over to Megan and extended a hand to help her to her feet. "Looks like Sam's glad to bust this joint."

She grinned. "Looks like."

Jack curled his warm hand around hers and, with a powerful tug, hauled her to her feet...so fast she stumbled up against his wide chest. Megan steadied herself with a hand on his shoulder, while Jack splayed a hand at her waist, holding her close.

Rather than finding her equilibrium, Jack's touch, his proximity and his spicy scent made the room tilt. A dizzying rush of blood pounded in Megan's ears. For a few dazed moments, she didn't move, couldn't think. She tipped her head back to peer up at him, and his lips twitched into a grin.

"Got your sea legs now?"

She gave him a jerky nod.

But he didn't let go, didn't step back.

Jack's eyes darkened, and his gaze drifted to her mouth. When she nervously moistened her bottom lip, his pupils grew with desire. He slid his hand from her waist to her back, anchoring her in his arms.

Slowly he dipped his head. Closer. Closer.

Megan's breath snagged in her throat. Her lips tingled in anticipation. Waiting...

"Can we get my cat now?" Caitlyn chirped, wedging herself between them.

Jack jerked his head back and cleared his throat. "Sure, munchkin."

As Jack stepped away from her, the stark emptiness that washed over her in his absence rocked her, and a dull ache lodged in her chest. She blinked, mentally scrambling to compose herself.

Disappointment. That's what this ache was. She'd *wanted* Jack to kiss her. The realization spiraled through her with a stunning force.

As Jack let Caitlyn drag him toward the cat room, he looked back over his shoulder. His gaze was still hot, hungry, piercing. *Later,* he promised without saying a thing.

Heart knocking against her ribs, Megan watched Jack disappear as the door to the next room closed.

Maybe pretending she was romantically involved with Jack wouldn't be so difficult after all.

Chapter 8

Jack stood on Megan's front porch, images playing in his head of their near-kiss, and heat flashed through his veins. When Caitlyn had suggested visiting Megan so his daughter could deliver her gift, he hadn't needed much convincing. He had his own reason for wanting to talk to his neighbor. Although, if he were honest, he'd been looking for an excuse to see Megan for the past two days. For the past fifty or so hours, his captivating neighbor and the changing tenor of their relationship had frequently filled his mind. Distracting him from his work. Providing sensual material for his dreams. Keeping his body taut and humming with sexual energy.

When no one answered his knock, he tugged Caitlyn's braid: "Doesn't look like she's home, munchkin."

His daughter's crestfallen brown eyes peered up at him, matching the pinch of disappointment inside him. "Where is she?"

He shrugged. "Don't know."

Caitlyn poked out her lip. "When *will* she be home?"

Jack put a hand on Caitlyn's shoulder and steered her down the porch steps. "Again...I don't know."

His daughter dragged her feet, barely keeping up. But as they neared the sidewalk, Caitlyn broke ranks and race toward the street. "There they are!"

Just as he opened his mouth to shout a warning, Caitlyn staggered to a stop, gave the street a quick left-right-left look, then hurried across to meet Megan and Sam on their way in from a walk.

"Good girl," he said quietly as he too crossed the street to greet Megan.

She'd swept her hair up in a bouncy ponytail, leaving the graceful curve of her throat more visible. *More fodder for tonight's dreams.* His lips itched to trail kisses along the slim column of her neck and nuzzle the tender spot behind her ear. Ever since Saturday's unexpected moment, when he'd had her in his arms and been poleaxed by the urge to kiss her, thoughts of kissing Megan had taunted him.

When he factored in his discouragingly slow progress on his feature concerning the Gentleman Rapist case, the past couple days had been exceedingly frustrating.

While Caitlyn received a tail-wagging, dog-slobbery greeting from Sam, Jack focused on Megan.

The late afternoon sun made her hair shine like spun gold, and exercise had flushed her face a light pink. She gave him a bewitching, Mona Lisa-type smile and wiped perspiration from her forehead with the back of her hand. "We really have to stop meeting like this. You always catch me looking my worst."

He let his gaze wander lazily over her curves. "Darlin', if that is your worst, I'm not sure my heart will survive Saturday night when you're in form."

Mention of Saturday stole some of the color from her cheeks. Her smile faltered, though not for long. She marshaled herself and restored her grin. But that split second told him all he needed to know. She was anxious about their "date." Perhaps even having second thoughts. Her reluctance struck too close to home, and a knot lodged in his chest.

He hadn't read the warning signs with Lauren in time to save his marriage, but he'd be damned if he'd plunge headlong into something with Megan without knowing where he stood. Not even if every male fiber of him wanted nothing more than to pursue the sizzling connection he'd felt with her too briefly on Saturday.

He cleared his throat. "We are still on for this weekend, aren't we?"

She seemed startled by his question and tipped her head. "Why wouldn't we be?"

Jack's smile spread, and the cords of caution tangling him up inside loosened their hold. He shrugged. "No reason."

"Daddy, where's Sam's award?" Caitlyn asked, tugging on his arm.

"Right here, munchkin." Jack reached in his breast pocket and pulled out the small aluminum-foil medallion on a hair ribbon Caitlyn had fashioned for Sam.

"What's this?" Megan squatted beside her dog as Caitlyn, limited by her arm cast, struggled to slip the homemade medal over Sam's head.

"His hero award for savin' me. I made it myself."

Megan helped slide the ribbon over the dog's ears under the pretext of examining the award more carefully. "This is wonderful, Caitlyn. Sam is so happy to have your hero award."

Caity beamed, and fatherly pride puddled in Jack's gut.

"How's your kitty? Have you named her yet?" Megan asked.

"Uh-huh. I named her Ashley 'cause Ashley was my best friend when we were in Texas. Now my cat is my best friend, so her name is Ashley. 'Cept Ashley sleeps all the time, and Daddy says I shouldn't bother her when she's sleepin'." Megan's eyes and smile widened as Caitlyn jabbered on without stopping for breath. "Wanna see her? My new friend Hanna says black cats are bad luck, but Daddy said that's just stuper…soopish…su…" Caitlyn gave a dramatic sigh. "What's that word again, Daddy?"

"Superstition."

"Yeah, stuperdition."

Jack chuckled. "Close enough."

As she pushed to her feet, Megan caught her bottom lip with her teeth to cover her amusement, and that was all the provocation needed to draw Jack's eyes to her mouth. Another shot of desire slammed into him, along with nerve-stretching regret that he hadn't kissed her at the animal shelter when he'd had the chance.

Remembering his second purpose for seeking Megan out, Jack rubbed the muscles at the back of his neck. "I have another favor to ask."

Angling her head to meet his gaze, Megan arched a sculpted eyebrow. "Another favor? Dare I ask what?"

A light breeze stirred the muggy evening air, carrying to him a hint of the sweet scent he'd come to know as Megan's. The wisps of hair that had escaped her ponytail danced in the gentle wind and caressed her cheek.

He forcefully quashed the urge to touch her face himself.

"I have a meeting tomorrow, an interview I set up with the lawyers who are defending the guy they arrested in connection to the Gentleman Rapist case."

Was it his imagination or had Megan just tensed?

"I don't know if you're following that case or not, but right now, the cops think the man they've got is the copycat, not the original rapist. While they've got some pretty conclusive forensics and a few victim IDs to finger him in a couple of the cases, they've got nothing to tie him to the first few reported rapes."

Megan drew a deep breath and gave him a jerky nod. She dropped her gaze to Sam and stroked his fur. "That's what I hear. On the news, I mean. I— What does this have to do with the favor you need?"

"Well, the interview may run long. I may need someone to watch Caitlyn for a little while tomorrow afternoon." Jack scrubbed a hand down his face. He hated to impose on Megan but had run out of other options. "I know I've seen you home by four most days and thought maybe…"

She flashed him a quick grin then shifted her attention back to Sam. "Sure."

"The preschool van brings her home at about ten till four. Is that too early?"

"No problem. I'll be home by then." Megan gave Sam a final pat then lifted a puzzled gaze to Jack. "Doesn't Caitlyn's preschool have an after-hours program for the kids whose parents work?"

Jack nodded. "She's on the waiting list. Meantime, I have a lead on a high school girl who lives around the corner and might cover afternoons in the interim. But Lisa's got a dentist appointment tomorrow."

Megan glanced down the street. "Lisa Thibedeaux?"

"You know her?"

Her smile returned. "Yeah. Lisa's a good kid. Smart. Responsible."

"Good to hear. She's gonna keep Caity on Saturday. We thought we'd see how that goes before either of us commit to a regular gig."

A car pulled into his driveway, and a man bearing two flat boxes climbed out.

"Our pizza!" Caitlyn squealed and skipped down the sidewalk toward their house.

Megan motioned the direction his daughter had gone. "Well, I'll let you get to your dinner."

"Join us? We have plenty."

As Megan backed toward the street, she gave him a forced smile and shook her head. "Maybe another time. Tell Caitlyn thanks again for Sam's medal. That was sweet of her."

Jack watched Megan retreat, swamped again by the sense that Megan's refusal had more to do with some emotional barrier she'd erected than any conflict on her calendar. Yet she showed no such reservations around Caitlyn.

So was it him? Or was the distance she kept between them the legacy of the fiancé who hadn't loved her enough to see her through a rough time?

Remembering the shadows that had crossed Megan's face when she answered Caitlyn's tactless question Saturday, Jack gritted his teeth. He wanted five minutes alone with her bastard ex-fiancé for hurting and abandoning Megan.

Jamming his hands in his pockets, he strolled toward his house, where Caitlyn was introducing her new black cat to the pizza deliveryman.

Saturday couldn't get here fast enough. Maybe without Caitlyn in tow, he could get a better read on how his neighbor truly felt about him. He was sure he hadn't imagined the earlier sparks between them. Come Saturday, he'd have Megan to himself, and he intended to kindle that heat between them to full flame.

When Megan met Jack at her door Saturday night, he greeted her with a small bouquet of daisies and one of his knock-your-socks-off grins. His sexy smile started a slow burn in her belly, and the flowers melted her heart.

She gripped the edge of the door and took a deep breath. Jack had just arrived and already she was feeling overwhelmed by his roguish charm and sensual magnetism.

"Wow, you look beautiful." The approving gaze he swept over her jade-green sundress echoed his compliment and left her skin tingling.

"Thanks." She fidgeted with one pearl-stud earring, suddenly glad she'd taken a little extra time getting ready tonight.

"Ready to go?"

She took the flowers and sniffed their delicate scent. "Thank you for these, Jack. This was sweet, but…"

"You don't like daisies?"

"I love daisies. Really. I just…" She turned and poked the bouquet in a vase with another arrangement of cut flowers she had on her mantel. With her back to him, not looking in his liquid hazel eyes, it was easier to be honest. "I guess I'm just nervous about tonight. We said this wasn't a real date. I'm just *pretending* to be your girlfriend. I guess the flowers just make it feel, too…." *Real.*

When she hesitated, Jack filled the void. "Call them a thank you then. For coming to my rescue. Twice this week alone. You're a good neighbor, a good friend, and I appreciate that. Flowers are the least I can do."

"About tonight…" She glanced over her shoulder, frowning her worry. "I know this party is important to you, since the host is your boss and all."

"Mmm. Yeah, making a good impression outside the office couldn't hurt. But you have nothing to worry about."

She heard him move up behind her, but she still wasn't prepared for the warm touch of his hand on her bare shoulder. Her pulse scampered, and a low thrum started deep in her core.

"Just be yourself, and you'll enchant everyone there. Just like you've enchanted me."

He gently stroked her arm, and a dizzying rush of pleasure swept through her. She pivoted slowly to face him, trying to collect her thoughts, while his fingers provided a tantalizing distraction.

"What I mean is, we're supposed to pretend we're…seriously involved. Isn't that what you told your boss's wife? That implies a certain level of intimacy and we…" Her voice caught in her throat.

His eyes had darkened to a mossy brown, and heat flared in his gaze.

She cleared the tightness constricting her lungs and finished. "We've never even kissed. How are we supposed to convince everyone that—"

He shifted closer to her, and again her voice failed her.

"Well, maybe we should practice," he murmured, his voice low and seductive. "We should make sure we can pull this thing off."

Chapter 9

Jack's tender touch and the piercing intensity in his eyes sent tremors of anticipation racing through Megan. He grasped her elbow firmly and drew her body up against his, confirming for Megan his intention to kiss her. She fell into the depths of his hazel eyes, swimming in the desire she saw reflected in their warmth.

Holding her breath, she let him cup her chin and raise her mouth toward his. For the first time since her attack, she wanted, truly wanted, the intimacy this man offered. Could she block out the frightening memories long enough to share a kiss with this stunningly handsome man?

As he lowered his mouth toward hers, she didn't take time to ponder. She merely closed her eyes and savored the soft caress as he brushed his lips across hers.

Jack sucked in a sharp breath that mirrored her reaction to the shocking sensation that crackled through her. With feathery strokes, his thumb traced the curve of her throat, circled the fluttering pulse at the base of her neck and skimmed back up to nudge her chin higher, deepening the kiss. He angled his head to draw more fully on her mouth, and the sweet suction left her senses reeling.

Megan raised her hands to his shoulders to steady herself, uncertain how much longer her legs would support her. No kiss had ever affected her quite so powerfully. She'd been unprepared for the way her knees wobbled as if they'd melted from the flames licking her veins. If the kiss had melted anything in his body, she certainly couldn't tell. Every inch of him she pressed against told her how firmly muscled he was, how solid all over. He peered down at her with heavy-lidded eyes but kept her body anchored securely against his.

"I don't know," he said, his voice a husky growl. "I think we might pull this evening off. I know I'm going to find it difficult to keep my hands off you."

His hold on her tightened, and he dipped his head to kiss her again. He didn't linger this time. Instead, he pulled away, heaved a deep sigh, and dragged a hand through his hair. "Geez, we'd better get going before I change my mind about this party and haul you back to your bedroom to have my way with you."

A sudden frisson of cold tripped up her spine. She knew he didn't mean the comment the way it sounded. The teasing light in his eyes said he was joking.

But Megan couldn't laugh. In a blinding flash of reality, the seductive haze that had wrapped around her was swept away. She shivered and struggled to push images from five years ago back into the closets in her mind. Out of sight. Locked away.

"Megan?" Jack's puzzled expression told her she hadn't masked her reaction to his comment well enough.

She drew a slow breath for calm and rallied herself. "I...I just need to get my purse, and I'll be ready to go."

Flashing a wobbly smile, she hurried back to her bedroom for her purse.

Jack's concerned gaze followed her from the room and unnerved her further. She didn't need to pique his journalistic instincts and curiosity with her mood swings and odd behavior.

Before she left the house, she let Sam in from the backyard. She sank her fingers in the warmth of his thick coat and hugged his neck, stealing a little reassurance from her furry guardian before rejoining Jack. "Watch the house, boy."

Sam gave his tail a quick swish as if to say, *Roger that.*

On the drive to Burt Harwood's house, Megan kept the conversation as light as possible. Her class trip to the zoo. The continuing heat wave. The crayon drawing Caitlyn had brought over to her house earlier that day.

Jack parked in front of a well-lit, two-story red brick mansion then rounded the truck to open her door. He escorted her inside with his hand resting lightly at the small of her back. She couldn't be sure if the possessive gesture was for show or not, but the heat of his hand gave her a sense of comfort and security that she liked. Probably too much.

Ginny already accused her of relying on emotional crutches to give her a feeling of security. Sam. Her handgun. Even her lonely and predictable routine. She didn't need to let Jack become another crutch. It would be too easy to depend on him for the strength and protection he represented.

Your security has to come from within, Ginny had said until Megan could recite it in her sleep.

A barrel-chested man with a hearty laugh and twinkling blue eyes answered Jack's knock. "Jack! Et tu, Brutus? How long have you known my wife was cooking up this soiree?"

"Evenin', Burt. Happy birthday, old man." Jack pumped

their host's hand and nudged Megan forward. "This is Megan Hoffman. Megan, my boss Burt Harwood."

"Hey, hey! Jack, you've been holding out on us." Burt pushed Jack aside and flirtatiously took Megan's hand for a kiss. "You didn't tell me you were dating such a beautiful young lady. Megan, welcome. Can I fix you a drink?"

Abigail Harwood, a vivacious redhead who could have passed for half her age, joined them in the spacious foyer and was included in the next round of introductions. Megan immediately felt at home thanks to the gracious charm of their hosts.

As the parade of faces and lengthy introductions continued, Megan struggled to assimilate the new names. She'd developed a system for remembering the names of her students at the start of each school year and relied on the same method of association to keep the other party guests straight. David Rawlins wore the red shirt. *R* for Rawlins. *R* for red.

The sports reporter, Tim, was kind enough to wear a tie with a football team logo. His wife Betsy looked like she could well have been a cheerleader on the sidelines of the sporting events Tim covered.

Associations came easily until they reached Burt's brother and his wife. Frank and Patrice.

While she smiled and shook each of their hands, she scrounged in her brain for some tag to remember them. Patrice reminded her of a timid mouse, while her husband was as big as two men. Before moving to Texas several years ago, Frank had lived in Lagniappe, operating a home security systems installation business. Yet nothing about the man made Megan feel safe. Frank was slimmer than his brother, but he towered over his petite wife and had the shoulders and chest of a linebacker. His military-short haircut and piercing, gunmetal grey eyes called images of a battle-ready warrior to mind.

And his face seemed disturbingly familiar. Megan's pulse plucked an uneasy staccato rhythm.

When Frank shook Megan's hand, his welcoming smile faltered slightly. "Have we met?"

His question caught her off guard, and she cast a quick, uneasy glance toward Jack. What if this man knew her from before her attack, remembered her from the days she went by Sara? She thought of the TV report from five years ago when her name got leaked to the public, and jitters did a dance in her stomach. "I…don't think so."

Yet she couldn't shake the sense that she *should* know him. Something about him sent tremors skittering through her.

"I suppose you're right. I'd remember a face as pretty as yours." Frank gave her a wink, while Patrice frowned and drifted away toward the kitchen without another word.

Jack wrapped an arm around her waist and pulled her closer. "I see flirting runs in the family. Well, give it up, Frank. The lady only has eyes for me. Right, honey?"

Putting on a brave face, she patted Jack's cheek. "Just keep telling yourself that, darling."

Her jibe won a roar of laughter from the crowd. Frank Harwood was among the loudest. The braying, nasal-like quality of his laugh sent a prickly sensation down her spine, much like the sound of fingernails on a blackboard.

She knew that hideous laugh. But why?

"Smart aleck." Jack flashed a grin that gave no warning before he stole a kiss, stole her breath. Disengaging herself from Jack's arm, she escaped into the kitchen to offer Abigail help with preparing the food.

"Why that's mighty sweet of you. Tell you what, grab the oyster dip out of the fridge and follow me in here to the table with it." With that, Abigail exited to join Patrice in the dining room, leaving a cloud of exotic-smelling perfume in her wake.

Megan stood in the silence of the kitchen for a moment to catch her breath, before she turned to open the fridge and hunt for the dip. The shelves were packed with party food, but Megan saw nothing resembling a bowl of dip. Scowling, she shoved a few platters of fruit and shaped sandwiches around, determined not to let her hostess down on such a simple task.

"Can I help you find something, Megan?" Frank Harwood asked from right behind her. His low-pitched voice sent her pulse skyrocketing again.

She turned with a gasp, only to come up short when she encountered the man's massive chest trapping her in the corner of the refrigerator and its door. He reached around Megan to pluck an olive off a relish tray, intentionally brushing up against her.

"I...uh, Abigail wanted the oyster dip for the table."

Why did this man's size and piercing silver eyes fluster her so, when Jack's broad shoulders and height made her feel safe? She'd insisted to Ginny numerous times that she wasn't afraid of men, and she'd have sworn it was true. Her principal didn't scare her, nor did the postman. She met her students' fathers at PTA meetings without batting an eye.

But none of those men cornered her in the chilly blast of a refrigerator and gave her leering looks.

"Excuse me," Megan rasped as she tried to squeeze past the behemoth of a man.

Frank lowered his arm to hip level and braced his hand so that she couldn't pass. "Going somewhere, Megan?"

He kept her cornered like a cat playing with a mouse and gave a low chuckle at her expense. Though quieter than before, the chuckle had the same nasal sound.

The shiver that raced through her had nothing to do with the cold air pouring from the fridge.

"I should...tell Abigail I can't find the dip."

"Maybe we should look together?" He stepped closer and glanced briefly to the shelves behind her before pinning her again with his steely eyes. "Are you sure we've never met?"

She shook her head, growing increasingly panicked by his odd behavior.

He reached for her shoulder and rubbed the bare skin along the base of her throat, much the way Jack had earlier that evening. But Jack's touch hadn't sent the taste of bile to her throat.

"Don't." She shrugged away from his hand, and he smirked. He seemed to enjoy her distress.

That thought brought a whimper to her throat.

He chuckled again and ran a finger under the stringlike shoulder strap of her dress. "Do I frighten you, Megan? Hmm? Don't be scared. I'm a pussycat. Really."

The clatter of high heels on the tiled kitchen floor jolted her from the rumble of her captor's murmured taunts.

"Frank? Is there a problem?" Abigail's voice sounded sharp and tense.

Of course, with Megan's every nerve drawn taut, even the sound of her heartbeat thudding in her ears sounded harsh.

"No problem. Just helping Megan find the oyster dip you seem to have hidden." The affable tone he used with his sister-in-law grated almost as much as his untoward advances. He stepped out of the way and waved a hand toward Abigail. "Maybe you can show us where it is? I told Megan how delicious your oyster dip is. I hope you can find it."

He smiled smoothly and sauntered out of the kitchen, snagging a beer from the cooler at the foot of the counter as he left.

Megan shuddered and rubbed the goose bumps on her arms.

"Gracious, love. I didn't mean for you to catch a cold looking for the dip!" Abigail grinned and nudged her out of the way. "Now, where…? Oh! Of course. Silly me. I put it in the spare fridge in the garage. I'll get it." Her heels clattered across the floor again, and she motioned to the wine and beer at the end of the counter. "Help yourself to a drink. I'll be right back."

Megan stood in the middle of the kitchen debating her options. Rejoin the party where Frank had gone, or stay in the kitchen where he could trap her alone again? Calling herself a coward, she decided to stick as close as possible to Jack throughout the night. With him, she hoped, she'd be safe from any more of Frank's unwelcome advances. The idea of depending on Jack to shield her from Frank left an achy, hollow feeling in her soul. She was already falling into the trap she'd sworn not to.

Why hadn't she stood up for herself when Frank cornered her? She'd learned self-defense since her attack, and Frank had certainly deserved a knee in the crotch.

But she'd frozen, backed down. *Pitiful.*

You have a long way to go before you can call yourself self-reliant again. Spirits sagging, Megan found Jack and hovered at his side.

For the remainder of the evening, she made a point of steering Jack away from Frank, though she felt the large man's presence even when he was in another room. Frank's unusual laugh drifted in to disrupt her conversation with the other guests. At dinner, she hung back until she saw where Frank sat, so she could take a seat at the opposite end of the table. But the weight of his gaze haunted her through the meal, robbing her of any appetite.

Later, while the rest of the ladies congregated in the family room to swap stories and play cards, she stayed at Jack's side, savoring the safety of his arm around her shoulders. Though his nearness helped her survive the nerve-racking night, she began to wonder if she didn't have other motives for staying so close to him.

The warmth of his body near hers and the light in his eyes when he looked at her stirred a peculiar warmth inside her. She listened to him talk politics and sports, laugh at jokes and make a few of his own. She gained a new perspective of the man she knew primarily as a harried but loving father.

More than once he smiled at her, and her attention shifted to his mouth. His lips. Memories of his tender kiss earlier that evening stormed her senses, making her body thrum with longings she thought she'd never feel again for a man.

With one kiss, Jack had turned her world upside down. This glimpse of his many facets left her wondering what else she might miss if she didn't take the opportunity to get to know him better. When he'd asked her for a date—a real, let's-see-if-we-want-a-relationship date—she'd thought getting involved with him would be a mistake. But now she wondered if the real mistake had been in passing up the chance to make Jack a part of her life.

If we start dating while he's reporting on the Gentleman Rapist, and he finds out that I was one of the women attacked...

So tell him about your rape before he finds out some other way.

"Isn't that right, Megan?" Jack's question yanked her thoughts from her debate with Ginny concerning Jack.

"Um, I'm sorry. My mind was wandering. What was the question?"

"Are we boring you, sweetheart?" Jack squeezed her hand, and the sensation of warm honey flowed through her veins.

"No, I just..." *Was thinking how much I wanted to kiss you again.* Her heart thudded loud enough that she was sure Jack would hear it.

He checked his watch and raised an eyebrow. "Wow. It's late. I told my babysitter we'd be home an hour ago. Megan, are you 'bout ready to go?"

"Here's a better idea," Burt said with a mischievous grin. "You go on home and leave Megan here with us." Jack's boss winked playfully, reminding her how his brother had trapped her by the fridge earlier. Had she just overreacted to harmless flirting, characteristic of the family?

Jack laughed off his editor's comment, but he slid his hand to her waist and hugged her closer in a clearly territorial gesture.

Jack's woman. How sweet would it be to truly belong in this man's arms?

Burt and Abigail showed them to the door, and Megan looked around the coatrack for her purse.

"I moved your pocketbook to my bedroom," Abigail volunteered, seeming to read her mind. "I'll run and get it."

Frank joined them in the foyer as his sister-in-law ran up the stairs toward the master suite.

Megan saw his gunmetal gaze zero in on her, even though he spoke to his brother.

"Burt, you have a call from the office. Phone's off the hook in the kitchen. Some big pileup on the interstate involving a chemical spill."

Burt nodded and said his goodbyes. "Duty calls."

"Guess that means traffic will be bad. We'd better go through town to avoid the tie-up," Jack said.

Megan sidled a bit closer to her date, doing her best to avoid Frank's heavy stare.

"But first, I'm going to make a pit stop." Jack turned up a palm inviting Frank to direct him to the closest bathroom.

"First door to the right at the head of the stairs."

Megan's pulse jumped as she realized Jack was going to

leave her alone with Frank and his leering gaze, his suggestive smirks and hideous laugh.

"I'll be right back," Jack promised, kissing her forehead when he pulled away.

She tried to swallow the nervous tightness in her throat, but her mouth had grown arid. It was silly to get so uptight over being alone with Frank for a few seconds until Abigail or Jack returned. Her gaze shifted from Jack's retreating back to the floor. To the beveled mirror by the door. The Oriental vase that doubled as an umbrella stand. Anywhere but Frank's unrelenting silver eyes. She sighed and shifted restlessly.

The nasal rasp of his laugh slithered through the dearth of conversation and coiled around her lungs, squeezing the breath from her.

"You don't like me. Do you, Megan? You've avoided me all night."

Her gaze darted up to his. Had she been that obvious? For a moment she worried what Frank would say to Burt. Would her rudeness to Frank affect Jack's position with Burt and his job at the paper? She'd wanted to help him impress his boss, give Jack the edge he so clearly wanted.

Though her every muscle was strung tight with tension, she forced a smile that felt as if it could crack her face. "Don't be silly. Wh-why would you say that?"

"Don't feel bad, Megan. You're not the first woman to take my teasing the wrong way. I'm actually perfectly harmless."

He'd said almost the same thing before Abigail had returned to the kitchen and rescued her from the refrigerator disaster.

Don't be scared. I'm a pussycat. Really.

Yet the more he assured her he was no threat, the more frightening he seemed.

I won't hurt you, if you cooperate, a voice from five years earlier taunted in her memory.

"Here you go, hon. Love this purse by the way. Where did you get it?" Abigail's voice called Megan's gaze to the stairs. Relief swept through her.

"I…don't remember. I've had it for years." Megan hugged her purse to her chest and flashed a grateful smile to Abigail.

Frank shoved his hands in his pockets and glared at Abigail. She returned a cool stare to her brother-in-law.

Odd.

Burt's brother faced Megan again and extended a hand toward her. "Well, then I guess this is good night."

Not wanting to so blatantly appear rude by rebuffing his handshake, Megan reluctantly offered her hand.

Then froze.

The cuff of Frank's dress shirt rode up on his arm, several inches above his wrist. Partially exposed on his forearm was the jagged design of a lightning bolt tattoo.

Images swam before her. Dark leering eyes. Linebacker shoulders. A policeman's uniform.

Megan's every nerve screamed. The earth seemed to tilt. Her legs buckled.

"Megan?" She heard Jack's voice. Turned toward it.

"It's him!" she rasped before she fainted in Jack's arms.

Chapter 10

Jack hovered beside the bed in the Harwoods' guest room, where he'd carried Megan when she wilted in his arms.

Ronald Grigsby, a guest at the party who was a local internist, checked Megan's vital signs with a frown puckering his brow. "Everything looks good but… Are you sure you won't go into the E.R., just for a check?"

Stubborn to the end, Megan shook her head. "I'm fine. Really. I just want to go home."

She turned toward Jack, and her pleading eyes turned him inside out.

"Are your legs steady now?" Jack asked. "I can carry you down to—"

Before he could finish his sentence, she swung her legs off the bed and lunged to her feet. She wobbled a bit, and he hurried to shove a shoulder under her arm and brace a hand on her waist. Her fingers fisted in his knit shirt for a moment then relaxed as she steadied herself.

"I can walk. I'm fine. Let's just go, please."

She still seemed desperately pale to him, but the urgency behind her insistence to leave the party tugged at him.

"All right. But I'm taking you to my house. I don't think you should be alone tonight." When she grunted and opened her mouth to protest, he laid a finger across her lips to silence her. "My house or the E.R. Those are your choices."

She scowled at him, her eyes flaring with discontent. The gentle caress of her breath on his hand reminded him he'd yet to remove his hand from her lips.

Her soft, full lips. Lips slightly pursed in frustration. Lips he'd kissed earlier that night and thought of nonstop ever since.

Was it safe to take her back to his house? The temptation to carry her straight to his bed was almost overwhelming.

But the same vulnerability he'd witnessed in Caitlyn's hospital room clouded her eyes again. Along with shock. Sadness. Fright.

The need to protect and take care of her clawed at him with a fierceness that stole his breath.

Grabbing his wrist, she pulled his hand away from her mouth. "I won't be alone at my house. I have Sam."

"Sam can't call 911 if you pass out on the way to the bathroom in the middle of the night."

She scooped her purse off the bed. "Why are you being so obstinate?"

"I'm obstinate?" He chuckled and playfully swiped at her chin with his knuckles. "Look who's talkin'."

Megan released a shuddering sigh. "Can we debate this in the car? I'm ready to go."

"Oh, I see a wedding in the future," Abigail cooed from

the doorway where she hovered like a mother hen. "You're already fussing at each other like old married folk!"

Jack exchanged a startled look with Megan. *Marry Megan?* The idea kick-started a low hum at his core. Yesterday he'd have denied ever considering another marriage. But that was before the kiss he'd shared with Megan tonight, the possessiveness he'd felt when other men at the party flirted with her, and the simple pleasure he'd known having her at his side as they chatted with the other guests. At the moment, the idea of marrying Megan didn't sound half bad to him.

But Abigail's comment had caused Megan to blanch a shade whiter. Apparently marrying him didn't hold the same appeal for his date. The hum deep inside him shifted to a dull ache. A hollowness.

Megan didn't want him. He had to get that through his thick head, or he was on course for another heartache.

Thanking the Harwoods profusely for their hospitality and for their concern and assistance when Megan fainted, Jack and Megan made their way to his truck.

As they drove back into town, Megan leaned her head back and closed her eyes. Jack regarded her weary profile while a host of questions spun through his reporter's mind. "What did you mean when you said 'It's him' right before you fainted?"

She angled toward him, her eyes dark and wide in the dimly lit car. "You…must have misunderstood me. I don't know what you mean."

But the bright-eyed, terrified expression she wore said otherwise.

Jack shook his head. "Maybe you don't remember, but I distinctly heard you say 'It's him'."

Turning away, Megan sighed, a broken, fluttery exhale that arrowed through his heart.

The furrow in her brow and her telltale fidgeting with her earring told him she knew exactly what he meant. Yet she didn't answer him, didn't share anything else she knew with him.

Just one more flashing neon sign that she wasn't interested in getting involved with him. No, sir, no shared confidences here.

Whatever he'd experienced in their kiss and however right having Megan at his side tonight had felt for him, it had clearly been one-sided. She was intentionally keeping him at bay, maintaining a distance. In light of her warmth and receptiveness earlier that evening, her turnabout both puzzled him and chafed the raw wounds Lauren had left with her desertion.

Jack clenched his teeth and stared at the road.

When they got back to his house, they peeked into Caitlyn's room together, just like he'd always imagined he and Lauren would. Megan's desire to assure herself his daughter was sleeping safely in her bed strengthened the picture he was forming of a selfless and caring woman.

Ashley, Caitlyn's new cat, slept curled beside his daughter, and when Jack leaned down to kiss Caity's forehead, the cat peeked up and meowed.

He scratched the cat behind the ear. "Yeah, 'night to you, too."

He recalled Megan's cuddling-in-bed argument in favor of a cat over a goldfish, and he chuckled when Megan gave him a side glance that said *I told you so.*

Jack eased out of the bedroom to pay the babysitter and see Lisa out to her car, while Megan lingered in Caitlyn's room, a tender expression on her face as she watched his daughter sleep.

When he stopped to lock the front door on his way back inside, Megan met him in the foyer. "Thank you."

He arched an eyebrow. "For what?"

"For…being there when I needed you this evening." She ducked her head and wrinkled her brow. Her hands stirred at her sides, restless and trembling. "I really don't want to be alone tonight."

Jack stepped closer and lifted her chin with his thumb. He splayed his fingers across her cheek and searched her eyes. "What happened? Why did you pass out like that? And why won't you talk to me about it?"

She backed away from his touch, a gesture that left a cold twist in his gut. "It was nothing. I just didn't eat enough at dinner, I guess, and…my blood sugar must have dropped."

"Hmm, maybe."

She was right about dinner. She'd eaten like a bird, but he'd dismissed her lack of appetite as nerves or a dislike of roasted pork. Now he had to wonder…

"Despite the inauspicious ending, I hope you at least had a little fun tonight. I appreciate your going with me."

She flashed a polite smile that didn't reach her eyes and gave a stiff nod. "It was fun."

"You lie."

His bluntness wiped the forced civility from her face. She blinked at him in stunned silence.

He curled up a corner of his mouth. "Admit it. You were bored stiff by all our shoptalk and rambling about football."

For a minute he thought she was going to deny it, keep the distancing politeness and dishonesty between them. But after a moment of wavering, she eked out a small smile and nodded. "A little bored, yeah."

"You were a good sport, though. Thanks." He reached for her arm and stroked his hand from her shoulder to her wrist. When she trembled, he grasped her hand to pull her closer. A hug was all he intended. Just a comforting embrace to thank her for her patience at the party.

But once she was in his arms, he didn't want to let go. For a moment, she remained stiff and tense. Finally, with a weary sigh, she sagged against him, circling his waist with her arms and clinging tightly. He tucked her under his chin, held her firmly against his chest, felt the shudder that raced through her.

His own body sang with a desire to remove the barriers between them. He ached to peel away not only their clothes, but also her reservations and his old hurts so they could face each other heart-to-heart.

He kissed the top of her head, inhaling the peach orchard scent of her, and she tipped her face up to his. The damnable vulnerability still shadowed her eyes, but he saw need there, too. Longing. Passion.

He couldn't have stopped himself from kissing her if he'd wanted. But he didn't want to stop. He wanted to drink her in, fill himself with her sweetness. He wanted to chase away her doubts and crumble the walls she kept between them.

Her kiss was tender and hesitant at first. Exploring, much as it had been earlier tonight. As desire flamed inside Jack, he swept his tongue along the seam of her lips, gaining access to her mouth. He teased her tongue gently, coaxing her to duel with him. He moaned in bliss as he sampled the velvety texture of her, reveled in the crush of her softness against his body. Taut and vibrating with growing arousal, he pulled her closer, anchoring her hips against his with one arm.

But a little bit of Megan wasn't nearly enough. He became greedy, wanting both hands free to plunder her silky hair, stroke her breasts, indulge in the curve of her bottom. He shuffled a few steps until he'd pinned her against the wall. His hands moved restlessly over her, exploring, savoring.

His body, his soul begged for more. *More!*

She wiggled and writhed, her breathing as ragged as his

own. The friction of her hips and scrambling hands inflamed him. She whimpered, and he sealed his lips more tightly against hers, swallowing her provocative gasp.

Fire crackled and snapped in his blood, and her enthusiasm fueled his own eagerness to be buried inside her, to lose himself in the promised nirvana of her body gripping him.

The bite of her fingernails in his back shocked him, gave him pause. He hadn't imagined Megan would be the sort to mix pain with pleasure, but he'd endure the discomfort for now. He drew the line at inflicting pain on her though. No way could he enjoy, even tolerate, hurting Megan for any reason.

When she bit down on his lip, lightning flashed through his jaw, and he jerked his head back, tasting blood.

"Ow! What'd you do that for?" His tone was sharper than intended, tinged with frustration and thwarted passion.

"No," she gasped. A wild panic filled her eyes. Shoving against his chest, she raised her knee toward his groin.

Thankfully he saw the move coming in time to spare his family jewels a direct hit. "Geez, Megan! What's wrong?"

"Let go of me!" she cried as she tore free of his grasp. She staggered several steps away before she wrapped arms around her chest and heaved a broken sob.

Jack dabbed at his swollen and bleeding lip. He struggled to clear his lust-muddled mind enough to figure out where he'd gone wrong. She'd been fine, returning his kiss, opening to him and leaning into his embrace one minute and then…

"I'm…g-going home now." She pivoted toward the living room and hurried to the couch for her purse, her breathing still an uneven rasp that shredded his soul. When she faced him, her dubious expression said. *I'm coming past you now. Don't try to touch me.*

Did she really think he'd been trying to hurt her? The possibility galled him, slashed through him with a razorlike pain.

"Wait, Megan, talk to me!"

She stormed past him, her movements jerky and tense.

"Tell me what just happened. What did I do wrong?"

"It's me. I'm sorry...but I can't—" Her voice warbled, and the poignant sound shattered his heart as well.

"Was I going too fast? Pushing too hard?" He pursued her out the front door and down his sidewalk. "Please, Megan, tell me what frightened you!"

Had he misinterpreted her interest? Her desire? He'd been so sure he'd seen an equal hunger blazing in her eyes.

But he'd thought he knew Lauren before she walked out, too. He'd been wrong.

Megan didn't so much as look back at him until she reached the street. "I...I thought I was ready. But I'm not. I'm sorry, Jack."

The remorse weighting her voice ripped a wide swath through him. She was *sorry?* What did he do with *sorry?* Even Lauren had said she was sorry—as she walked out on their marriage, abandoning him and Caitlyn.

Confusion and frustration tangled around the agony of desertion and betrayal Lauren had gouged in his soul, the guilt he felt over unintentionally hurting Megan tonight.

Jack slammed his palm against the door frame and growled an obscenity. He'd let himself fall for Megan, despite the warning signs, despite the walls she put between them. So what did he do with the emotions and passions Megan had awakened in him tonight?

And why had fate led him to another fickle female, another woman who didn't know what she wanted?

Hell, even Lisa, the babysitter, had told him tonight that she couldn't commit to watching Caitlyn every afternoon, didn't want to be tied down by the daily obligation.

Jack gritted his teeth and huffed a sigh. He'd had his fill, was choking on women's excuses and cop-outs and changed minds. His heart had been broken one time too many, his life torn apart and—

"Daddy?"

Caitlyn's sleepy voice slammed into him like a fist. He sucked in a slow breath, shook the tension and frustration from his hands. Jack faced her with what he hoped was a convincing smile. "Hey, munchkin. What are you doing out of bed?"

"I heard a loud noise, and I got scared."

Great. Now he'd frightened his daughter, too. "It's okay, baby. Nothing's wrong."

"I'm not a baby."

"Hmm?"

"You called me a baby again. I'm *not*."

Because he didn't know what else to do, he dropped to his knees and pulled Caitlyn into a bear hug. He squeezed her to his chest and rocked. Rocked and prayed.

God help him. What was he doing?

His daughter was everything to him. Forget his own wounds and feelings of betrayal. How could he justify putting Caity's heart on the line, risk hurting her on the off chance Megan decided he was what she wanted?

No matter what promise he'd sensed in their kiss earlier that night or the hope he'd nurtured for a relationship with Megan, he just didn't have room for error in his life. Or room for a woman who couldn't commit.

He had to protect his daughter, had to put Caity first.

For now that meant untangling Megan from their lives.

"Wow, sounds like you had a busy night." Ginny tucked her feet beneath her on Megan's love seat and smoothed a flyaway wisp of white-blond hair behind her ear.

Megan paced to her living room window and paused a moment to look through the blinds at Jack's house. She chewed her bottom lip, remembering the heat of Jack's kiss…and her panic when he'd pressed her against the wall, his body confining hers.

"What do I do, Gin?"

"About what? Your suspicions of Frank Harwood? Or… the feelings you've developed for Jack?" She paused, the silent moment full of significance. "Those are both pretty big issues. Which do you want to deal with first?"

Turning from the window, Megan crossed the floor again and rubbed her arms. "I don't know. You're supposed to help me make sense of all this. You tell me what to do."

"Ah, shifting responsibility to me?"

Megan scowled at Ginny then buried her face in her hands. "I don't want to deal with any of it! I want to leave town."

"Mmm-hmm, running from your problems."

She growled at Ginny. "Are you gonna help me figure this out?"

Sam followed her as she paced back to the window and glanced outside again. When he whined, she knelt beside her furry friend and hugged his neck.

Ginny swung her feet to the floor and stretched. They'd been up all night following Megan's late-night call for help, and fatigue showed on Ginny's face. Along with infinite patience.

Once again, Ginny had proven a rock in the middle of Megan's latest storm.

"You know exactly what you need to do. About Jack. About Frank Harwood. About everything. But you're holding back." Ginny's voice held no censure, only loving support.

Megan pushed her nose deeper into Sam's thick coat. Sam was warm and comforting, but he was nothing like the heat and solace she'd known all too briefly wrapped in Jack's embrace.

Before she'd freaked. Before she'd blown everything by panicking. But on the heels of confronting the man she believed was her rapist, Jack's tight hold and aggressive kiss had been too much. Too soon.

"Why are you afraid to do what you know you have to do?" Ginny pressed.

Afraid. Megan cringed at the word. For too long, fear and uncertainty had imprisoned her more securely than the handcuffs her rapist had used to fetter her to her old brass headboard. *Old*, as in she'd gotten rid of the headboard right after her attack.

Now she had a sleigh bed—a beautiful antique piece made from a solid slab of varnished walnut. No beams, bars or holes where anyone could tie or bind her down again. But lovely as it was, her new bed frame was a testament to the extremes she'd gone to since her attack. The changes she made in her life. Because of fear. Because of *him*.

She'd changed jobs, left graduate school, moved to a new house. And she'd let Greg walk away without a fight. She'd left behind everything that had been a part of her life at the time of the rape. As if she could escape the memories of her attack, outrun the fear and anger and heartache.

But through her fear, the rapist still held her captive. If she needed any more evidence, her drastic reaction to Jack's sexual overtures proved that. And she was tired, so tired of running. Being with Jack had shown her that, too. She wanted all the things she'd been denying herself. A real home, with a husband and children and a black cat, who'd curl up on the bed at night.

"Megan?" Ginny tilted her head, her gaze full of compassion. "You know what you need to do about Harwood. It's a no-brainer."

Megan rubbed her dry, weary eyes with the heels of her

hands. Ginny was right. As always. The time had come to stop running away. By putting a name to the face that had haunted her for years, she now had a chance to take a stand and put an end to the years of fear and uncertainty. Anger stirred in her gut as she thought about all she'd lost, all the pain she'd endured because of Frank Harwood.

Pushing to her feet, she curled her hands into fists and raised her chin. "I need to call the police. Tell them what I remembered, what I suspect. That I think Frank Harwood is the man that raped me."

Ginny's pale eyebrows knitted in a deep frown. "It'll be hard, honey. You need to prepare yourself. There'll be lots of questions, lots of media attention, lots of yucky stuff from the past dragged up and reexamined."

Megan wrapped her arms around her middle, willing herself to stop trembling. She'd done nothing but shake since she'd seen that glimpse of Frank's tattoo and made the devastating connection. "I know. But…he raped me. He has to be brought in so he can't hurt anyone else."

Ginny smiled her encouragement. "That's my girl. Now… what are you going to do about Jack?"

Megan rolled her eyes and flopped down on the sofa to stare at the ceiling. She was so tired. "Isn't one monumental decision per day enough? Do I have to think about how I screwed up with Jack, too? How confused I am about him?"

"No. You don't *have* to. But sounds to me like you left an awful lot unresolved with him." Ginny got up and strolled into the kitchen for another cup of coffee. "What would you like to see happen? Best-case scenario."

"I want another chance. I blew it tonight. I just don't know how to explain to him what happened." Megan snagged a pillow from the sofa and hugged it to her chest. "How do I make him understand?"

"Here's a novel approach…*tell him the truth!*" Ginny raised the coffeepot and swished the contents. "There's one cup left. Want it?"

"No. And no." Megan rolled up to sit cross-legged, and Sam scrunched over to put his chin in her lap. She idly scratched his ears, bracing for Ginny's arguments.

"He's bound to find out eventually. If you two become serious, you owe it to him to tell the truth. Would you rather he find out through his investigation of the story? How do you think *that* will make him feel?"

Megan rubbed her temple. Her head hadn't stopped pounding for the past six hours. So much had happened. So much had changed. So much was about to change.

She had a duty to turn Frank in, despite what it would do to her privacy, her quiet life.

And she had an opportunity to give Jack the exclusive of his life.

But what would Jack think of her once he knew the truth? Would he turn and run the way Greg had?

"Ginny, Frank Harwood is the brother of Jack's boss."

"Mmm-hmm. And?"

"What is it going to do to Jack's career if his boss finds out I'm the one who turned in his brother? And how is Jack supposed to report a story that exposes a member of his boss's family as a criminal?"

"You're sure Frank Harwood is the one?"

How many times had she been over this in her mind? A hundred? A million?

"Well, there are discrepancies in his appearance. Frank's eyes were silver, not dark brown. But he could have worn colored contacts." Megan rubbed the chill on her arms.

"And you said your attacker didn't have much hair, that he was balding." Ginny tipped her head.

"With a razor, Frank could easily have gotten rid of his military haircut."

Ginny nodded. "True. Appearance is easily changed."

"Burt said his brother owned a home security system business when he lived here in Lagniappe. He wasn't a cop. So where did he get the uniform, the badge?"

Ginny shrugged and waved a hand. "Anywhere. Where'd the stripper the teachers from your school hired for your birthday get his uniform? The ones you can rent from a costume shop look pretty realistic. Or he borrowed it or stole it or ordered it off the Internet."

Megan nodded. "Yeah, you're right." She sucked in a deep breath and closed her eyes. "Everything else fits what I remember. His formidable size, his eerie laugh. His predatory stare and subtle intimidation. The tattoo."

Her instincts had told her all night he was the one, but she hadn't recognized him with certainty until she'd glimpsed the tattoo on his forearm. Only then had the floodgate to her past opened and the pieces clicked.

Megan drew another shaky breath. "I'm sure. He's the one."

"Then the chips are gonna fall regardless. It's your job to see this guy gets turned in. It's Jack's job to report it. The family connection to Jack's boss is not your fault. So don't you dare feel guilty about it. Not for one minute. You hear me?" Ginny squatted in front of her. "Ready to head down to the police station with me?"

Megan grimaced as she looked at her counselor, her advocate and friend. "Any chance we can protect my identity…at least until I can talk to Jack?"

Ginny offered her a hand up from the couch. "I'll do my damnedest."

Chapter 11

Jack glowered at his pancakes late Sunday morning and tried not to think about Megan's abrupt departure the night before. He'd spent most of the night tossing and turning, his body aching for her and his mind tumbling with recriminations and warnings. His fervent hope that the morning would bring relief and clarity to the situation hadn't been fulfilled. His head still throbbed with fatigue and confusion, his blood still sang with a need more intense than ever.

"Look, Daddy! Ashley likes chocolate chip pancakes, too!"

Jack turned his bleary gaze to the floor beside Caitlyn's chair. "Don't feed your breakfast to the cat, munchkin."

"Why?"

"'Cause the chocolate could make her sick."

Caitlyn blinked and gave Ashley a worried look. "It will? But…she already ate it. Should we take her to the doctor?"

Jack groaned. How much chocolate did it take to make a cat sick? Jack wasn't sure.

Megan might know. Maybe he could call her or—

Grunting, he slammed his mug down a bit too hard. Coffee sloshed out on the table. He would handle his daughter and her cat by himself. He wouldn't involve Megan in their lives anymore. She clearly wanted no part of what he had to offer, so why torture himself? He couldn't let his kid grow attached—

"Can we invite Megan to go with us to the park today, Daddy?"

Clenching his jaw to bite back a curse, Jack stabbed a bite of pancake. "I'm sure Megan's too busy today to go to the park, Caity. Why don't we just make it a family thing?"

"We could make Megan part of our family. She doesn't have any kids to play with."

Caitlyn could have stabbed him with the butter knife and it would have hurt less. How did he extricate Megan from their lives when she'd so thoroughly charmed his daughter? Hell, she'd charmed *him*. And it had happened so fast.

"Megan's got Sam, and that's all she wants right now." Her retreat had said as much last night. Jack squeezed his coffee mug harder. "Finish your milk, Caity."

"Can we get a dog like Sam?"

Jack scrubbed a hand down his face. "We got a cat instead, remember? The deal was if I got you a cat that you'd stop asking for a dog."

Caitlyn pouted. "But I still want a dog. Can I have both?"

The telephone's ring spared him the dog debate…again. He scraped his chair back, dumped the rest of his pancake in the sink and snagged the receiver before the answering machine picked up.

"Jack, our source at the P.D. just called," Burt said without preamble. "Something's breaking in the Gentleman Rapist thing. One of the victims came in early this morning and said she'd IDed the guy this weekend or some such. I need you to get down to the police station and see what you can find out."

Jack frowned at the table where his daughter was finishing her brunch. "I'll have to call around for a sitter. It may take a little while."

"Jack, this is big. Should I send someone else?"

"No! I'll be there. I will." He jammed a hand through his hair. He still hadn't showered and the odds of finding someone to babysit on such short notice were slim. "This is my story, Burt. I'll be there."

He pressed the switchhook then dialed Lisa Thibedeaux's number. And got no answer. His elderly next-door neighbor was just leaving for church. A day care Megan had recommended was closed on Sunday.

Huffing his frustration, he snatched his coffee from the table and quickly rinsed the mug at the sink. "Caitlyn, get dressed. I may need you to go with me on an errand for work."

"What about the park?" she whined.

"We'll go to the park later. Hurry, munchkin."

Caitlyn stomped her foot. "But you pwomised we could go to the park today!"

His gut wrenched. He had *pwomised*. "I'm sorry, baby. I—"

"I'm not a baby!" she shouted.

Jack stopped himself just shy of yelling back. Instead he drew a deep breath.

He'd call Megan. He was running out of options and time. The Gentleman Rapist case could be busting wide open while he debated the park with Caitlyn.

"Go get dressed, and I'll see if Megan can take you to the park. Deal?"

A wide grin split Caitlyn's face. "Deal!"

Blowing a long breath through pursed lips, Jack lifted the receiver once more and called Megan.

What would he say to her? He drummed his fingers on the wall anxiously, listening to her phone ring once, twice. Three times.

An image of her emerald eyes glowing at him as he'd dipped his head to kiss her last night flickered in his memory. His gut twisted, and he resolutely shoved the vision aside.

"Caitlyn, are you dressing?" he called as much for distraction as to check on her progress. In his ear, Megan's phone continued to ring.

"I can't find Barbie's bicycle!"

Jack groaned and hung up the phone. "You don't need Barbie's bike to get dressed. Put some clothes on. Quick. We're in a hurry!"

Striding over to the table, he groaned at the mess Caitlyn had made of the table and floor. When he remembered Caity was trying to eat left-handed because of her cast, he cut her a little slack. Just the same, a dog like Sam would come in handy sometimes.

Five minutes later, after a quick shower, Jack redialed Megan's number. He strode into the living room where Caitlyn was watching *Cinderella* and peered out his window to Megan's house. Her car was just pulling into her driveway.

Where had she gone this morning? Did Megan attend church?

He realized there was a lot he didn't know about Megan. A lot he wanted to learn. He let the phone continue to ring, giving her time to get inside and answer.

"Hello?" she said breathlessly a moment later. His pulse

lurched, imagining that same voice, winded after vigorous sex, whispering confidences as they huddled naked in his bed.

"Uh, Megan. It's Jack." His own voice sounded hoarse thanks to his obsession with picturing himself and Megan writhing in the sheets. He huffed, frustrated with himself.

"Jack. I—" Megan fell silent.

"I'm sorry to bother you, but…something's come up." He grimaced. He hated asking for her help. Again. Hated being in debt to her. Hated feeling so overwhelmed. "I have to work. There's been a big break in the Gentleman Rapist case, and I need to get to the police station. Is there any chance you can watch Caitlyn for me this afternoon?"

A pregnant silence filled the phone line, and Jack closed his eyes, seeing her face, seeing the pain and fright that had clouded her eyes last night. He had no right to ask anything of her. But without Megan's help, he'd miss the biggest story to break in months. His career would crash and burn.

"Please, Megan. I'm…sorry about last night." He paced the floor, past the spot in the foyer where he'd crushed her to the wall and groped her like a randy teenager. No wonder she was angry. She deserved better. Much better. "It won't happen again, I swear. Right now, though, I'm desperate. I—"

"Give me five minutes to change clothes, and I'll…be right over."

The pressure in his lungs eased in a whoosh. "Thank you." The words seemed inadequate. "See you in five."

He tossed the phone on the couch and raced back to his room to dress before Megan arrived.

Jack was late. He'd sworn to Megan he wouldn't need more than a few hours to collect the information he needed at the police station and return home. But it had already grown dark outside. She'd long ago fed Caitlyn supper and put her to bed.

The waiting was killing her. What had he found out? What was taking so long? How did she face him when he got home? When the phone rang, she snatched it up, eager for news from Jack.

"Yes?"

"Hey, it's me. I'm sorry this is taking so long. I know you must have had plans today that I messed up."

"Just cutting out pictures for the bulletin board in my classroom. I got that done with Caity's help after we got back from the park."

"You took her to the park?"

"She said you'd promised her she could go today. I hope that it's okay—"

"It's great! I just meant… Thanks, Megan. I know it meant a lot to her."

"So…how's it going?" She forced the question out through a throat tightening with apprehension. She pressed a hand to her whirling stomach and tried to breath normally.

"Bad. Worse." He growled. "There's been some sort of gag order issued, and the usual sources at the police department aren't talking. And get this. Burt called a while ago. His brother—you remember meeting Frank last night, right?"

Bile surged up in her throat, and Megan had to swallow hard before she could speak. "I remember."

"Well, the Dallas police showed up at his house tonight and have taken him in for questioning regarding some case here in Louisiana. Crazy, huh? When it rains, it pours. So Burt has left town to see what's going on with Frank, and I'm here at the newspaper office waiting for a call back from a third-party source that might give me something to go on. It could be a while before I can get away." He sighed. "I'm sorry. I didn't expect this to take so long. How are things there?"

Megan released a slow breath, fighting for composure. "Fine." *Except that I'm going nuts, knowing that my whole life is about to be torn apart.* "Caitlyn's fed and asleep. I…uh, made a pot of gumbo. I'll leave it on the stove for you to reheat when you get in."

"Hmm. Sounds wonderful. A lot better than the stale sweetroll I got out of the vending machine."

He said nothing for a moment, and an awkward tension hummed between them. But it was nothing compared to the hurricane about to hit.

"How can I thank you for everything you've done for me?" His voice rasped with a fatigue that matched her own. "I owe you big-time. You name it, and it is yours."

Tears sprang unexpectedly to her eyes, and she clamped a hand over her mouth to muffle the catch in her breath. God, if only he could grant her what she wanted.

Make this all go away. Give me back the last five years. Give me a future with your beautiful daughter and your warm smile.

Or just hold me. Hold me and tell me everything will work out all right.

Even clearing her throat before she began, her voice came out a croak. "It's nothing. You don't…owe me a thing. We had fun today."

That much was true. She'd had a wonderful time pretending Jack's daughter might some day be hers, too. She'd thrown herself into every minute of playing dolls and braiding hair.

Once Jack knew she'd hidden her connection to the case from him, once he learned what had happened to her, how damaged she was, would he want anything to do with her again?

"I, uh…don't suppose I had any calls there, did I?" The hopefulness in his tone wrenched inside her. This story was so important to him. She'd seen his enthusiasm for his job and his zeal for this assignment before and managed to push it aside, ignoring the obvious.

Now her reckoning had come, and she couldn't neglect the impossible conflict of their positions.

Raking her hair off her forehead, she squeezed her eyes shut while silent tears leaked down her cheeks.

"Megan, any calls for me?"

"No." Then she remembered the message taped to the refrigerator. "I mean yes. I almost forgot…your in-laws called. Your ex-in-laws rather. They wanted to talk to Caitlyn and asked me to remind you that next weekend was their visitation weekend."

"Yeah, I remember." He sighed. "I don't know how much longer I'll be."

"I'm okay. But I need to let Sam out. I'll probably bring him over here…if that's all right with you."

"Yeah, sure. And Megan?" He hesitated, and Megan held her breath. "Later, when all this rape case stuff settles down for me…and I've had some sleep so I can think straight—" He gave a short, weary chuckle then paused another beat. "Can we talk?"

If you're still speaking to me… "Okay."

He sighed. "Good. Listen, the other line just lit up. This may finally be the info I've been waiting for. I gotta run. Thanks again."

She heard the click as he disconnected, then the buzz telling her he was gone. For several moments, she stared at the receiver in her hand. Listening to the drone of the dial tone. Wishing she could bring him back on the line a little longer. Missing the sound of his voice.

You know exactly what you want to do. But you're holding back. Ginny's voice nudged her, but the wrenching ache in her chest when she considered losing Jack decided her course for her. She knew what she had to do.

Slowly she punched in Ginny's number and put her plan in motion.

Chapter 12

Tiny fingers pried Jack's eyes open, dragging him into consciousness. "Daddy, are you awake?"

"I am now," he grumbled. He rubbed his gritty eyes and peered at the clock by his bed. Five forty-three. "Caity, what are you doing up so early?"

When she clicked on his lamp, he threw his arm over his face to block out the offensive light.

"Where's Miss Megan?"

His heart tripped. *Megan.* Even hearing her name made him miss her.

"She's at home. Sleeping. Like you should be." Jack pulled the pillow over his head.

Caitlyn shook his shoulder. "Is Megan gonna be my new mommy?"

That woke Jack up. His pulse jackhammered as he sat up and squinted against the bright lamp light. "Why do you ask that?"

His daughter tried to climb on the bed with him, struggling with her cast. Jack caught her under the arms and hauled her up to the empty pillow beside him.

"I like her. She played with me all day and took me to the park and pushed my swing and everything! And when I went to bed, she made all the voices when she read my story, just like you do. That's how I know she'd be a good mommy."

Jack gave Caitlyn a wistful smile. "Megan would be a good mommy, wouldn't she? I bet she gets lots of practice making voices when she reads to the kids she teaches at her school."

"Will I go to her school when I'm a big kid?"

Jack yawned. "No, ba—Uh, munchkin. We're not zoned for her school."

"What's *zoned?*"

Jack rubbed the stubble on his jaw and sighed. "That's what I'll be all day if you don't let me get a little more sleep." He tickled her under her arm. "Zoned out!"

Caitlyn giggled then scooted off his bed. "I know…don't wake you up till the numbers say six, four, five!"

"Right." Jack clicked off his lamp but only stared at the ceiling. Who was he kidding? He wouldn't be sleeping anymore between now and six forty-five. Not that he'd slept much since 2:00 a.m. when he'd finally tumbled into bed.

He wondered if Megan had slept any better than he had. They'd both been dead on their feet by the time he dragged in from the office at midnight. Despite that, he'd paced for two hours, replaying everything he knew about the Gentleman Rapist case. And letting his thoughts stray over and again to his situation with Megan.

Clearly the time they'd spent together yesterday had bonded Megan and Caitlyn even more.

Is Megan gonna be my new mommy?

Jack's gut pitched.

The mothering Megan had given Caitlyn yesterday was what his daughter deserved on a permanent basis. And Megan was everything he wanted in a wife. But the signals she sent out couldn't be clearer. She didn't want anything permanent, wasn't ready for commitment. His kiss sent her running for cover.

Jack scratched his morning beard and sighed. The mess of his relationship with Megan would have to wait. He had to get Caitlyn ready for school and prepare for another day of deciphering the mysterious turn of events in the Gentleman Rapist case.

"This is insane!" Burt slapped a manilla file folder down on his desk and shoved his chair back with a grunt. "My brother is no rapist! For God's sake, he doesn't even live in Lagniappe anymore. It's got to be a case of mistaken identity."

Jack hadn't been at work for five minutes before his boss had charged into his office with the latest twist in the constantly changing serial rape case. The woman who'd come forward late Saturday night had identified Frank Harwood, by name.

Now in Burt's office, Jack scrubbed a hand over his jaw and shook his head. "If we back off the story, it looks like biased journalism. The television stations have already reported Frank's connection to you and your position here at the paper."

Jack watched his boss storm back and forth in the tiny confines of the editorial office like a caged tiger. He understood Burt's restlessness. Jack felt like an army of fire ants had invaded *his* body, stinging his stomach and crawling through his veins. The stakes in this story just got higher and higher. He had to stay focused and get his job done.

But how did he report the facts without dragging his boss's family down?

"Do you want to go on the record voicing your support for Frank or should we play down the family connection?"

"What I want—" Burt spun to face him, jabbing a finger toward his reporter to punctuate his point. "—is for you to find this woman. Shield law or not, I want to know who she is and why she's crucifying an innocent man!" Veins on Burt's forehead throbbed as he raged. "Find out what her story is. Is this an attempt at blackmail? Is she a druggie? Does she have a history of arrests herself? This charge against Frank is bogus, and I want you to prove it!"

Jack pinched the bridge of his nose, where a massive headache was building. "Burt, your flouting the shield law aside, I'm not sure we want to report anything that would look like we were attacking the woman for coming forward. She was raped by someone five years ago, even if it wasn't Frank." Jack couched his remarks carefully, not wanting to rile his boss any further but needing to make his point clear. "The public's sympathy is going to be with *her* as the victim of a brutal crime. The paper shouldn't antagonize the public by taking any position that opposes her claim."

In addition, though Burt dismissed the information, everything Jack *had* gotten from the police station supported the mysterious woman's claim. Other Gentleman Rapist victims, who hadn't already IDed Smith, the copycat, as their attacker, had been shown pictures of Frank. And while none could identify him with any certainty, they all agreed there was a strong resemblance, each pointing out different features they recognized in Frank's mug shot.

"Well, we're sure as hell not going to imply my brother is guilty like the TV stations are!"

Jack filled his lungs slowly, gave Burt a chance to take a

breath, too. "All I'm saying is, we should stick with the facts. That's our job. Not building a case meant to tear down this woman. We don't know why she's accusing Frank."

Burt braced his arms on the desk and leaned forward, getting in Jack's face. "So find out why."

"Like you said, it's probably just mistaken identity. Have you talked to Frank? Can he recount every place he went while he was in town this weekend? Who might have seen him? Where might he have run in to this woman?"

Burt groaned and ran a hand over his face. "He went all over town running errands for the party. He ate lunch at a popular deli crammed full of customers. He flashed his credit card with his name and wrote checks buying stuff for my birthday dinner all day."

Jack sighed. "I still think our best option is to talk to the detectives on the case again."

"Good luck getting those hard-asses to crack." Burt's scowl deepened. "This gag order she demanded really makes me suspicious. What's the woman hiding?"

Jack's hands fisted, and he gave himself a second to think before he said something to his boss he'd regret. "Who's to say she's hiding anything?"

"Isn't the timing a bit pat for you? The story has been in the papers for the past couple weeks, and suddenly she's seen her rapist walking around town—" Burt gestured with a sweep of his arm "—and turns him in?"

Jack shook his head. "I'd say it took a lot of courage to come forward about her rape in the first place, and even more to report her new suspicions."

Burt slapped the desk with the flat of his hand. "Damn it, Jack! Whose side are you on? Why are you defending her?"

He raised a conciliatory hand. "I'm just trying to see all the sides of this. This whole situation doesn't make sense. But just because she named the wrong guy doesn't mean she's maliciously going after Frank. We just have to figure out where the mistake was made and get to the truth. We'll clear Frank with the facts."

Burt grumbled something under his breath and threw a pen down on his desk.

Jack couldn't imagine what his boss must be going through, having his brother arrested for such a heinous crime. The tension radiating from his editor was thicker than the gumbo Megan had kept warm for him last night.

With a huff of frustration, Jack stood. "Well, I'm not getting anywhere sitting in here. Let me see what I can find out. I'll keep you posted. When is Frank's arraignment?"

"This afternoon." Burt dropped wearily into his desk chair again and narrowed a hard gaze on Jack. "I'm counting on you to get to the bottom of this. Beg, borrow or steal. We gotta prove she's accused the wrong man."

"Yes, sir." Jack marched back to his own office, steeling himself for a tedious day of tightrope-walking, red tape and searching for the truth.

Perched on the edge of her chair, Megan fidgeted with her hands in her lap as she listened to Ginny negotiate by phone with Jack.

Megan hadn't spoken to Jack in two days. Two tense days of wondering what he knew. Two anxious days of worrying about the choice she'd made. Two painful days of wishing she had the comfort of Jack's arms around her and wondering if she'd ever feel his warm embrace again.

No matter how things fell in place now, she had to believe she'd made the best choice. The right choice. The only choice she could.

"No." Ginny jabbed the notepad in front of her with her

pen. "For her safety, we must insist that her name not be used, and no pictures be taken. Only you and your editor are to know anything about the meeting. This is a deal breaker, Mr. Calhoun. Take it or leave it. I'm sure the *Lagniappe Herald* would be happy to—" Ginny glanced at Megan and gave her a small smile. Obviously the idle threat of taking their exclusive elsewhere had brought Jack around to her terms. "Good. I'll tell her."

Ginny closed her notebook. "Friday afternoon. At the newspaper office. No, she works and doesn't want to take time off for this. Four o'clock? Good." Ginny gave Megan a thumbs-up and a nod.

Restless, Megan lurched out of her chair and stalked the hardwood floor of Ginny's spartan office at the Lagniappe Women's Center. Cheery motivational posters decorated the walls and door, and Megan tried to focus her attention on them instead of the details Ginny was working out with Jack. To no avail. Her gaze and her interest shifted back to Ginny's end of the phone conversation.

"I'll be there, too. That's right. I've been her rape counselor since she first went to the police five years ago. She's agreed to answer any questions she can pertaining to her case." Ginny paused, and her eyes met Megan's. "Why you?"

For the first time that afternoon, her friend seemed at a loss for words. Her gaze seemed to ask Megan what she should answer.

Megan's heart thudded so hard the blood rushed past her ears in a whoosh. Above her clamoring pulse, she heard Ginny say, "You'll understand everything soon enough. We'll see you Friday, Mr. Calhoun. Goodbye."

Ginny hung up, but her piercing blue eyes held with Megan's. "I know this is scary. I know it's hard. But you're doing the right thing."

Megan only nodded weakly. Already she was having second thoughts. Her stomach rioted and roiled.

But for Jack, for any hope of having a future with him, for the chance to finally begin to rebuild the life she wanted, she had to do this.

So much for baby steps, for testing the waters. She was diving in headfirst.

Friday afternoon, Jack tapped his pencil on his notepad, waiting anxiously for the anonymous woman to arrive for their interview. The week had crept by at a snail's pace, despite everything he'd had to keep him busy.

Lauren's parents had arrived that morning as arranged to pick up Caitlyn for the weekend. His ex-mother-in-law had frowned at the disorder in his house and sniffed in disdain when he'd tried to explain about the chaos at the newspaper with the breaking story and Frank's arraignment. He'd bitten his tongue and not hurled any barbs about his clutter being less harmful to his daughter than Lauren's desertion.

Jack sipped the cold coffee beside his notepad. The bitter brew did little for the acid churning in his gut. What was keeping Ginny West and the woman accusing Frank? Had the victim changed her mind about giving him the exclusive on her side of events?

He dragged in a large breath and searched for patience.

Burt paced the small, sparsely furnished conference room, jangling the keys in his pocket, clearly as eager to get started as Jack. He, of course, had more at stake, since the woman was accusing Burt's brother of a vicious crime.

"How's Frank holding up?" Jack asked.

Burt shrugged. "As well as can be expected. I still can't believe how high the judge set his bail. Frank's not a flight risk. He has family here. He wants to clear himself of these

charges." Burt shook his head. "It took a better part of his re-
tirement savings to post bail, but at least he's home with us
until this mess gets cleared up."

Jack nodded. "Let me know if I can do anything."

Any answer Burt might have made was preempted as the
door to the conference room opened with a creak. Ginny
West poked her head in. "Mr. Calhoun?"

"Yes, Ms. West, come in please." Jack stood to greet the
rape counselor. "We're all set. This is Burt Harwood, my
editor."

Ginny pushed the door open wider to enter. Jack's gaze
shifted expectantly to the woman who entered behind her.

And his heart lurched.

Chapter 13

Megan? What the—?

"Hello, Mr. Harwood." Ginny offered her hand to Burt while both men gaped at Megan. "I believe you've already met Ms. Hoffman?"

"Uh, yes. Yes, I have. Hello, Megan, good to see you again." Burt sent a puzzled look to Jack, and Jack gave him an equally baffled look in return.

Turning his attention to Megan, Jack tried to catch her eye, but she avoided his gaze. She wiped her palms on her neatly pleated slacks before shaking hands with Burt. She drew a deep breath and released it slowly, her complexion pale.

An eerie prickling started at the nape of Jack's neck when Ginny pulled out a chair across the wide table from him and motioned for Megan to sit.

"What…what's going on? Where's the woman I'm supposed to interview? The rape victim that identified Frank

Harwood?" Even as Jack asked the question, praying his suspicions were wrong, a sick feeling in his gut told him the answer was staring at him with frightened green eyes.

Megan flattened her palms on the table as if steadying herself and raised her chin a notch. Her haunted eyes told the horrifying truth. "It's me, Jack. I'm Sara Hoffman."

The room tilted. Shock knocked the air from Jack's lungs and rendered his legs useless. He dropped heavily into his chair, his thoughts spinning. His mind flatly rejected the idea that Megan could have been raped.

Please, God, not Megan!

Ginny nodded. "Remember, she's here on the condition of complete anonymity. That's the deal. Oh, and we prefer the term rape *survivor*. Victim sounds so defeatist. We want to emphasize the fact that a woman *can* come back from an attack and lead a productive life," Ginny said, though to Jack her voice seemed distant and indistinct, as if it came from a deep well. "It may be a matter of semantics to you, but the spin on the positive is important to us. Shall we get started?"

"Megan?" he whispered hoarsely. His gut squeezed, and he stared, willing her to tell him there'd been a mistake.

Ginny reached over and squeezed Megan's hand. "You can do it, sweetie. Whenever you're ready."

Megan closed her eyes, presumably steeling herself, and Jack clutched the arms of his chair, bracing *himself* for what seemed inevitable.

When he'd thought the woman telling her story would be a stranger, he'd told himself he could keep an emotional distance in order to write his story. Sympathy for her pain, yes. But also the professional detachment a doctor might use in treating terminally ill patients.

But he knew Megan. He cared about her. She made this scenario personal. Deeply personal. Good God, how was he supposed to sit here and listen to Megan detail something so horrific? His mind shrank from the notion, and an odd buzzing started in his ears.

"It happened five years ago. I was twenty-five, living alone, in graduate school, engaged to a man I'd dated for four years."

Jack detected the tremble in Megan's voice right away, and a sharp pain twisted in his chest. This had to be incredibly difficult for her. He longed to wrap her in his arms, wanted to scream at her to stop.

He glanced at Burt, who nodded his head toward the tape recorder sitting forgotten on the table. Numbly, Jack reached for the machine and punched the record button.

Megan's gaze flicked nervously to the tape recorder then to him. His breath stilled, and a coil of guilt tightened his chest.

Of course the recorder made her more uncomfortable. How thoughtless of him! He reached for the tape machine again, but she shook her head.

"No, it's…it's okay. I want you to get it right. And I don't want to have to repeat myself. Leave it on."

Her eyes held a dark distress that grabbed him by the throat.

"Megan…" he muttered, not sure what to say to her.

She continued before he could say more. "It was a Tuesday night. I was home fixing dinner when my doorbell rang. The man at the door wore a police uniform, and he…told me that the police department was doing courtesy checks in the neighborhood to find weaknesses in residents' home security." She paused and drew a breath, her gaze shifting to focus on the table. Her fidgeting fingers traced the pattern of the wood grain. "He walked around outside the house inspecting my windows and bushes and door locks. Then asked…to go inside to see my bedroom windows. I…I led him back to my room and…while I was raising the blinds, he…" She stopped and cleared her throat. Staring down at her hands, she fumbled with the ring on her right hand.

Bile rose in Jack's throat. He longed to squeeze her hands between his, press her trembling fingers to his lips. He wanted to tell her he'd changed his mind, that he'd find a different angle for his story. *Anything*, as long as she didn't say the gruesome words he knew she would.

Ginny covered Megan's fidgeting hands with hers and nodded her support.

"He pulled out a pair of handcuffs and…before I knew what was happening, he'd locked my hands to my bed frame." Megan shuddered. "Then he laughed at me. A strange, nasal sort of laugh and told me…how stupid I was to have let a strange man in my house." Her voice cracked. "That I deserved whatever happened to me." She bit her bottom lip and scrunched her eyes shut. A fat tear squeezed from the corner of her eye.

That single tear landed a sucker punch in Jack's gut. His hand fisted, itching to slam into the nose of the man who'd hurt Megan. Not just physically hurt her, but mentally, emotionally. Her anguish ripped through his chest, wreaking havoc on his soul. No man had a right to crush a woman this way, shatter her life.

"He ripped open my blouse and started pawing at me, saying crude things…asking me if…if I liked what he was doing."

With a rock lodged firmly in his gut, Jack pictured Megan, frightened and helpless, being manhandled by this creep. He forced the image away, sickened and enraged. He needed to say something to comfort Megan, to make the ugliness go away, but his voice seemed to have fled. Like some kind of useless hack, he sat frozen, stunned. But inside, he writhed, screamed, raged.

"He kept laughing at me in that same nasal-sounding way. It was his laugh that I recognized first…at the birthday party." Megan glanced up now, casting a quick, almost apologetic look to Burt.

In his shock, learning of Megan's attack, Jack had forgotten for a moment that she'd identified Burt's brother as her assailant. A white-hot fury blazed through Jack's veins, and he turned an accusing glare toward Burt.

"Plenty of people have a nasal laugh. You can't point a finger at Frank based just on *that*." Burt's tone was bitter, and Megan jerked her gaze away.

"Let her finish," Ginny said. "Go on, Megan. You're doing fine." Ginny rubbed Megan's arm, and again Jack longed to be the one consoling her.

Megan drew a shallow breath. Jack held his. For several excruciating minutes, he listened to her elaborate in heart-wrenching detail about her attacker's cruelty and brutality. He suffered through the mind-numbing baseness of what the slimebag had put Megan through. A sick, sinking sensation dragged him deeper and deeper into a pit of rage and despair and horror. He wanted to apologize on behalf of all men for the despicable indignity the man inflicted on her. The urge to throw back his head and howl with frustration and agony swirled through him.

If hearing her testimony affected him this deeply, then what must she be going through? What kind of terror had *she* lived with these past five years?

"I was so numb when he finally left that I…I didn't do anything but huddle on my bed for hours. Finally…when I got up, I…made a common mistake. I showered. I washed all the evidence away. But I felt so dirty, so guilty." Megan's face had a ghostly pallor. "Then I didn't report it...until morning because...I couldn't forget what he said. That I deserved what had happened because I was foolish enough to let a man in my house."

Jack felt as if the floor gave way beneath him. How could Megan blame herself? Why...?

Horror flamed in his gut with an acid bite. It was too much. He couldn't hear any more without going ballistic. He shoved back his chair and lurched to his feet. His sudden movement drew the eyes of all in the room, but his gaze connected only with Megan's. He tried to speak, tried to say something to ease her pain.

But what could he say that would mean squat in the face of her tragedy? Never in his life had he felt so inadequate, so helpless. His throat squeezed, and he struggled to force a breath into his lungs.

Turning abruptly, he knocked his chair over as he lumbered away from the table to pace. The clatter as the chair crashed to the floor jarred his taut nerves.

"So you have no real proof that Frank did this. No way to substantiate your story?"

Jack spun toward Burt. What the hell was he doing? The point of this interview was not to grill Megan or challenge her account. Where was Burt's objectivity as a reporter? Jack scoffed. Where was *his* objectivity? It had flown out the window the second Megan stepped through the door.

"Mr. Harwood, we didn't come here to—"

"He recognized me at that party, too. He asked if we had met," Megan interrupted Ginny, her voice steely now. Cold. Hard. Bitter. "He even cornered me in the kitchen when no one was around and tried to intimidate me again. I've seen his face in my mind, in my nightmares, every time I've closed my eyes for the last five years. I *know* it was him."

"The court won't convict him based on your *hunch*," Burt challenged.

Megan flinched, her face growing paler.

Jack's jaw tightened until his teeth hurt. "Damn it, Burt! What are you doing? Back off!"

Ginny stood and faced Burt. "Other women have come forward and confirmed her ID. I guarantee the physical evidence from their cases will support their testimony."

"I'm not a liar, Mr. Harwood. I'm not making this up to persecute your brother." Megan lifted her chin and met Burt's challenging gaze with a dignity and aplomb that caused Jack's heart to swell with pride. "He hurt me, and I have to stop him from hurting anyone else."

Damn, but the woman had pluck. He could easily fall in love with a woman with the grit and inner strength Megan clearly had. Maybe he'd already fallen in love with her. Maybe that's why he felt the pain and terror of her attack to his marrow.

"We'll see whether the evidence supports your claims or not." Burt drilled a hard look at the women, and Jack had the overwhelming urge to slam his boss against the wall. But at the moment his first priority was Megan, not his fury with Burt's callousness.

He moved around the table toward Megan, his heart in his throat. He reached for her when she rose from her chair.

"Don't," she whispered, ducking away from his touch.

With a hollow pang inside him, a black uncertainty and sickness took his breath.

Jack watched Ginny hustle Megan from the room. Ginny tipped her head to him as they exited. "Good luck with your article, Jack. I hope you got what you needed."

His article. *Damn.* How could he write his article now? The newspaper, his career, meant nothing compared to Megan.

The door to the conference room closed with a click that reverberated in the aching corners of his heart.

She might not want him, but Megan needed him now. He didn't know what he could do, what he would say, how to ease her pain. But he knew for certain he had to try.

Chapter 14

Jack pulled into his driveway and sat for a long time with his engine idling, replaying Megan's account of her attack, torturing himself with details of the ugly truth. He saw the past several weeks in a new light. Her panic when her guard dog had been taken from her. Her ambivalence when he kissed her. Her reluctance to take their relationship to a deeper level.

And why his clumsy groping on Saturday had frightened her. He'd let his pain over Lauren's abandonment color his perceptions of his relationship with Megan. Yet Megan had needed his patience and understanding instead of his leftover baggage from Lauren.

Damn, he'd screwed up. But he intended to make amends. Somehow.

He looked up when a Jeep Cherokee pulled in Megan's driveway and she climbed out. She walked stiffly to her door, turned and shook her head to answer something the driver of the Cherokee, probably Ginny, had said. She gave a little wave, and the Cherokee pulled away.

Jack jumped out of his truck and ran across the street, trying to catch her before she went inside. "Megan!"

She turned when he called, then quickly opened her door and disappeared inside. Obviously, she didn't want to see him, talk to him. But he wouldn't leave her alone. Not now. He had to hold her, had to make sure she was all right.

"Megan!" He pounded his fist on her door, determined to get inside one way or another.

Inside, Sam barked, and Megan hushed him.

Guilt, frustration and grief balled inside Jack, fueling his desperation.

"Open the door. Please, Megan." He paused to listen, pressing his ear to the door. Nothing. Not so much as a whine from Sam. "There's no way in hell I'm leaving you in there alone tonight, Megan, so you might as well let me in."

A movement in the periphery of his vision caught his attention. Megan's next-door neighbor, an older woman, fixed a shrewd, narrow gaze on him and shuffled to the edge of her porch. Jack gave the woman a little wave then dragged a hand over his face, sighing.

"Megan, I'm serious. I'll break the door down, if I have to, but I'm not leaving." He slammed the flat of his hand against the door. When she continued to ignore his summons, he rested his forehead against the door. Dejected, he slumped against the frame and squeezed his eyes shut.

He recalled the agony in her voice while she testified, saw the misery in her eyes when she looked at him across the table. With every second that she ignored his plea to open her door, his heart split wider, aching with regret.

"Megan!" A desperate, soulful quality filled his voice. Raising his hand, he slapped the door again. And again. Then he banged his forehead on the unyielding door, castigating his blindness. "Please, Megan! I didn't know. I should have figured it out, but I...I was selfish. I'm sorry. Please, let me—"

The door opened abruptly. Jack lost his balance and stumbled forward through the portal. Megan put up her hands to stop his awkward sprawl, and he caught her shoulders for balance. As he straightened, he met her stony expression.

Her mouth, pressed in a firm, straight line, matched her rigid stance. Only her eyes, the color of a storm-tossed sea, gave away the depth of her pain.

"Go away," she growled through clenched teeth. "I want to be alone."

When she tried to back away, he tightened his grip on her shoulders. He sensed that if he left her now, he would lose her forever. He drew her stiff body against his chest and wrapped his arms around her. "Not a chance. You're stuck with me tonight."

"Let go! Damn it, Jack, go away!" She fought his grip, shoving away with a jerk.

Remembering how his tight hold had frightened her before, and understanding the source of that fear, he opened his arms and stepped back. He held his hands up, surrendering, granting her freedom. "I won't touch you unless it is what you want, but I'm not leaving you alone."

Claws clicking on the hardwood floor, Sam appeared around the corner from her kitchen and eyed the situation, his muscles tense.

Megan sighed, and her shoulders slumped. "Please, go home."

"No." He whispered the word, but his tone reflected his determination to stay. He continued to hold his arms out. "I want to hold you, Megan. Just hold you."

She turned her back, hugging herself. Without looking at him, she shook her head and headed toward the back of the house.

"Please. I need to hold you."

His voice stopped her. She stood still. Silent. Alone.

Slowly, he closed the distance between them. Touched her shoulder. Heard her draw a ragged breath.

He tugged her arm, turning her toward him. When he pulled her close and pressed her face to his chest, she stiffened. Though her spine remained defensively straight, her fingers dug into him, clutching the fabric of his shirt. The warmth of her labored breaths penetrated his shirt, steaming his skin and sending a rush of heat through his blood.

The ticking of the grandfather clock in her foyer counted out the guilt-burdened beats of his heart.

With a yawn, Sam stretched out on the foyer floor and put his head on his outstretched paws.

Jack nuzzled the top of Megan's head, drowning in the sweet, peach scent of her shampoo. His chest throbbed with rage for the violation she'd suffered, the isolation she'd imposed on herself. When his throat tightened, he swallowed the taste of bile and despair. A quiver started deep inside him and slowly traveled until his whole body quaked with uncertain emotions.

They might have stood in the front hall for a minute or an eon. He didn't know, didn't care. He was where he belonged and wouldn't leave until Megan was as certain of this as he.

The tension and rigidity of her muscles melted by degrees, until she sagged in his arms, leaning on him for support.

"Jack." The jagged weariness of her whisper shredded his heart.

"I'm not going anywhere, baby. I swear."

Her knees buckled, and as she crumpled in his arms, a sob tore from her chest.

In one smooth movement, he scooped up her legs and cradled her against his body. He carried her into the living room, where he settled on her couch. He held her on his lap, and she huddled against his chest while her shoulders shook as she cried.

After a few moments, she raised tearful eyes, and a *V* of worry creased her brow. "Wh—where is Caitlyn? Is she all right?"

In that instant, he recognized the emotion weighing his chest, clambering inside him. He loved this woman with a reckless abandon. Deeply and irrevocably.

Despite her own misery, in the midst of her crisis, Megan's thoughts were for his daughter. Her selflessness and concern for Caitlyn's welfare sliced through layers of self-preservation and denial.

She was everything he needed to heal the wounds Lauren had left in his soul. Tears rushed to his eyes, and he took a deep breath to regain control of his runaway emotions.

"She's with Lauren's parents for the weekend." Jack stroked the side of her face. "She's safe."

Relief flooded her face, relaxing the knit of worry in her brow. She nodded, licked the tears from the corner of her mouth. "Oh…right. Now I remember."

Drilling his gaze into hers, he sank his fingers in her hair and clasped her head between his hands. "I'm all yours tonight, and I'm not going anywhere."

Shadows skittered across her face, and sadness darkened her eyes. "I don't need—" Her voice was tight and choked, and she stopped short, closing her eyes.

He felt the tremor that shook her body.

"I'll be all r—" She started, but a hiccuping sob interrupted her.

"Ah, baby." He pulled her head down to his shoulder and

rubbed the tense muscles at the back of her neck. "Of course, you'll be all right. You're strong. But you've earned the right to cry tonight. Let it out."

She nestled closer, as if trying to climb inside of him. Heavy sobs, laden with her anguish, racked her body. Her sorrow left him raw.

He'd seen her pain and vulnerability from the beginning. Why hadn't he connected the dots?

Silently, he swore to make up to her for his inattention and thickheadedness.

Outside, the sun sank below the horizon, and the dark of night seeped through Megan's house. He held her while the shadows in her living room grew and shifted. He held her while she emptied herself of tears. He held her while the hands of her grandfather clock marked hour after hour, and her watchdog snored at their feet.

Jack's body became stiff and sore from cradling her in the same position for so long. But he didn't move and risk breaking the serenity of the moment. He suffered the ache in silence while she grieved.

Eventually, her sobs quieted, and her breathing assumed the deep, even rhythm of sleep. But he didn't wake her, not even when his own eyelids drooped.

Instead, he stood carefully, lifting her in his arms and swallowing a groan when his numb muscles protested.

Sam sprang to his feet, his tags jangling, and he galloped to the door, where he whined and thumped his tail against the wall.

"Just a minute, pal. I'll be right back," Jack told the dog quietly.

He carried Megan to her bedroom and laid her on her bed. When he draped an afghan over her, she stirred.

"Jack?" she mumbled, sleep heavy in her voice.

"Shh. Sleep now." He pressed a kiss on her cheek and tiptoed toward the door.

Megan yawned, and the bed creaked as she rolled over. "Jack?"

He paused in the doorway and glanced back at her. She looked sexy as hell with her makeup gone, her hair rumpled and her eyes half-closed. Megan personified the cozy warmth and lazy comfort of a favorite quilt in winter. The temptation to wrap himself in her body snaked through him, and a sweet, forbidden craving heated his blood.

Snap out of it! She needs your support tonight, not your lust.

"'Night, Megan." His voice rasped like sandpaper, and he hoped she didn't hear the repressed longing that he did. She needed patience, and he'd give her that patience if it killed him.

"Don't go." The whispered plea had a desperate edge, despite the thick layer of grogginess.

"I'm not leaving, sweetheart. If you need me, I'll be on the couch. Just call."

She sighed her fatigue, and her eyelids drooped a tad more. "Don't go. Stay here."

Her voice was barely louder than the rustling of bedcovers, and he wasn't sure he'd heard her correctly. Her eyelashes fluttered against her cheeks as she fought to keep her eyes open. "I like…having your arms…around me."

The thud in his ears as his pulse kicked up almost drowned out her murmured request. She punctuated the invitation to sleep beside her by sliding her hand over the half-empty bed and tugging the bedspread back from the pillow with groggy fingers.

Jack swallowed hard. "I—"

Her eyelids closed, and her chest rose and fell on a deep breath. He knew she'd fallen back to sleep, knew he could leave the room and pretend she hadn't asked him to stay. Would she remember her request in the morning? Would she wake in the night, frightened, and reach for him?

He wanted to be there, if she did. Hell, he wanted to be beside her, regardless.

But was it wise? He debated his options as he walked to the foyer and locked the front door.

Sam stared at him expectantly, then at the door.

"Let's go out back, boy." He walked through Megan's kitchen to the back door and gave a soft whistle. Sam came loping in and danced around him while he unlocked and opened the door. The German shepherd charged outside, where Jack noticed a large doghouse and bowls of food and water by the stoop. Satisfied the dog was provided for, he closed the door again and relocked it.

He paused in the hallway, gave a look to the short sofa in Megan's living room and considered her invitation to sleep with her. *Sleep* was the operative word. She needed restraint from him. But after holding her for hours, stroking her soft skin, her sweet scent surrounding him, his body ached with wanting.

He gritted his teeth. He'd find self-control and shove down his desires if it killed him, which it might. Kicking off his shoes, he crept silently back into her room. Moonlight spilled in from the window and lit her pale skin with an ivory glow. The sight made his chest hurt.

Patience and self-control. Simple.

Jack unknotted his tie and a pulled it off, hanging it and his belt over the end of her bedframe. Lifting a corner of the afghan, he crawled under the cover next to her.

I like having your arms around me.

Her warmth seeped through his dress shirt, surrounding him like a hug, and he muffled a groan.

Patience and self-control.

* * *

Sam was snoring louder than usual tonight.

Megan rolled over to nudge him. But the body beside her was not soft and furry. Smooth cloth over hard muscle greeted her touch, and the incongruity prodded her awake.

Jack.

The dim memory of his arms holding her while she blubbered like a baby stirred in her sleep-hazed mind.

Stay here.

And he had stayed. He'd pulled her against his solid, reassuring strength and wrapped her in his loving arms as she'd asked. Remembering it, a peacefulness stole through her.

His kindness, support and patience as she bawled had been exactly what she needed. He'd stayed with her as he promised, letting her use him for a pillow, his shirt absorbing her tears as she'd sobbed on his shoulder.

His broad, strong, dependable shoulder.

Good for crying on. Good for clinging to. Good for sharing the burdensome yoke of her fears.

Why hadn't she trusted him before? He'd shown her in many ways how different he was from Greg. His loyalty and love for his daughter. His dedication to his job. Even his evident pain from his divorce. Everything she knew about Jack Calhoun pointed to a man who took commitments seriously, who had the depth of love to stick with the people he cared about through the tough times.

All his blustering and blindness could be chalked up to his own scars and self-protection in the wake of his ex-wife's desertion. He needed reassurance, too. She'd seen fear in her mirror for too many years not to understand the shadows lurking in his gaze. Lauren had really done a number on him, battered his ability to trust.

Jack snuffled and snorted in an undignified manner, and

Megan grinned. He'd be appalled to know she'd heard him snoring so indiscreetly.

Listening to him snore, her heart melted for the man who'd been a rock of comfort and strength to her the day before. His presence in the conference room had pulled her through the impossible, the terrifying. His presence last night had been a beacon in the darkness of her loneliness and grief. His presence now, beside her, in her bed, sawing wood like a lumberjack, gave her a glimpse of him she'd missed before.

In the past weeks, he'd impressed her with his charm and virile sex appeal. Now she saw *Jack*. Not just another man with the potential to hurt her. Not a reporter who could expose her darkest hour to the world. Not an obstacle to her recovery or another potential crutch to keep her from finding her own strength and independence.

His snoring reminded her that he was human. He had his flaws, his own hurts and doubts. But she could trust a man, open enough to expose his imperfections. She could rely on a man who suffered through hours of her self-indulgent weeping without complaint…without any dinner. She could love a man whose expression revealed his heart every time he looked at his daughter.

Love.

Her breath snagged on the word. Did she love him? She knew she could, if…

If she could get past her own crippling self-doubt. She wouldn't give herself to him until she could do it without reservation, without the ghosts of her past, without the uncertainty of her future. Giving her testimony, telling him her secret had been a start. But she had more work to do.

She had to get past the memory of her violation. She had to find the missing piece of her self-assurance that would quash the niggling fears once and for all.

With a deep, sleepy sigh, Jack shifted, stretched and rolled toward her. His arm fell across her hip, draped limply, his hand brushing her bottom. The intimate contact, though casual—accidental, really—started a flutter in her stomach. She held her breath, waiting for the surge of panic, the coil of tension.

But it never came. The deep, even rasp of his breathing filled her ears. Filled her mind. Filled her heart.

In the darkness, she studied the sexy curve of his lips, the rugged plains of his face and the set of his square jaw. She extended a finger to touch the shadow of stubble on his cheek, savoring the abrasion on her fingertip. Jack was testosterone and muscle, breathtaking appeal and intensity, pure alpha masculinity and strength.

But was he *too male?*

Her heartbeat grew stronger, faster. Her breath whispered in the stillness, quick and light, in contrast to the heavy, restful pattern of his. Her body craved his, even if her memories had stood in the way until now. And she had her answer.

"I'm ready." She whispered the words, feeling them tumble from her lips, hearing them with her whole body, shining them in the dark recesses of her soul.

Jack was the right man. The next step in her healing had to be taken. She seized her courage with both hands. The decision felt good, felt right.

A tingle spiraled through her, and she smiled. The sensation sprang from anticipation. Not fear.

The time had come.

"Good morning." Megan's face hovered over his, and Jack blinked to clear the blurry image. A smile, too sweet to be called sultry and too sexy to be called innocent, curved her mouth and sent a surge of heated blood straight to his groin.

"Good morning, yourself." The grin he returned came effortlessly to his lips, rooted in the sheer pleasure of waking to such a beautiful sight.

"You snore."

He heard no condemnation in her pronouncement, but the bluntness of her statement caught him off guard.

"So I've been told." He studied her expression for any hint of censure. "Sorry. Did I keep you awake?"

"Sam snores, too. I'm used to it."

Jack made a deep rumbling noise in his throat and narrowed his eyes on her. "I'm not sure I like being compared to your dog."

Her smiled brightened and laughter bubbled from her. "I think you'll like what your snoring helped me realize."

She reached for him and stroked his cheek with one finger. Was it his wishful imagination, or did she intend her touch to be seductive? She continued smiling at him with that angel-imp grin. More blood rushed south.

He worked to infuse his tone with casual curiosity and gentlemanly concern. "What did you realize?"

She rolled onto her back and stared up at the ceiling. "That you were…human."

A short, dry laugh erupted from him. "You doubted this before now?" Sarcastic amusement colored his tone. "Have I acted that beastly?"

She tipped her head to look at him. "Not at all. In fact, hearing you snore made you seem…less scary."

His chest tightened. "I scare you?"

"No." She scowled and looked away. "No. It's just you're so…male."

Jack sobered, realizing she was trying to express something much deeper and more important than whether he'd snored or not.

He propped up on an elbow, resting his cheek on his hand and gazed down at her. "Megan?"

She stared across the room, deep in thought. "Your snoring made the idea of being…intimate with you less…intimidating."

Finally her eyes met his, and his pulsed stumbled when he saw the bright intensity in their green depths. "I want you to make love to me, Jack."

Chapter 15

Jack's heart slammed against his ribs as if Megan had pitched it there like a fastball. He fumbled for a reply that didn't sound crude or gauche. Words were his livelihood, but they failed him now.

"O-okay." His croaked response, straight out of the annals of sophomoric-sounding answers, brought a tiny grin to her lips.

She drew a deep, fluttery breath. "I can't let my fear govern me forever. If I don't do this, then he's still in control. I have to get past the bad memories."

Jack's chest clenched as her need dawned on him. She was asking for more than sex, more than affection, more than physical fulfillment. The prospect of playing such an important role in her spiritual recovery both flattered and daunted him. What she asked of him was an awesome responsibility, a significant rite of passage and a duty with no margin for error.

He couldn't screw up this time. He had to get things right for her sake.

A chill ran through him. Could he give her what she needed without frightening her again?

Her warm hand touched his cheek, rousing him from his self-scrutiny.

"Megan, I—Are you sure? I didn't stay here last night with any intention of pressuring you to—"

"I know. You were wonderful. You were sweet and understanding and the perfect gentleman."

He thought about the steamy scenarios that he'd indulged in while he held her, and guilt pricked his conscience. He pulled away from her caress and sat up in the bed. Drawing his legs up, he propped his arms on his bent knees. "I know I came on too strongly before. I frightened you. So if you'd rather we just work our way up to this slowly, give it more time—"

Grabbing his shoulder, she pulled herself up and braced on one arm. "I've already spent too long cowering in the wake of bad memories. I want new memories to take their place. I don't want to be scared anymore."

Turning to her, he stared into her fathomless eyes for long seconds. "God knows, there is nothing I want more than to make love to you."

"Then you will?" The hope he heard in her voice belied the flicker of anxiety he saw lurking behind her eyes.

"Oh, baby," he whispered on a sigh, pulling her into his arms. He pressed her close to his body and felt the scampering beat of her heart against the unsteady thud of his own. "You know I will."

His body sang with a strange combination of anticipation and apprehension. While all of his nerve endings crackled with expectation and desire, the weight of his responsibility mired his mood in uncertainty.

He pressed a kiss to her forehead and leaned back to find her gaze. "I didn't come prepared for this."

The quick knit of her brow reflected her bewilderment.

"I have condoms back at the house. I can go get them and be back in just a minute or two."

Before he even finished, she was shaking her head. "No. You don't need them. I've been on the pill for years. Since Greg and I were first engaged. And you don't have to worry about, well— Since the rape, I've been tested for everything, many times. I'm healthy."

"Ditto."

She tugged her lips up in an awkward smile that twisted his heart as surely as she was knotting the sheet in her fingers.

Jack shook his head. "I didn't mean to imply that I thought—"

"I know." A shy smile tugged the corner of her mouth before she sobered again. "Without condoms, I'll feel more like…we're making love. And—" She ducked her chin and knitted her brow. She paused long enough to wet her lips.

Her moist mouth looked as sweet and tempting as a ripe raspberry, and the hunger to take a bite of them punched him so hard he almost missed the rest of her sentence.

"Thing is…*he* used a condom. So that he wouldn't leave evidence, I guess."

He tensed, grappling with the enormity of her statement. "Then we won't use one. Whatever you want. Whatever you need."

Her mouth curved in an appreciative grin. "Well…if that's settled, then I just need a minute to freshen up." She scooted to the edge of the bed and slid her feet to the floor. "I'm not much of a morning person and…"

Nervous tension built in her voice.

Of course, she was scared. He had to think of some way to put her at ease.

"Sure, take your time."

Megan disappeared into the bathroom, and he dragged a hand over his face. He should probably do a little maintenance himself.

Digging in the pocket of his pants, he found a piece of cinnamon gum and popped it in his mouth. He chewed vigorously, hoping to eradicate any morning breath that plagued him, then stumbled out of bed. He caught his reflection in her dresser mirror.

His hair suffered from a major case of bed-head. Hardly sexy. The stubble on his chin made him look like a thug. Stroking his jaw, he sighed. Not the impression he wanted to make, but what choice did he have?

He started undoing his shirt, and on the last button he stalled. Did he want to be undressed when she came out? Would she still be dressed? The idea of Megan naked recharged the heavy ache in his groin.

Easy, buddy. She'll need to take it slow.

Releasing a slow breath, he fumbled to rebutton his shirt.

The sound of water rushing from the bathroom faucet filtered in from the next room. He pictured her brushing her teeth or washing her face. Even the simplicity, the intimacy of the mundane tasks caused a warmth to swell in his chest. The idea of sharing such simple tasks with Megan for years to come appealed to him. He didn't just want her in his bed, he wanted her in his home, in his family, in his life.

Anticipation made his fingers clumsy, and he tried three times before he got one of the buttons to cooperate. He finished refastening his shirt and started back to the bed. Should he sit on it? Stand beside it?

He tried to recall exactly what she'd testified that Frank

had done. Whatever the scum had done to her, he had to avoid at all cost. No way did he want to trigger any painful flashes of memory.

His jaw tightened, thinking of the dirtwad looming over her while he dropped his pants.

Muttering a curse, he spun away from the bed and virtually ripped his shirt off. He unzipped his pants, shoved them down and kicked them off. She'd seen her attacker undress, suffered the knowledge of what he was preparing to do, waited helplessly.

"Damn," he grumbled, realizing again the importance of what she'd asked him to do. What if he failed? What if he frightened her?

He stood bedside the bed in nothing but his boxers and black dress socks and raked his fingers through his hair.

Just think things through. She's counting on you.

The key was to not frighten her. Not to be intimidating. Not to be too…male. Whatever *that* meant. He stared down at his feet. Boxers and black socks.

"Now there's a sexy look," he mumbled. *Not.*

Hooking his thumbs in his boxers, he slid them off in a flash and tossed them on the pile with the rest of his discarded clothes. He'd just bent to rip his socks off, when he heard the click of the doorknob. He whirled around to face the opening bathroom door.

The sight of Megan wearing a pale blue, satin robe, belted at the waist, her cheeks flushed and dewy, her hair shining, her lips puckered in a moue of surprise, made everything in him grow still, rigid.

Everything.

Right down to his ridiculous black socks.

Megan stopped in the doorway, startled and stunned by the sight that greeted her. Her breath caught in her lungs.

She scanned down Jack's hard chest and flat stomach to the prominent male organ that stood as stiffly as the man did.

Large. Ready. Terrifying.

A tremor spiraled through her, and her mouth went dry. Her nerves stretched, taut and ready to snap. She couldn't do it. Couldn't…

Dropping her gaze from the intimidating sight, she glanced at his feet. He wore black socks. She blinked. Still shaken by the previous image, the new one took a moment to register. Then her gaze swept up the length of him and back down.

He was wearing black socks. *Only* black socks. *What…?*

He looked…well, *silly*.

"Hi." The rumble of his deep voice interrupted the question forming in her mind and brought her eyes up to meet his. She tugged on the ends of her belt, pulling it tighter.

"Ready?" he asked.

The jangling inside her intensified. "I—Yeah."

He sat on the edge of the bed and pulled off both socks. "My, uh, feet got cold."

He stood again, and her gaze drifted to his bare feet.

From the depths of her quaking body, the urge to laugh sprang up like the clown from a jack-in-the-box. Quickly, she bit the inside of her cheek and swallowed hard. She *couldn't* laugh. Not when he was naked. Talk about tactical errors!

Her anxiety unwound in an instant, as if someone had snipped the strings that had pulled her insides into knots. Her tense muscles relaxed, and breathing became less of a task. She took another good look at Jack.

Cold feet, my fanny! She knew exactly why he had dressed in such a ludicrous manner. Warmth blossomed inside her, and a smile burgeoned on her face.

Bless his sweet, sexy heart. He'd done it for her. To distract her from her worry. To ease the stress she battled. To appear less intimidating.

And it worked.

She stepped closer to him, the corner of her mouth twitching. Lifting a hand to his chest, she flexed her fingers against his warm skin. "Thank you."

Her eyes locked with his, telling him without words that she understood his ploy, his motivation, the sacrifice to his tough-guy image.

He raised his hands to her waist and nudged her closer. "Forget it."

She could feel the heat of him through the thin fabric of her robe, pressing against her belly. A different sort of shimmer started deep inside her. Wanting.

"Not likely. This, I want to remember."

She slid her hands to his shoulders then stood on her toes to lift her lips to his.

With the contact of his mouth to hers, tingling expectation streaked through her. His kiss tasted like cinnamon, and she heard the whisper of his pleasured sigh. Despite the gentle caress of his lips, she sensed his restraint in the quiver of his muscles under her palms. Knowing how hard he worked not to frighten her encouraged her to trust him even more. He had her interests at heart. She was safe with him.

That assurance sparked her confidence, and she pressed closer, deepening their kiss.

Jack slid his arms around her and hugged her closer. His mouth explored hers with leisurely patience. The sweet, slow seduction of his lips lulled her, and she melted into the heat of his embrace. Her blood seemed to thicken, flowing like warm honey through her veins. She savored the intoxicating sensation. If she could only close her mind to the memories, focus on the physical…

With no warning, Jack swept an arm down behind her knees and scooped her off the floor. She gasped and clutched his neck. The abrupt loss of her balance startled her from the sensual track her thoughts had been on.

"Easy," he murmured. "I've gotcha."

She sought out his eyes as he set her down on the bed. His pupils were wide, dark pools of desire, his gaze hard and hungry.

As he lowered himself next to her, he trapped her thigh under one of his legs. His weight pinned her to the bed as he stretched across her. A frisson of anxious doubt spiraled through her, and her pulse skittered.

When he captured her lips again, she closed her eyes, sought the stirring of pleasure once more. She willed herself to enjoy the pressure of his mouth, the suction and heat.

His fingers skimmed over the curve of her hip, along the dip of her waist to settle possessively on her breast. Rather than the size and strength of the hand squeezing her intimately, she struggled to focus on the tenderness of his touch.

He kissed her harder, deeper, stealing her breath. The first hint of alarm prickled the back of her neck. She called the image of him in his socks back to her mind, and her tension eased some.

When his palm brushed across her nipple, it budded and ached with arousal. A low, appreciative moan rumbled from his throat, and he gently pinched her taut nipple and rolled it between his finger and his thumb. A crackling heat teased her breast then rippled through her body, and a soft mewl of surprise caught in her throat. Jack's touch made her body throb with erotic bliss.

He broke their kiss, his breath a warm caress as he hovered over her. "You're beautiful, Megan."

The familiarity and kindness in the voice whispering her

name washed over her like a balmy breeze. Her eyes fluttered open, and she met the hazel gaze peering down at her.

Jack.

His dimple dented his cheek briefly as he flashed her a quick reassuring smile.

Her ragged breathing calmed.

"Are you okay?"

She nodded then realized her body contradicted her. All her muscles were tense, her fingers curled into the bedspread with a death grip, her jaw clamped tight.

His brow puckered with concern. "Any time you want to stop, just give the word. We'll stop. Okay?"

She nodded again, stiffly, and drew in oxygen.

"Talk to me. Tell me what you want, what you need, what feels good. Okay?"

This time when she nodded, she tried to give him a smile, but her cheek only twitched.

"You are in control here, baby. You're in charge. You're safe." He stroked the side of her face, and the tenderness of the gesture tore a sob from deep within her.

"Oh, Jack." Burying her face in the crook of his neck, she wrapped her arms around his neck and clung to him. The night before she'd clutched him this way for hours, purging her soul of repressed grief. The memory of his patience and comforting friendship filled her with a heartening peace.

He shifted his weight so that he no longer pinned her down, and immediately she missed the warmth of him on top of her. The heavy encumbrance of his body no longer seemed restrictive. His strong, solid presence gave her a sense of security that she cherished.

With bold determination, she slid her hands into his thick hair and brought his head down until she could take his mouth again with hers. She kissed him with a desperate fervor, open-mouthed and greedy, and he responded with an equal hunger. Again, her body awakened by degrees.

When the tip of his tongue swept her lips, sparks of desire flickered to life in her blood. She lost herself in the moment, closing her mind to everything but the rush of thrilling sensations. This was what she wanted, what she *needed* to numb her to the dark memories, and she reveled in the blossoming exhilaration.

She allowed her tongue to tangle with his in a mating dance. Participating in the love play gave her a sense of freedom, a feeling of power that heightened her enjoyment. Jack traced her swollen lips and stroked into her mouth. She gloried in the exquisite, damp heat as he moved his gentle exploration down the curve of her throat. Alternately licking and kissing, he blazed a wet path down the valley between her breasts, and a dizzying pleasure coursed through her.

"Oh, yes." She hadn't meant to whisper the words that filtered through her mind. He answered with a low hum of satisfaction that rumbled from his throat.

Megan watched Jack edge lower, and she wound her fingers into his tousled hair. When he dipped his face to nuzzle her breasts, the intimacy of the act caused a quick prick of ill-ease. But he peeked up at her as he hooked his thumbs under the lapels of her robe, and well-known hazel eyes, glowing with affection and encouragement, replaced her misgivings with an urgency that throbbed inside her.

This was Jack. Not a stranger. *Jack.*

His name echoed in her thoughts, and her pulse fluttered in response.

Nudging the edges of her robe, he nipped the soft swell of one breast then the other, teasing her without ever moving to their sensitized peaks. He loosened her belt, and the silky robe slithered down her sides, baring her to his eager gaze.

"Sweet Megan," he murmured.

She followed the movement of his eyes as he drank in the sight of her, naked except for a lacy scrap of panties. His fingers trailed lightly over her ribs and stomach, tickling her and sending shivery waves of pleasure shimmying all the way to her toes. The vulnerability she should have felt under his careful scrutiny never came. Instead, his lingering gaze, his wandering hands, his gentle touch, aroused her even more. A drunken heaviness suffused her limbs, and she savored the blissful lethargy.

When he finally seized a nipple, sucking it into his mouth, bolts of electricity raced through her, and she sighed her enjoyment. He rubbed her other breast with his palm, abrading the stiff tip as he moved his mouth back to hers. She kissed him hard, and he matched her fervor.

He moved his leg over hers again, and the weight of it on top of hers nudged her legs slightly apart. The friction of his thigh at the juncture of her legs caused a sweet agony to bloom there, and she began to grow impatient with his slow and cautious ministrations.

Anticipation heightened her awareness of every inch of contact between his body and hers. The coarse dusting of hair on his stomach tickled her abdomen as he hovered over her, and his wide wrist propped against her shoulder while his fingers toyed with the hair near her ear.

Raising her hips, she increased the pressure where his thigh grazed her and moaned softly.

"That's it, baby," he crooned to her. "You're doing just fine."

Her subtle urging seemed all that was necessary for Jack to increase the pace of his attentions. His warm hands moved faster, skimming across her skin, roaming her body and eliciting sensations that stirred an erotic frenzy inside her.

He rolled over, pulling her along to straddle him, and the new position boosted her perception of control and freedom. He cupped her breasts in his hands and teased her nipples until she writhed in ecstasy. She collapsed against his chest and found his mouth, wanting to taste him, feel him, experience everything she could about him. The way her body sang, vibrated with arousal, was beyond her expectations, and she basked in the sweetness.

Her skin became dewy with perspiration as they stroked and kissed, nuzzled and licked. When he eased her onto her back again, her body quivered with craving and burned for fulfillment. With a smooth stroke, he slid his hand down her stomach and under her panties to find the wet heat that cried for his touch. He rubbed the tender flesh, and she gasped for breath as his caress made her mindless with need.

"Easy, babe." He kissed her belly, inched lower. Lower. "That's it." His fingers curled around the edge of her panties, and he rose to his knees to draw them down.

Lifting her bottom, she helped him slide the wisp of satin down her legs. A cool draft on her newly exposed skin reminded her with a stark clarity how defenseless and unprotected she was.

A chill crept through her, raising goose bumps on her skin and dampening the flames of desire.

Her gaze scanned up to the man towering above her, but the bright morning sun, streaming in the window behind him, backlit him and hid his face in shadows. Her pulse scampered, and she crossed her arms over her chest. Feeling vulnerable, she clamped her legs together.

Frantically she searched for the lifeline that had brought her this far. She tried to recall the sensations rocking her moments ago. But, instead, a sense of helplessness swamped her as he turned and placed his hands on her knees. He pushed her legs, prying them apart, and she tensed. His wide shoulders and shadowed countenance loomed over her, and with a whimper, she squeezed her eyes shut. Sinking in doubt, she fought his attempt to open her legs and scrunched up the bed away from him.

"Megan?" The thick rasp of arousal darkened his voice.

But the passion that had carried her to this moment had been swept away with the resurgence of her deep-seated fears. Despite the shivers skirting through her, she tried to part her legs, even a little, for him.

"It's okay, baby. You're doing fine." His large hands stroked inside her trembling thighs, and he lowered himself into position. With a finger, he circled and caressed her then delved deeper into her flesh.

Her muscles bunched with a jerk, and a whimper caught in her throat. Tears leaked to her lashes, and she scrunched her eyes tighter shut.

She couldn't do it.

"Megan." The male voice, colored with concern, demanded her attention. "Megan, open your eyes."

A tremor ravaged her body. Sucking in air, she fought for calm.

"Megan, please! Open your eyes, baby. You're safe."

She complied to his order, peeking out timidly at first before finally raising her gaze to meet the one watching from only inches above. *Jack.*

A ribbon of warmth unfurled inside her.

"It's okay, sweetheart. We can stop. You're all right."

When he brushed her cheek with his hand, she realized he'd moved off her to lie at her side. Except for his tender caress of her face, his body didn't touch her anywhere. Fat tears rolled onto her cheeks, but her shaking subsided.

"I'm sorry," she squeaked.

"Shh. Don't apologize." He heaved a deep sigh. "What happened? What did I do wrong?"

"N-nothing. I—" She bit her lip to stop it from quivering. "I…I couldn't see your face. It was stupid of me. I panicked and—" She paused and swallowed hard, pushing down the frightening images.

"You'd see me better if your eyes weren't closed." A grin flickered over his lips. She started to explain about the sun that backlit him, the shadows hiding his face, but she didn't.

What did it matter now? She'd failed him again. She'd let herself down. The fears had won again.

Frustrations and resentment surged through her. *He* had won. "Damn it!"

She slammed a balled fist down on the mattress and clenched her jaw as she turned her face away from Jack.

"Aw, baby. It's all right." He combed his fingers through her hair, tucking the wisps behind her ear the way she'd seen him do for Caitlyn many times when he consoled her.

"It's *not* all right. I'm tired of living like this." Her voice sounded hoarse, raw with emotion, much the way her heart felt.

He wrapped his arms around her and cuddled her close, his body heat seeping into the chill that permeated her bones. *Jack.*

For several minutes, he held her, still and silent, his chin resting lightly on her shoulder, while she castigated herself for her weakness.

After a few moments, she whispered, "I want to try again."

He didn't answer right away. "Don't do this to yourself. You don't have to—"

"I want to try again!"

"Megan…"

She heard the worry in his voice, and it firmed her

resolve. She didn't want to be pitied. She'd pitied herself long enough. She'd run from the pity of her friends and co-workers once before.

Rolling to face him, she met his hazel gaze. "I want to try again. I have to do this."

"Tonight…or tomorrow. Don't torture yourself if—"

"No, now." She framed his face with her hands and closed her eyes as she kissed him.

Turning his head, he pulled away from her kiss. Disappointment stabbed her, and she raised a wounded gaze to his. His eyes held a fire, an intensity that bore down to her soul.

"Why, Megan? Why me?"

His question caught her off guard. She blinked. "Well, because…" She searched for a way to explain what she'd come to understand herself just the night before. "Because you've been so good to me. You've been understanding, and kind, and patient, and—"

"So could any number of other guys. Why did you ask *me* to make love to you?"

"I have to get past the memories that—"

"No." He shook his head, his gaze still locked on hers. "Why *me?*"

"Are you saying you don't want to do this?"

"Just answer the question."

She drew a deep breath. "I don't want anyone else." Her heart thumped wildly in her chest, and her blood grew warm. "You're the one I trust, the one I care about, Jack."

He shifted, moving so that he covered half of her body with his own. Still his gaze held hers, penetrated her defenses with the honesty radiating from his eyes. "Say it again."

Her mouth felt dry, her tongue thick. "I trust you, Jack. I want to make love to you."

His hand settled on her cheek, and the warmth of it soothed

her ragged nerves. Her eyes drifted closed as she savored the comforting heat from his skin.

"Open your eyes, Megan. Look at me."

She did.

"Say my name."

"Jack."

"Again."

She focused on the loving glow in his eyes.

"Jack." Her voice cracked.

"I want to make love to you, too, Megan." The echo of multifaceted emotions reverberated in his words.

Her chest tightened. His image blurred as moisture crept to her eyes. "I do trust you, Jack."

Something akin to pain puckered his brow, and he ducked his head to kiss her forehead. "All right. Then keep your eyes open. Keep them on me."

She nodded.

He wedged his leg between hers, and she held her breath.

"Say my name."

She had to release the pent-up air to speak. "Jack."

A smile graced his lips, and he rewarded her efforts with a gentle kiss.

When her eyes drifted shut, he broke the kiss. "Look at me, Megan."

She did. And a wave of tender emotion flooded her heart. *Jack.*

She could do this, would do this. She *wanted* this.

Because she was with Jack.

That thought took root and wound itself around the dark memories deep in her core. This was Jack. She opened her legs…and her soul to him.

Smiling his support, he moved on top of her.

"Jack." She breathed his name on a sigh, the one word a

profession of her faith in him. Sliding her arms around his neck, she wove her fingers through the hair at the nape of his neck. Happiness flowered inside her and bloomed in a smile on her lips.

He kissed her deeply, filling her with the sweet, hot taste of his mouth. The velvet warmth of his lips claimed her, seared her, stirred a passion within her that flickered to life. His mouth moved over hers in a caress, a gentle seduction that eased her into a weightless bliss where only the melting of his lips on hers mattered.

"Jack," she whispered between kisses. A promise filled with hope.

He seized her parted lips and drew her breath into his lungs. As he lingered, he sucked her swollen lip between his teeth and soothed it with his tongue. Her world spun, and shooting sparks raced through her veins. He sealed his mouth to hers, pulling her deeper into the vortex of dazzling ecstasy until she never wanted to climb out.

She slid her hands down the curve of his back, then splayed them at the base of his spine. She tugged his hips closer, rose to meet him, knowing only that she yearned for more. Her body ached for him to fill her.

"Jack," she whispered breathlessly. A plea for fulfillment, beseeching him to answer the aching need that thrummed in her blood.

His arms tightened around her, and he bound her lips to his with a soul-shattering kiss as he penetrated her. The hot, hard length of him filled her, and she dug her fingers into his back.

"Are you still with me, babe?" he asked, his voice no more than a rasp.

"Yes. Oh, Jack." She gasped her response, her breath coming in pants as she teetered on the edge of glorious oblivion.

He moved, slowly at first, his heat stroking her, and she clung tighter to him.

"Jack…"

His moan answered her, his breath hot in her ear. He drove harder, pressing deeper into her, carrying her higher, higher. She wrapped her legs around him, surging to meet his thrusts.

"Jack!" With the cry, she found her release amidst the star-burst of a million glimmering sparks. Pulsing waves of liquid fire rocked her to her core.

"Jack!" She wept his name. Tears of joy leaked from her eyes.

"Ah, baby," he sighed, clutching her closer. He bucked and shuddered, and with a satisfied groan, he collapsed on her, his skin slick with sweat. "Oh, Megan, sweet Megan."

Kissing her damp cheeks, he cradled her in his embrace, their bodies still fused.

I did it. Her mind struggled to encompass the truth. *I really did it.*

She buried her face in the crisp hair on Jack's chest and breathed in the warm, musky smell of man and sex. She lounged, limp and sated, in the comfort of his arms for long minutes. Savoring. Smiling. Rejoicing.

She'd made it over the first hurdle toward reclaiming her life, and she owed it all to this man. She owed it to his patience, his snore. His black socks. It would be so easy to fall in love with Jack. Too easy.

Just like it would be easy to depend on him for the security and happiness she felt right now, snuggled in his arms. She couldn't do that. Couldn't allow him to become another crutch.

Now was not the time to rest on her laurels or become complacent in her recovery. She'd made a good start, but the key to her freedom from fear still lay deep inside her.

The realization shot a cold nip of reality into her idyll. She might be falling in love with this man, but until she found that elusive *something* that still held her back, any plans for a future with Jack would have to wait.

Chapter 16

They could get married next weekend. No reason to wait.

That thought made Jack smile. He hugged her closer and kissed the top of her head. "Soooo…?"

She tipped her head back to look up at him. "Sooooo, what?"

"You okay?"

She grinned and kissed his chin. "I'm better than okay. In fact, I'm very good." Nestling against him again with her head on his chest, she sighed. "Too bad we can't stay here all day."

"Who says we can't? Caitlyn's with Lauren's parents, Sam's got a bowl—"

She stiffened with a jerk and sat up, groaning. "Oh, no! Poor Sam!" She was half out of bed, distracting him with her beautiful derriere, before he caught her hand to pull her back.

"Hey, whoa! Where you goin'?"

"I never fed Sam last night or let him out. Lord! He's probably wet the floor by now." She tugged against his grip.

"Sam's okay. He's in the backyard with food and water. I let him out last night."

She blinked at him, clearly trying to recall that detail of the night before. "When did—?"

"Right after I brought you back to bed." He tugged again on her arm. "Come here. It's cold without you cuddled next to me."

A warm grin slid across her lips. "You took care of my dog."

"Mmm-hmm."

She stared at him with that funny little smile for a few more seconds, as if he'd hung the moon, and he felt a little like he'd won the Pulitzer instead of just having fed her mutt.

Crawling back onto the bed, she slipped under the sheet. "Thanks."

"No problem." He trailed nibbling kisses along her shoulder as she settled next to him. "So maybe we *can* stay here all day."

Megan grew very still. "But you...still have to write your article."

He shook his head. "No way. I can't write that article now. Not knowing—"

"What!" She propped on an arm and scowled down at him. "Of course you're going to write it. That was the deal! I give you my story, my side of what happened to me, and you tell the world what that monster did to me!"

Her vehemence surprised him. She *wanted* him to write the piece?

"Megan, come on! You don't think after everything that's happened that I could exploit your pain and trauma to sell newspapers or advance my career, do you? What kind of jerk would that make me?"

She scoffed. "You were willing to write that article when you didn't know it was me. What difference does it make whose pain it was? Mine or some other faceless woman you don't know? The story is the same."

Ouch. She was right. Guilt jabbed him in the gut, and he looked away while she continued passionately arguing her case.

"He gained our trust by playing the gentleman, being the helpful civil servant or the policeman there to protect us. Then he destroyed that trust without a hint of remorse. That…that *psychopath* on a power trip hurt and humiliated me. He shattered the very sanctity of my home—" She clapped her hand to her chest to punctuate her point, her anger and frustration sharpening her tone. "And he's had me looking over my shoulder, scared of my own shadow, second-guessing myself for five years!"

"Megan, honey, I know. I—"

She didn't give him a chance to speak but sat up and plowed on. Deciding she needed to get this off her chest, he shut up and listened.

"It's time for it to stop. He has to be stopped. Other women have to be protected."

"I agree."

"But thanks to his expensive lawyers, his social position, the way the media have reported his arrest, he's created a groundswell of support from the public. Heck, he even got a judge to release him on bail! There's enough doubt about his guilt that if his trial were today, he…he might get off! I can't let that happen."

She gripped his shoulders, and her eyes blazed with conviction. "You have to tell the truth, Jack. Tell the public what he did to me. Damn it, coming to you, spilling my guts, telling you everything that happened was the hardest thing

I've ever done. Bar none. But I did it because he has to be stopped. He has to be convicted. You can't back out on our deal now, Jack. Please. Write the article."

He cradled her cheek in his hand and met her fierce gaze. "When I think of him touching you, hurting you...I—" Fury choked him, and he had to swallow hard before he could speak again. "It makes me sick. Sick to my stomach, sick at heart, sick to the bone with rage and pain for you."

She nodded weakly. "Yeah, it kinda makes me sick, too."

Hands shaking, he curled his fingers in the thick curtain of her hair, pulling her closer. "I want to kill him. I want just five minutes alone with him...."

She gave him a short, humorless laugh. "That's where we differ. I don't ever want to be alone in a room with him again. At the party, when he cornered me—"

He yanked her head down and silenced her with a deep kiss. "I'm so sorry this happened to you. I wish I could do something to take away the hurt and fear and horrible memories."

"You have." She tipped her head toward the rumpled sheets. "This was a pretty good start."

"But it's not enough." Frustration tightened his voice.

She gave him a level look. "So write the article."

He opened his mouth to protest again, but the passion and pleading in her voice told him how important this was to her. How could he say *no?* "All right. For you."

She closed her eyes and released a deep breath. "Good."

She stretched out beside him again, her hand resting lightly over his heart.

Jack tucked one arm around Megan and one arm behind his head to stare up at the ceiling, his thoughts spinning. How did he write an impartial account of something where his emotions were tangled all through the truth? He couldn't. The piece he wrote had to express all the emotion and depth and humanity that Megan's story deserved. Could he write a piece that did justice to the pain and fear and turmoil Megan had endured, the hell she'd survived? And once he wrote that piece, would the *Daily Journal*, where the accused's brother was news editor, really print it?

The subject of his concerns rhythmically strummed her fingers across his skin. Soon the hypnotic stroking distracted him from the daunting task facing him with this article.

His body responded to her touch in a most predictable way, every nerve ending snapping to life and his blood zinging through him. He gritted his teeth and tried to calm his zealous reaction to her stroking. *Patience and self-control.*

"Jack?" Her dulcet voice was a sensual caress itself.

"Mmm?"

"Before you rush off to your laptop, do you think you have time to…make some more good memories?" The corner of her mouth lifted, and his heart turned over.

"Baby, for you I have all the time in the world."

They made love again. Slowly. Carefully. Tenderly.

Paying attention to detail. Learning each other. Finding the perfect balance between his endurance and her need to linger. The resulting union shook Jack to the core, eroding any remaining doubts that he wanted this woman in his life. Forever.

"What's your calendar look like next weekend?" Jack asked as he pressed a nibbling kiss to the hollow of Megan's throat.

"I don't know. Nothing special planned. Why?"

"I figure we can get our blood tests this week and make us official next Saturday."

She angled her head to give him a baffled, even suspicious, scrutiny. "Official? What…what are you saying?"

He flashed her a lopsided grin. "I'm saying I want to marry you. I want to wake up with you every morning for the rest of—"

Before he could finish, she was shaking her head, her face pale. "No, Jack. I can't. It's too soon…."

"Next weekend is too soon?" He thunked himself on the head. "Of course. How stupid of me. It's your first wedding, and you want a big to-do. Dress and cake and flowers, right? We can do that. I just thought maybe—"

Frowning, she rolled away from him, finger-raking her tousled hair from her face. "Jack…"

Uneasiness stirred in his chest. "Megan, what's wrong? You do want to get married, don't you? Don't tell me I'm the only one who felt what was happening here." He waved a hand across the bed where they'd just had the best sex of his life.

More than sex. They'd made love. They'd spiritually connected.

Hadn't they?

He'd been blown away by everything that had happened in the past eighteen hours. So why was she looking at him as if he had two heads?

She worried her teeth over her bottom lip, her eyes turning the color of a deep lake. Deep water hid all sorts of potential dangers, and he had no doubt her expression meant trouble for him. A familiar tension slowly coiled in his chest. "Megan?"

Quietly, she slid out of bed and pulled on the silky robe she'd worn out of the bathroom. Her silence turned the pressure inside him a notch higher.

"I think you've misread what happened here. I never intended to—" Her fingers trembled as she reached for her earlobe. Finding no earring, her hand fell heavily at her side.

She met his gaze with sad, apologetic eyes. "I can't marry you. Not now. And maybe…not ever. I'm not ready to—"

He muttered an obscenity as he sighed. Somehow each time she pulled away from him it hurt even more. Right now his chest felt as if it would split wide open. Frustration and disappointment knotted around the pain of rejection, a mammoth sense of loss.

"I'm sorry, Jack. I—"

He held up a hand to stop her. "No, don't. My mistake. No explanations needed."

He cringed at the bitterness that colored his tone. Emotions churned a first-class ulcer in his gut. *Hell!*

Tears welled in her eyes. "I thought you understood…"

Jack slammed his feet to the floor and snatched up his pants. "Yeah, I thought I did, too. Seems no matter how many times you tell me to take a hike, that you don't want anything permanent, I can't get it through my thick skull."

Megan trembled, and her hand clutched the lapels of her robe closed. "What we just shared was special to me, Jack. You're very important to me…."

He huffed and shook his head. "I don't need any pretty words to make me feel better. It's my mistake, and I'll deal with it. I assumed when we—" With a snort, he dragged his hand through his hair. "I assumed. Damn it, that's a bad habit I really gotta break. Not a good trait for a reporter, huh?"

He attempted a smile, but he knew it fell short of the mark, probably coming off as more of a grimace. He shoved his feet into his shoes and snagged his shirt from the end of the bed.

Megan watched him dress, her chin quivering, and her eyes puddling with tears. "I should have thought about how you would interpret my request. And I'm sorry if I misled you. I—"

Her voice cracked, and she drew a slow breath, squeezing

the robe tighter. Her efforts not to cry gouged his heart all the more. He knew she felt *something* for him.

But he didn't know how to translate that something into the kind of commitment and future he saw for them. He didn't know how to give Megan what she needed without investing so much of himself he couldn't survive her leaving unscathed. And he sure as hell hadn't known how to keep Lauren from walking away.

He'd given his heart without any assurances that his feelings were reciprocated. So really this was his own fault.

A pain so sharp it stole his breath sliced through his chest. He stalked to the bedroom door, not bothering to button his shirt. He couldn't breathe, had to get out of there before he did something stupid like slam his hand through the wall or fall at her feet begging for another chance.

"Jack, wait!" she cried.

He stopped in the hall but didn't turn. The soft padding of her barefoot steps whispered behind him, warning him of her approach. Still he wasn't prepared for her to slip her arms around his waist and bury her face in his back. Warm moisture penetrated the fabric of his shirt. Her tears, he realized as his gut wrenched.

"I want to be with you, Jack," she whispered so softly he had to strain to hear. "I feel safe with you. I feel loved and protected and cherished. You're everything I want."

It took every ounce of his strength not to turn and pull her into his arms. His body shook, his hands fisted and tensed.

"I would marry you today if I could, but…you'd be a crutch."

"A crutch? What—"

"That's what Ginny calls Sam. And the gun I bought. And all the locks on my door. They all make me feel safer, but I'll never have the true peace-of-mind I need, the real healing to my psyche until I can find that sense of security and confidence within myself. She says as long as I rely on my crutches, I'll never really face down my true fear."

She moved around him, her arms still circling his waist. "Before I can marry you, before I can promise you any kind of future, I have to find that inner peace. Telling you about what happened was a start. Making love to you was an important step. I'm on the right track finally. But I need more time."

"How long?" he asked, his voice a thick rasp. He hated the flicker of hope that teased him.

She shook her head. "I don't know. Maybe a month or two."

"Or a year. Or forever," he said darkly.

Her brow creased, and her eyes grew stormy. "Maybe. It's taken me five years to come this far. I can't make any promises."

He seized her wrists, disengaged himself from her arms. The rock sitting on his lungs made it hard to speak. "And I can't do this halfway."

He moved to the front door giving himself the distance he needed, the time necessary to catch his breath and firm his resolve. "I need more than *maybe*. I can't put my life and Caitlyn's on hold indefinitely. Caity needs someone she can count on, not someone who can't commit. And so do I." He took a deep breath, shoving down the bitter taste of disappointment in his throat. "I need certainty. I need one hundred percent."

Her wounded expression ripped through his gut. Didn't she know this was killing him?

But he had to protect his daughter. His heart. A clean break healed fastest.

"I don't want you seeing Caity anymore. She doesn't need to build any more false hopes or dreams about you being her new mommy."

Megan inhaled sharply, and the first tear fell. Her face crumpled in misery, and she swiped at her cheek as more tears joined the first. "I understand."

He turned away quickly and snatched open the front door. He was doing the right thing. Letting Megan string him along indefinitely would be a mistake. Letting himself and his daughter hope for something that might never be would be a mistake. Letting himself love a woman who might never love him back was a huge mistake.

His heart in his throat, he glanced back at her one last time. "Goodbye, Megan. I wish you all best."

As he closed her door behind him and crossed her yard toward his house, he couldn't help but wonder if he hadn't just made the biggest mistake of all.

Chapter 17

Jack spent the rest of Saturday working on the article that would expose Megan's attack and heartache to the public. But for every word he typed, it seemed he deleted two. By that evening he was beyond frustrated.

His words simply couldn't convey the wrenching sound of Megan sobbing in his arms Friday night, the haunted expression in her eyes as she related the graphic details of her assault, or the years of emotional limbo she'd lived since the attack.

Dwelling on those details as he worked was slowly driving Jack insane.

He would have loved to cram his laptop down Frank's throat.

Near midnight, he gave up on getting any work done. He spent the rest of the night staring at his bedroom ceiling, missing Megan, and alternately regretting his harsh ultimatum that she stay away and reminding himself that he'd made the only choice he could. He and Caity would hurt less by cutting all ties with her now than they would if Megan got cold feet and walked away a few months down the road.

Jack rolled out of bed early Sunday morning, bleary-eyed from lack of sleep, numb from flogging himself with the same recriminations and sick of repeating the same reassurances.

He made himself a pot of coffee with chicory, a strong enough brew to make any Cajun connoisseur proud, and got to work again. But even the mega-dose of caffeine didn't help get his writing on track.

After beating his head against the same writer's block for hours, he opted for a change of scenery by late morning.

Caitlyn was gone until early tomorrow morning with Lauren's parents, so he might as well head to the newspaper office to work. Maybe the office atmosphere, the clack of keyboards and jangling phones, would inspire him. Or at least get his mind off the look on Megan's face as he'd walked out her door.

He snatched his keys from the counter and marched out to his truck. He needed something to distract him from the incredible sex he'd shared with Megan and the crushing disappointment of learning he'd merely been a tool for her recovery. She was no closer to giving him her heart, her life or a commitment than she'd been the first day they met.

He backed out of his driveway and jabbed the accelerator harder than necessary. His tires squealed, and an elderly neighbor watering her flowers frowned at him.

Damn it, it wasn't that he didn't *want* to help Megan heal and regain her confidence. But he'd wanted so much more than a one-night stand from her.

Being a Sunday morning, traffic was light, and he reached the *Daily Journal* office in record time. Shuffling a stack of papers off his desk, he slapped down his notes from Megan's interview and got to work. He'd stay all night if he had to in order to finish the piece.

Megan had trusted him with her story, her deepest hurt. She was counting on him to help balance the public opinion toward the Gentleman Rapist and tell the truth about the man claiming to be falsely charged.

Whatever it took, he wouldn't let Megan down.

Jack had come through for her at every turn in the last few convoluted days. Yet she'd cut him off at the knees when he'd made his spontaneous marriage proposal, squashed his hopes and sent him running for the door. Knowing how Lauren had hurt him, knowing that marrying Jack—someday—was just the sort of dream come true she craved, why had she been so brutal, so negative? What had she been thinking?

Megan mentally kicked herself. Maybe marriage was a big, scary step at this point, but she could have given him something to hold onto. She should have told him how she felt. That she was falling in love with him.

Now she'd likely lost him for good.

Megan jogged to keep up with Sam's brisk pace on their Sunday morning walk. She'd hoped the fresh air and exercise would clear her mind, but she couldn't get thoughts of Jack out of her head.

When Sam's ears perked up, and he gave a whine, she followed the direction of the shepherd's gaze in time to see Jack hop in his truck and race out of his driveway.

"No, Sammy, we're not going to see Jack today." She ruffled Sam's thick coat. "Made friends with him the other night, did you?"

Sam's tail wagged twice, and he started toward Jack's

house. All day Saturday, she'd managed to avoid gazing wistfully out her window at Jack's house and had purposely chosen a route for their walk that did not go past it. Obviously Sam had other ideas.

She tugged Sam's leash, urging him to follow her in the opposite direction.

Megan sighed. She'd run the same excuses and reasoning for her refusal of Jack's proposal over and over, but what she kept coming back to were the reasons she should have said *yes*. The warmth of his arms around her. The heat of his body buried deep inside hers. The fire in his eyes when he talked of waking each morning beside her.

Her spirits flagging, she stroked Sam's head as they headed back up her driveway. Was she kidding herself about getting any semblance of her old life back? Was she passing up a life full of Jack's love and family on the chance that she could find some unspecific something inside her that would give her a personal peace-of-mind? Perhaps she'd never truly feel safe again. Except in Jack's arms.

She gave her head a hard shake. *No!* That was defeatist, dependent thinking. She *had* to get her life back on track *by herself* or her spiritual recovery would never be complete.

She needed to talk to Ginny. Ginny would help her make sense of things. Sort out the truths from the wishful thinking.

After unhooking Sam's leash and sending him out to the backyard to roam and bark at squirrels, she called Ginny.

"I'm just about to head out to church," Ginny said. "Want to come? We'll get lunch afterward, and you can talk about whatever you want."

Church. Years before, she'd attended church regularly. She'd cherished the weekly revival of her spirit and refocusing of her attitude, the mental centering of her priorities. Just one more area of her life where she'd gotten off track. Today, she couldn't think of anything she wanted or needed more for her weary heart and muddled mind.

Megan looked down at the grungy sweats she wore. "I have to shower and get dressed, so I'll probably miss the first hymn, but…yeah. I'll meet you. Sit toward the back so I can slip in late."

"Sure thing."

Just the promise of a worthy distraction energized Megan. Maybe, just maybe, between a booster shot of her religious convictions and Ginny's sage advice, she could come to some practical decisions about Jack that would ease her mind.

Goodness knows talking to Sam and rewinding her own circular thoughts had done no good so far.

"You slept with him, didn't you?"

Megan nearly choked on her bite of baked potato when Ginny tossed the question at her over lunch. She glanced around the other tables at the crowded family steak house, feeling heat sting her face.

"I'll take that adorable flush in your cheeks as a 'yes'." Ginny flashed a gloating grin and wiggled her eyebrows. "Spill. I want details. Since I haven't had a man in longer than I care to remember, I have to live vicariously through your conquests."

Megan snorted. "I'd hardly call it a conquest. I was nervous, awkward, inept…ugh!" She pressed fingers to her temple. "It would be embarrassing if Jack weren't so sweet and understanding about everything."

"I figured he would be. But you did it, and he was…good? Great? Hunka burning love?"

Megan tore off a piece of yeast roll to throw at Ginny as she scoffed. "You're shameful!"

"And you're blushing again. I'm guessing that means he gets high marks."

Megan's only response was a noncommittal grin. She stabbed a bite of steak and stared at it a few seconds before dropping her bomb. "He asked me to marry him."

That wiped the sassy grin off Ginny's face. Her eyes widened, and she leaned forward, the ruffle on her blouse hitting the catsup on her plate. Ginny ignored her plate and her clothes. "What did you say?"

Megan scooted a bite of salad around her plate aimlessly. "I said *no*."

"Why? It's obvious how much you care for him."

Ginny's reaction stunned Megan. Surely Ginny of all people should understand her choice.

"Because I'm not ready. I still needed time to find my inner strength and peace-of-mind. I can't let him become another crutch."

"Would he be a crutch?" Ginny asked, her pale blue eyes narrowing to two piercing lasers cutting straight to the issue.

"I wouldn't mean for him to be, but it would be so easy to depend on him for security before I was truly healed. From deep inside."

"Do you love Jack?"

"I—" Megan huffed. "That's not—" Her shoulders drooped. "I could. He did everything right the other night. And I'm not talking about sex. He knew what I needed and gave me one hundred percent of himself." Now she leaned forward. "He even let Sam out and made sure he had food."

When Ginny gave her a dubious frown, Megan added, "He knew what needed to be done, what was important to me, and he took care of it. He's someone I can rely on." She flicked her hand in dismissal. "Which is why I can't marry him now. It would be too easy to grow dependent on him. I can't do that."

Ginny furrowed her brow and gave her an exaggerated

scowl. "Oh, right. Heaven forbid you marry a man you love and are happy with because he's *dependable*."

Shaking her head, Ginny flopped back in her chair and noticed the catsup on her shirt. "Aw, fudge! I just got this back from the cleaners."

While Ginny dabbed at the stain on her blouse, Megan played mental catch-up. "Are you saying you think I *should* marry Jack? But what about all your talk about crutches and finding my inner strength?"

Ginny paused from cleaning her blouse and peered up at Megan. "Getting an attack dog is a crutch. Having a pet you love and cherish is not. Getting a gun is a crutch. Taking self-defense classes and learning to use a gun safely is not. One gives you false confidence, the other helps you move on in your life. Positive steps toward leading a productive, happy life where you're confident in your own ability to protect yourself."

"But what if even after the self-defense and weapons classes, even with a pet I love and cherish, I still feel something is missing? What if I still feel I haven't found the secret to that personal satisfaction and security and peace?"

Ginny drew a slow deep breath, clearly choosing her words carefully. But careful or not, Ginny would be honest and cut to the chase. Megan appreciated that frankness, relished the pointed guidance.

"There is no magic formula. No proven course of action or miracle cure." Her face softened with regret. "I don't have any answers for you, Megan."

Megan's heart sank. Ginny couldn't fail her now. She needed advice, needed perspective, needed slap-in-the-face truth.

Ginny reached for Megan's hand and squeezed her fingers. "You've done everything right. You've told Jack the truth. You've talked through your fears, and you've worked with the police. You've confronted the issues and replaced bad memories of a violent act with new ones of a loving act. You've made real progress. I'm proud of you."

Frustration wound through Megan like a coil ready to spring. She slapped her hand on the table and fought to keep her tone low enough as not to cause a scene for the other diners. "Then why do I still feel at my wits' end? Why do I still feel so lost and vulnerable?"

"Maybe you've done everything except the most important thing of all."

Megan frowned. "What's that?"

"Forgive yourself."

Megan grunted in exasperation. "For what? I didn't ask to be raped. It wasn't my fault! We got past that much in the first months of my counseling." She shook her head and gave Ginny a baffled, disconcerted look. "I was targeted for an act of violence." She poked herself in the chest for emphasis. "And I survived. I'm a rape *survivor*, not a victim. I am not to blame."

Even as she said the words, an uneasiness swirled through her gut. Tears bloomed in her eyes, and her chest grew tight. The nagging doubt that held her back returned.

This time, though, she saw what she'd been avoiding for years.

"What is it, Megan? What is that look on your face about? Put it in words." Ginny wiggled her fingers in a *give-it-to-me* motion. "Don't push it down again. Get it out where we can look at it and get rid of it once and for all."

Megan closed her eyes and looked at the ugliness lurking behind her bravado and learned responses.

She'd failed. She'd trusted someone who should have been trustworthy and been burned. Not just the police uniform, not just her fiancé.

But herself.

She *did* blame herself. That was why she never felt truly

safe. She didn't trust herself to keep herself safe. Deep down, she believed she'd made a colossal error in judgment and had paid the price for her own mistake.

Throat knotted, she rasped, "I shouldn't have let him in my house. I should have called the police station to verify his badge number. I should have called a neighbor to walk through the house with us while he was there. I had plenty of chances to do the smart thing, and I failed. If I'd listened to my instincts, if I'd done what I knew I should, I'd have been okay. But I trusted him instead. Trusted his uniform. I was stupid, and I got hurt."

Ginny shook her head adamantly. "Not stupid. Human. We all make mistakes. Even if you'd made a million mistakes, I still wouldn't put the blame for what happened on you. Frank Harwood is solely and completely responsible for his actions. Not you! All you can take ownership of is poor judgment or misplaced trust. It sucks eggs that your mistake caused you so much grief and pain, but you have to forgive yourself. You learn from your mistake, you grow, you move on. Next time, God forbid there ever is a next time, you will not make the same mistake."

Sharp-edged apprehension sliced through her chest. Ginny had hit on the key to her doubts. Curling her fingers into her palm, Megan growled, "How do I know that? If I was dumb enough to mess up once, how do I know it won't happen again?" Tears burned her throat and stung her eyes. "How do I trust myself to do the right thing ever again?"

With a confident grin, Ginny covered Megan's trembling hand. "Do you really think you'll ever forget what happened? Do you really think moving on in your life means forgetting what happened, setting yourself up to make the same mistake?" She shook her head and gave Megan a warm smile. "Honey, moving on means being

stronger, being happy again, being ready to embrace life—
whatever it brings. I don't know anyone more ready than
you. Give yourself permission to be happy. Stop punishing
yourself for a five-year-old mistake. You did not cause your
rape. You did not allow it to happen. It's okay to trust
yourself, because you've learned the hard way and are a
stronger woman for it."

Megan sat back in her chair, trying to absorb what Ginny
was telling her. Ginny had never steered her wrong in the past.
But how did she change five years of thinking otherwise, five
years of believing herself untrustworthy, unreliable for her
self-protection? For five years she'd felt vulnerable, scared.
Rewiring her brain to believe something else would take
time, wouldn't it? And how did Jack figure in all of this? She
wanted to believe he could be an active, present part of reclaiming her life and happiness.

The same questions still plagued her when she pulled into
her driveway after lunch. She sat in her car and stared out her
windshield long after she'd turned off the engine. As she de-
liberated, brooding over all Ginny had said and wondering
how to put her friend's advice into practice, the babble of a
child's voice drifted through her open car window. A familiar
child's voice. Caitlyn's chatter.

A car door slammed. Her heart in her throat, Megan
turned to watch a couple she assumed were Lauren's
parents walk Caitlyn to Jack's front door. A pang twisted
inside her. She missed Jack's daughter as much as she
missed Jack.

Heaving a deep sigh, she finally opened her car door and
hoisted herself from her front seat. Sam would be waiting
for his lunch.

"Hi, Miss Megan!" Caitlyn called.

When she looked up, she found Jack's daughter waving

her arm in an enthusiastic greeting. She returned a wave and blew Caitlyn a kiss. "Hi, sweetie. Did you have a good weekend with your grandparents?"

"Yeah, but we had to come back early 'cause somebody died."

Megan's chest gave a lurch. "Somebody died?"

Lauren's mother, a refined looking and well-coifed woman, turned at the front door. "Don't panic, dear. It was my Uncle Herbert. He was ninety-two. But we have to get back to Fort Worth for the funeral, so we've brought Caitlyn back earlier than planned. Do you have any idea where Jack is? He's not answering the door or his cell phone."

Megan remembered seeing Jack speed out of his driveway that morning. No telling where he'd gone or when he'd be back. "I'm sorry, I don't."

Even from across the street, Megan could tell the woman was displeased.

"Grandma, Megan can babysit me!" Caitlyn said loudly. "She's babysitted for me before, 'cause she's Daddy's new girlfriend! Can I stay with Megan?"

Lauren's mother hesitated then glanced toward Megan.

"Ma'am, is there any way you can watch Caitlyn until Jack gets back? We really must get on the road if we're going to get back to Fort Worth in time for the family visitation at the funeral home."

A combination of pleasure and anxiety wrapped around Megan's heart.

I don't want you seeing Caity anymore. Jack had been explicit and firm. How could she defy his wishes? But what else could she do? Lauren's father had already gotten back in the car and had it in Reverse. Lauren's mother looked ready to leave Caitlyn on the doorstep if needed. Maybe Lauren's lack of mothering instincts was an inherited trait. Irritation with the older couple's eagerness to be rid of their own grand-daughter spun through Megan, deciding the matter for her.

"I'll watch her. Bring her over."

Lauren's mother said something to Caitlyn, and Jack's daughter jumped for joy and raced across the lawn toward Megan's house.

"Stop!" Megan cried, hurrying toward the street to meet Caitlyn. "Look both ways!"

The child stumbled to a stop at the curb and did a quick look both directions. Megan double-checked the street for traffic then knelt to wrap Caitlyn in a bear hug as she barreled into her arms.

"We went to the zoo yesterday and saw monkeys and zebras and a really neat tiger!"

Caitlyn's eyes glowed with excitement, and Megan thought her heart would splinter right then and there. How could she ever tell this sweet little girl goodbye? How could she give up Jack and all he already meant in her life?

She couldn't. She'd find a way to move past the sense of vulnerability and fear and seize what her life had to offer with both hands. Or die trying.

"Have you had lunch yet?"

"Nuh-uh." Caitlyn tossed her braids as she shook her head.

"Come on inside, and I'll get you a sandwich. Unless you'd like to try some of Sam's dog food? I have to fix his lunch, too." Megan winked at Jack's daughter.

"Eww!" Caitlyn said, giggling.

Megan laughed and led Caitlyn to the front door.

When Lauren's mother reached the front porch, Megan took Caitlyn's bag and promised to leave a note on Jack's door telling him what had happened and where his daughter was.

The coiffured woman gave a satisfied nod, kissed

Caitlyn's cheek and rushed off with a finger wave. "Thanks, dear! 'Bye, Cait!"

Once her grandmother's car had disappeared down the street, Caitlyn tugged on the skirt Megan had donned to go to church. "Can we make cookies today?"

She looked down at the expressive dark eyes of Jack's daughter, knowing this could well be the last quality time she had with her. Especially once Jack found out she'd gone against his direct request that she stay away.

"Sure, sweetie, after lunch we'll make cookies."

"Chocolate chip?"

"Is there any other kind?" Megan playfully pulled on one braid and led Caitlyn into the kitchen. They started lunch with Sam inside, but Caitlyn decided it was more fun to feed her lunch to the dog than eat it herself. Megan eventually put Sam in the backyard in order to get Caitlyn to eat.

After lunch, she sent Caitlyn to wash her hands while she gathered the ingredients for chocolate chip cookies. Megan was deep in her pantry, juggling cans of peas and boxes of crackers when the doorbell rang. Probably Jack wanting his daughter back. Megan frowned. She'd been looking forward to baking with Caitlyn, spending the afternoon distracted from the restless thoughts Ginny had stirred.

"I'll get it!" Caitlyn chirped from the hall.

"Caitlyn, wait for me, sweetie," Megan called out of the pantry closet. "Don't open the door until I get—"

"Well, hello, little lady." The male voice from the foyer told her the warning had not been heard or had come too late. Caitlyn had let a man in the house with them.

The voice wasn't Jack's.

Megan's heart rate kicked up a notch.

"Who might you be?"

"I'm Caitlyn Calhoun."

Fumbling to reshelve the items in her arms as quickly as she could, Megan kept her ears tuned to what was transpiring in the foyer.

"Who are you?" Caitlyn asked.

"I'm a friend of Megan's. Is she home?"

A friend of hers? She didn't have any male friends. At least none that would come by her house. Megan dropped a can of corn and ignored it. Suddenly getting out to the foyer—now—was far more important.

"Uh-huh. We're going to make cookies! Chocolate chip!"

"Oh, yeah?"

Megan raced around the corner to the entry hall just as the man laughed at the little girl's enthusiastic pronouncement. Simultaneously her eyes and ears confirmed the stranger's identity. The linebacker stature and nasal laugh assaulted her, slashing through her with an icy blade of horror.

Her rapist had returned.

Chapter 18

A scream ripped from Megan's throat. Her legs threatened to give out. The walls in the foyer seemed to waver. She was going to pass out.

Caitlyn, startled by Megan's scream, wailed in fright.

That reminder that she had an innocent child to protect was all Megan needed to put the starch back in her legs. She rushed across the foyer and stepped protectively between her rapist and Caitlyn.

"Well, well. If it isn't Miss Megan Tell-all." Frank Harwood moved toward her, his silver eyes narrowed. "Surely you aren't surprised to see me? You didn't think I'd let you tell the world our secret without coming back to make you pay for your…indiscretion?"

"Get out of my house!" She aimed a remarkably steady finger at the front door as she edged backward with Caitlyn. Her priority was keeping the slimebag away from Jack's daughter, a child she loved as her own. No matter what it took, what it cost her, she would keep Frank from touching so much as one hair on the girl's head.

She could hear Sam barking and snarling at the back door. Her lethal protector was shut out in the yard.

And since she'd crossed the foyer to protect Caitlyn, Frank now stood between her and the kitchen. And Sam. And the phone.

But her gun and a second phone were in her bedroom. Pulse scampering, Megan sidled toward the hall, keeping Caitlyn behind her.

"Is this your daughter? Funny, you didn't mention children the other night at my brother's house." Evil lurked in the slanted grin Frank sent her.

"Stay the hell away from her!"

"Such a pretty child." Frank took a step toward them, and Megan's stomach lurched.

"Your beef is with me. Leave her alone!"

"Wait a minute. Your lover Jack said he had a daughter, didn't he?" Frank gave another of his twisted, nasal laughs. "A bonus I hadn't expected!"

She tried distracting Frank while her brain scrambled for a plan. "The police know who you are now."

"Thanks to you," he snarled, venom in his eyes.

Numerous scenarios flashed through Megan's head. In an instant she weighed each one's merits and drawbacks. She needed to act. Fast!

Send Caitlyn to let Sam inside? No. The door was locked and the key was too high for Caity to reach. And that assumed Caitlyn could get past Frank to the kitchen.

Eyes narrowed, teeth gritted, Megan curled her lip at Frank. "Don't you think they'll trace anything you do to me straight back to you?"

Frank's only response was to stalk closer.

Megan's chest tightened. Her priority was to get Caitlyn out of harm's way.

And if Frank did attack, she didn't want Caitlyn to see anything Frank might do to her.

Acid curdled in her stomach.

"If you hurt us, you'll only make things worse for yourself."

Frank made a tsking sound and moved closer, reaching under his shirt. He drew out a handgun, and Megan's blood froze.

How could she protect Caitlyn from a bullet?

"I'd say you're the one who made things worse for me. I can't let you get away with that."

Icy terror spun through her veins. Though fear strangled her, Megan managed to shove Caitlyn into the hall bathroom. "Stay in there, Caity! Lock the door. Don't come out for any reason!"

Her bottom lip quivering, Caitlyn blinked at her. "But why—"

Megan gave Caitlyn's back a push. "Please, sweetie, go!"

Facing Frank again, she blocked the hallway until she heard the bathroom door slam and a lock click.

Again she edged back. Toward her bedroom. Toward her own gun. Toward the phone.

As Frank followed Megan down the hall, his large gun trained on her, he paused when he reached the bathroom door.

Megan's heart rose to her throat.

Frank jiggled the locked doorknob then sent Megan a chilling grin. "That flimsy lock won't keep me out…once I've finished with you."

Protective rage flared in Megan. "You bastard! Don't you touch her!"

She whipped off a shoe and hurled it at Frank's head. The shoe smacked him in the face.

While Frank cradled his bloody nose, Megan spun around and raced to her bedroom. Snatching open her nightstand drawer, she grabbed her own gun.

Not loaded. Megan's gut clenched.

She'd removed all the ammunition, storing it in a separate drawer in deference to having Caitlyn visit on occasion over the past few weeks. Panicked, she scrambled to find the box of cartridges.

"You'll pay for that, bitch!" As Frank burst through the bedroom door, fire blazed in his eyes. He stalked toward her, his nose dripping blood on her floor.

She swung her gun toward him. "Stop! I know how to use this!"

He hesitated only a moment then laughed, waggling his own weapon in front of her. "Face it, sugar. You're out-gunned. I'm bigger. And smarter. And stronger. You haven't got a chance."

Megan swallowed hard, gulped for a breath.

He steadied his weapon and aimed.

Megan gasped and staggered back a step. She'd pushed too hard, let her own anguish color her judgment. Brutal intent darkened his eyes, and the cold slap of reality brought her senses back to the very real danger she was in, danger she'd exacerbated by letting her tainted emotions rule her actions.

As a loud pop reverberated through the room, Megan dived behind her bed.

The hardwood floor shook as he lumbered around the end of her mattress. He grinned at her, gloating, then lunged.

In a futile gut reaction, she pulled her trigger. Her gun gave a telltale click of impotence.

Frank cackled as he seized her legs. She kicked hard,

trying to free herself from his grasp. With brutal force, he brought the butt of his weapon down on her temple. Her head snapped back and thumped the hardwood floor, dazing her briefly.

Megan blinked to clear her vision.

Frank loomed over her, his weapon in her face. "You're gonna die, Megan Tell-all."

Dropping her own weapon, she grabbed for Frank's gun with both hands, shoving it away from her head. Her arms trembled as she struggled to keep his gun aimed away from her. She thrashed her body and strained with her legs, fighting to free herself from the weight of her attacker.

Frank landed a blow to her cheek.

Megan cried out in pain, struggled to stay conscious.

She had to protect Caitlyn. Had to get to the phone. Had to fight this madman until help arrived.

Adrenaline fueled her muscles as she flailed and fought randomly. Then training took over. The months of self-defense classes filtered back through her brain.

Go for his eyes. His knees. His throat.

Disable him.

With a feral cry, she gouged at his eyes with her finger-nails. He howled in pain and raised an arm to block her hands.

She used that moment of distraction to land a solid blow to the side of his wrist. Frank's gun fell and skittered under her bed.

Growling like a rabid animal, Frank pushed to his knees and swiped something from his ankle.

A bright flash of metal warned Megan of the blade swooping down at her. With a gasp, she rolled out of the way. The floor took the brunt of the stab, but a sharp ache in her shoulder told her she'd been cut.

The stabbing motion had shifted Frank's weight forward enough for her to free one leg. She raised her knee hard. But missed her target. Frank's groin took only a glancing blow that served only to enrage him.

Megan refused to give up. Mustering all her strength, she wedged her knee to her chest and used the leverage to land a swift kick in his chest.

Frank reeled back, gasping for breath. While he gulped for air, she wrenched away from his grasp. Crawling crablike, she inched across the floor, then clambered to her feet. Her shoulder throbbing, Megan scrambled over the bed and snatched up the phone. She managed to get 911 dialed before Frank tackled her from behind.

He knocked the phone from her hand. Breath whooshed from her lungs.

Roughly he flipped her to her back and pinned her with his body. With one large hand, he anchored both of her wrists over her head. Megan gasped for air to scream, but his body crushed her.

"Now, this is familiar," he taunted, his leering face hovering just above hers. Both his nose and the scratches she'd inflicted around his eyes bled and dripped on her cheeks. He cackled cruelly. "Don't you love it when history repeats itself?"

No! Her mind screamed. *Not again. Never again!*

His eyes glinted, their natural gunmetal gray this time, like at the party.

Bile rose in her throat. He would *not* rape her again.

"Nooo!" she roared.

Another slap stung her cheek, then the cold steel of his blade touched her neck.

She heard the squeak of door hinges.

"Megan? I'm scared. I want my Daddy!"

Frank looked over his shoulder toward the bedroom door. "Caitlyn, *no!* Get back in the bathroom! *Now!*" The vehemence of her cry caused the knife to dig into her skin. A warm trickle slid down her neck.

Frank turned back to her, smirking. "Maybe I should take care of the kid first…and let you watch."

"I'll kill you before I let you touch her, you monster," she rasped, tears filling her throat and eyes at the thought of this evil man hurting Jack's child.

Frank's grip tightened, and he shoved his battered face right up into hers, snarling. "Not if I kill you first."

Jack pulled into his driveway and killed the engine, sighing tiredly. It didn't take long at the newspaper office, listening to the tape-recorded interview with Megan, before the obvious solution became clear.

He had no right to translate or interpret Megan's words for the readers. He could never convey the emotion, the severity of what had happened to Megan the way she had. He had to let her words speak for themselves.

The rest of his time had been spent transcribing Megan's testimony word for word then editing it down to the most pertinent and poignant excerpts. He wrote a brief introduction and conclusion, but let Megan tell her own story. He was proud of the end result and hoped Megan found it adequate. Most of all, he prayed it won the response from the public that he intended. Prayed Burt had the guts to publish it.

If not, Jack would take the story elsewhere. Even if it cost him his job.

He pinched the bridge of his nose. Exhaustion pounded behind his eyes. He wished he could steal a nap but doubted sleep would be any more cooperative in coming this afternoon than it was last night. The way he'd left things with Megan still filled his every thought, every minute, every cell.

Somewhere during his eighth or ninth time listening to her

tell the story of her rape, his gut twisting over her anguish, it had dawned on him.

He'd done to Megan the very thing he lambasted Lauren for doing to him. The same thing Greg had done to Megan. When she'd needed his faith and love, his help getting through an emotional trauma, he'd bailed. She'd asked for understanding, for patience, for time, and he'd walked out.

For the hundredth time that day, Jack's chest wrenched with regret, with guilt. He'd blown it, big-time. Before he could ask Megan for the commitment he wanted, he had to be equally willing to risk everything, his whole heart and soul, to give her the love and loyalty, the time and support, she needed from him.

She'd trusted him with her darkest hour, and he'd run scared. Scared of the feelings she stirred in him. Scared of losing again. Scared of seeing his daughter hurt.

But Megan's love was obvious in her kiss and in her touch, in her concern for Caity, and in the sacrifice she'd made to bare her aching soul to him.

Damn. He could only pray that she loved him enough to give his hardheaded self a second chance.

As he climbed out of his car, a stack of folders in hand, he allowed himself to gaze across the road at her quaint brick home. He could hear Sam in the backyard, kicking up a fuss about something. A squirrel probably.

"Go get 'em, Sam," he called with a wry grin, trying to shake his grim mood. "Free the world of rodent tyranny."

Just as he turned to walk up his sidewalk, he saw Sam jump the five-foot fence around Megan's backyard. So *that* was how he got loose the day Caitlyn had been bitten. He'd suspected as much.

He'd have to warn Megan what Sam was capable of so she could take measures to keep him penned.

By now, Sam had reached Megan's front porch and

scratched furiously at the front door, snarling and barking for all he was worth.

Jack frowned. What had gotten into the dog? He stood on the sidewalk, his interest piqued, waiting to see if Megan let Sam inside.

Admit it, pal. You just want to catch a quick look at her. You miss her.

Sighing, he headed up the stairs to his front porch and dug his house key out of his pocket.

Ashley, Caitlyn's cat, strolled out of the bushes and trotted over to the door to be let in.

Then arched her back and hissed.

"Whoa, cat, what the—?"

Before he could finish the question, Sam charged up his porch steps, sending Ashley running for the bushes. The dog launched a series of sharp, strident barks.

"Sam? What's wrong?" Jack shook his head and laughed at himself. He was talking to a *dog*. "What's that? Timmy's fallen in a mine and has a broken leg?"

He caught Sam's collar and ruffled the fur on his neck. "Take it easy, boy."

As he keyed the front lock open, he noticed the small note taped to the brass knocker. *Jack* was written across the front in Megan's teacher-perfect handwriting. He pulled it down and opened the note.

Lauren's parents had a family emergency and brought Caitlyn home early. She's with me. Megan

An icy chill washed down his spine. He turned to Sam again, clearly urging Jack to follow him back to Megan's house. Circling and barking.

Something was wrong.

Jack didn't bother to take his files inside. He dropped them on the porch in a flurry of fluttering paper as he jumped down his front steps and ran across his lawn. Sam led the way as they charged across the street and up Megan's porch stairs.

As he raised his fist to pound on the door, a shrill scream rent the air. The hair on his neck rose in terror. He knew that frightened cry.

Caitlyn.

Caitlyn shrieked as Frank turned and lumbered toward her, the knife raised.

Megan's heart stilled, and horror turned her blood to ice. *"No!"*

She lunged off the bed and tackled Frank from behind. "Run, Caitlyn!"

With a whimper, Caitlyn raced back to the bathroom and slammed the door.

Frank flung Megan off with a vicious twist of his torso. He descended on her, rage blazing in his eyes.

A sharp blow knocked the wind from her lungs. Searing pain followed. Gasping for air and backed against the wall, Megan glanced down. A gash in her side seeped blood. Her chest burned as if on fire, and her head spun. Her limbs trembled. From the corner of her eye, Megan saw Frank lift his arm to strike again.

Mustering what strength she could, she grabbed his wrist with both hands and battled to keep the blade at bay. The knife slowly sank closer to her throat.

Tears filled her eyes when she thought of dying. She didn't fear death, but she mourned the opportunity she'd squandered. The chance to spend her life with Jack and his daughter. He'd offered her home, family, unconditional love.

And she'd turned him away.

Her strength ebbed. Her arms shook. Her legs struggled to keep her upright.

She whimpered in fatigue and discouragement.

Praying for strength, for courage, she fought back. She wanted to live, wanted a second chance to spend her life with Jack. With Caitlyn.

Her pulse pounded in her ears. Louder and louder.

Despite the pain, Megan sucked in a deep breath and focused every bit of energy, adrenaline and sheer willpower into shoving Frank's hands aside. The shift in his balance gave her the upper hand for a split second. Long enough for her to grind a heel into his instep.

Frank shouted in pain and backhanded her, sending Megan to her knees. The knife clattered to the floor and, following Megan down, Frank wrapped his hands around her throat. His thumbs dug into her neck and closed off her airway.

Megan struggled for a breath, clawing at his hands.

The pounding in her ears became a demanding cadence. But not of blood in her head. Someone was beating on her front door.

"Megan!"

Jack!

She didn't have the breath to answer, to call for his help.

With a vicious curse, Frank glanced toward the bedroom door and thrust her away.

Megan coughed and struggled to draw air into her burning lungs. She choked back the bile that rose in her throat as Frank edged toward the door, his back against the wall.

She heard the front door crash open, heard Sam barking.

A bittersweet combination of relief and anxiety twisted inside her. Jack didn't know the powder keg he'd entered.

The thought of anything happening to Jack sent a bone-deep horror slicing through her.

"Megan! Where are you?" Jack yelled.

As Frank disappeared out the bedroom door, Megan gasped enough air to scream, "Jack, he has a knife! Sam, attack!"

Chapter 19

"Daddy!"

Caitlyn charged toward him the instant Jack burst through the front door. Sam raced through the kitchen and living room searching for…what?

"Caity!" Jack scooped his daughter in his arms, and relief that she was safe brought tears to his eyes. "Where's Megan?"

"In the b-back," she sobbed. "The m-man hurted M-Miss Megan."

Jack's chest constricted, alarm streaking through him like an electric shock. "What man? Where's M—"

"Jack!" Megan's scream came from the back of the house. Her voice sounded strangled, weak. But she was alive.

The rest of what she shouted was lost in the cacophony of blood whooshing past his ears, Sam snarling as he bolted toward the back room, and Caitlyn sobbing about a bad man with a knife.

A knife?

He set Caitlyn on the floor and pushed her toward the open front door. "Caitlyn, go next door and stay there! Run!"

He rushed toward the back room, terror climbing his throat.

The blood chilling snarls of Sam's attack and a man's cursing echoed in the hall.

Adrenaline sharpened Jack's senses. Megan needed help. Caitlyn had said Megan was hurt. That the intruder had a knife. His thoughts spun, but fear for Megan's safety energized him, primed him for battle.

Rounding the corner toward Megan's bedroom, Jack found a large man on the floor, locked in combat with Sam. The German shepherd had the gasping man by the throat. A hunting knife lay on the floor just beyond the man's floundering hands.

In the second it took Jack to process the scene, the intruder's fingers closed around the weapon. The man swung his arm in a swift arc toward Sam.

"Nooo!" Jack bellowed, diving toward the dog.

Time moved in slow motion for Jack.

Sam yelped and lost his hold on the man's neck.

The attacker rolled away.

Sam struggled to his feet then collapsed again with a whine.

The man scrambled to his knees and poised the knife, ready to strike again.

Jack lunged, catching the man's jaw with a solid blow. The intruder went down, and Jack followed, grabbing the intruder's knife-wielding hand and pinning it to the floor.

"Megan!" Jack shouted once he'd subdued his attacker, the man's face to the floor. Using his own body weight, Jack held the man immobile. "Megan, are you all right?"

"Jack, be careful!"

She was hoarse, but she at least was conscious. He released the breath he held.

The intruder wasn't moving, but Jack felt the subtle rise and fall of his opponent's chest. Blood puddled on the floor from the man's throat.

"Caitlyn is—" Megan rasped from the bedroom.

"Outside," Jack assured her. "She's safe."

Sweet heaven, the woman always thought of his daughter first. A fierce mother and protector to the end. How could she doubt herself when he saw so clearly her strength and fighting spirit? If it was the last thing he did, he'd help Megan see it, too. He loved her too much to let her walk away from what they had together.

"Sam?" she asked weakly.

He glanced over his shoulder at the German shepherd, lying eerily still, a bloody gash in his side.

A sharp ache gripped Jack's heart. "He's down, sweetheart, but…" He detected movement from Sam's chest, indicating he was at least still breathing. "But he's alive."

The man beneath him grunted and shifted, turning his head to the side.

Jack focused his attention on controlling the man, who was coming around. He gazed down at the man's profile, and a new shock kicked him in the gut.

Frank Harwood, his face scratched and bleeding, his features twisted in a macabre mask of hatred, glowered at him. Realizing he had Megan's rapist in his grasp, a profound fury, overwhelming in its magnitude and power, swept through Jack like a hurricane. Never had the urge to kill another man been so strong, so staggering. So frightening.

His whole body shuddered. His temples pounded. His jaw tensed until his teeth ached.

Perhaps the ferocity of his own hatred and anger were what shook Jack from his vengeful haze. It shook Jack to his core.

"You had everything," he gritted through clenched teeth instead. "Family, wealth, success. Why do *this?* Why rape Megan? Why hurt all those other women?"

Frank scoffed, wheezed. "Family? What a joke. Spineless, pathetic Patrice. Holier-than-thou Burt. My father…let my mother walk…all over him until…he drank himself…to an early grave. Bunch of losers."

"That's your excuse? You were lashing out at *them* when you raped?"

Frank gave him a look of disgust. "Don't try to…psycho-analyze me. You don't know squat. Those women…got what they deserved. Anyone stupid enough, to fall for the lines I fed 'em…just asking for her comeuppance."

A fresh surge of anger sparked in his blood. "Megan didn't deserve to be raped, you miserable animal, and neither did any of those other women! What…did you need to hurt a woman to make you feel more in control of your own sorry life? Did it make you feel like more of a man to overpower and humiliate them? Well, news flash! You're no man. You're *scum*. You're a pig!"

Frank struggled beneath Jack, but Jack tightened his grip, held fast.

"Nobody…stopped me. They knew. But…they didn't tell."

Jack scowled and rolled Frank onto his back. He made certain he kept Frank's hands securely pinned then glared straight into the madman's evil eyes. "*Who* knew?"

Jack saw the extent of damage Sam had done to Frank's throat, possibly even puncturing his windpipe. "Even after I…finished with them," Frank rasped. "I…controlled them." He drew a ragged breath, but his dark grey eyes flared to life with a diabolic glint. "I controlled…their minds. Do you know how—" He coughed, wheezed, but continued. "—intoxicating power is? Once…wasn't enough. I grew addicted. Fed the hunger inside me."

"Hurting women doesn't make you powerful. It makes you a monster." Jack spat the words at Burt's brother. "It's a weakness, a depravity."

The flare of fury in Frank's eyes was Jack's only warning. The linebacker-size man beneath him heaved his body upward, catching Jack off guard with his remaining strength. With a quick twist, Frank wrenched away from Jack's hold and knocked Jack backward.

Recovering quickly, Jack jumped to his feet. He blocked Frank's first swing. But the crazed man still clutched the bloody knife. Jack focused his efforts on avoiding the wildly arcing blade. With a menacing growl, Frank lowered his head and plowed into Jack's gut with his shoulder.

The tackle brought Jack down with a tooth-jarring crash, momentarily disorienting him. A funny buzzing filled his ears, and his sight dimmed for a moment. As his vision sharpened into focus, he acclimated himself, quickly searching out his opponent's position.

Frank towered over him, the knife clutched over his head with two hands. Deadly intent glinted in his steely eyes.

Pain ripped through Megan's chest. Every move she made sent another scorching bolt through her. Despite the fiery throbbing, she dragged herself across the floor. She inched to the bed, where she fumbled beneath it for Frank's gun.

Her phone lay on the floor, and she could hear a woman's voice. "This is 911. Hello? What is your emergency? We're tracing your call and have police en route. Are you there? Hello? This is 911. Can you talk to me?"

She blinked hard when her vision wavered and fought to stay conscious. She had work to do. She *would not* pass out. Not when Jack needed her. Not when their lives were at stake.

She'd failed to protect herself once and paid the price.

But she would never go down again without a fight. And she would die before she let anyone harm the people she loved.

Picking up the phone, she muttered, "I'm here. We need an ambulance and the police." She gave her name and address then set the phone aside, despite the woman's directions to stay on the line.

Help was on the way, but she wouldn't sit back and wait when Jack needed her help *now*.

You can do it, she chanted in her head. *You have to do this.*

She could hear scuffling and grunting in the hall where Jack fought Frank for his life. Shoving down the pain, she crawled across her bedroom floor, her mind focused only on survival, on saving Jack. She crept toward the door, holding the bleeding gash under her ribs, then pushed to her knees. Megan watched in horror as Frank tackled Jack then raised his knife in both hands, ready to drive the blade into Jack's heart.

No!

Determination and certainty flowed through her veins as she leveled Frank's gun at him. A primal cry tore from her throat.

And she squeezed the trigger.

The concussion reverberated in her ears and rattled the hall chandelier.

In her weakened state, the recoil knocked her backward. A fresh explosion of pain splintered her chest when she landed. Spots danced before her eyes. She clamped a hand over her stinging wound.

Acrid smoke burnt her nostrils. An eerie moan, almost a

scream, rent the air. The sound of agony. But not hers. Chills spiraled through her.

She gasped for breath and dragged herself back to her knees. Only by clutching the door frame did she stay up. She didn't have the strength to raise the gun again.

Both Jack, on his back, and Frank, facedown, sprawled on the blood-smeared hardwood in the hall.

"Jack? Jack!" she called, her throat on fire. The whine of approaching sirens joined the ominous howl.

Jack moaned and slowly pushed up on one elbow. He narrowed his gaze on Frank then turned his attention to her.

"Megan! Are you…?" His face paled. "Good God, you're hurt!" He rolled to his side and pushed to his feet. Staggered to her side.

As she slid limply to the floor, her gaze found Sam, lying so still, bleeding from a wound similar to her own. A sob tore from her chest. "Sam!"

Feet pounded on the front porch. A loud male voice shouted, "Police! Drop your weapons! Put your hands in the air!"

Gratefully, Megan let the gun in her hand ease to the floor. Lifting her hands was not in the cards. When she released the door frame, she wobbled and Jack caught her.

"She needs an ambulance!" he shouted as he peeled her shirt from her bleeding side.

The black spots clustered before her again, and Jack's voice garbled as if passing through water.

"Damn it, Megan, don't you leave me!" His voice cracked, and he pressed the shreds of her shirt against her wound. "Hang on, Megan! Fight!"

"Put your hands up!" the new male voice repeated, this time from close range.

Jack balled her shirt to press against her wound. "She needs help. She's been stabbed!"

Panic rang in Jack's voice, and his worry wrenched inside her. "I'm…okay," she lied.

But her whisper was lost in the commotion of policemen filling her house, sirens shrieking outside.

"That's Frank Harwood." Jack jerked his head toward the man whose moans had subsided in volume if not in verve. "He broke in here. Tried to kill us."

Megan watched the policeman holster his gun, though the image wavered. Soon cops swarmed her tiny hall. EMTs set to work on both her and Frank. In the chaos surrounding her, Megan sought out Jack's face, found his gaze locked on her.

"Promise me…you'll save Sam…first."

"You're my priority, Megan. You've lost a lot of blood—"

"Promise!" She tried to shout, but the word merely croaked from her throat. Jack's features grew fuzzy. The sounds around her seemed to come through a tunnel. Even holding her eyes open took more effort than she could muster. "Jack?"

She had no idea if she spoke his name or thought it.

He sucked in a ragged breath. "I promise."

Satisfied with his answer, she gave in to the darkness that pulled at her.

Chapter 20

"No! Caitlyn, no!" Megan fought the suffocating panic. Tried to reason through the best escape.

Someone held her back, held her down. Sam was bleeding. Jack needed her. "Jack! Jack!"

"Shh, I'm right here."

She woke with a jolt and blinked as sweat dripped into her eyes. "Jack?"

"Easy, love," Jack said, brushing the hair from her cheek. His warm smile flowed over her and chased away the cold chill of her nightmare. "You're okay. You're safe now."

A whimper of pain and relief unfurled in her throat. A quick glance told her she was in the hospital. The fiery sting in her side and in her throat confirmed that her latest attack had been all too real. She closed her eyes again and shuddered at the images that flashed through her memory. "Oh, Jack! Frank Harwood…he came back."

Jack took her hand and squeezed. "I know."

"He came after me. To kill me." Panic surged through her, gripping her chest, stifling her breaths. "He—"

"Is in police custody. When he recovers enough to face the charges against him, he's going straight to jail." Jack stroked the side of her face with his free hand and hushed her again. "Now, you lie still, or you'll rip your stitches."

Hating the images she saw behind her closed eyes, she found Jack and searched his loving hazel gaze. "Caity? Wh—"

"Is with Ginny. She and I have taken turns watching munchkin and sitting with you. Caity was a little shaken, but Ginny's talked to her, had her laughing when I called a little while ago. Ginny says Caitlyn will be fine."

Megan felt the tension in her chest ease a bit. "Ginny's good at that. Talking. Knowing the right thing to say. Helping make sense of things."

Then a memory of Sam lying wounded and unmoving snaked through her mind. She bolted upright in the bed. A sharp pain sliced her abdomen...and her heart. "Where's Sam? Is he all right?"

Jack rubbed her arm and tried to coax her back to her pillow again. "I daresay he's a better patient than you are. He's under the watchful eye of one of the best vets in town. His cut wasn't deep. Barely more than a surface wound, but he was knocked unconscious when he hit the ground. Your mutt'll be back barking at squirrels in a couple days."

Relief whizzed through her and left her shaking. "Thank heavens."

"You, on the other hand..." He tapped her nose with his knuckle and gave her a smile that didn't hide the worry still shadowing his eyes. "You gave us a scare. Your wound required surgery. Fortunately, nothing vital was injured, but you lost a lot of blood."

Jack strummed her cheek with gentle hands and leaned close. "You've been asleep for a long time. How do you feel?"

Megan took a slow breath and released it. "A little tired. Sore. But pretty good overall. Considering…"

"The doc says you need bed rest and lots of TLC." Grinning, he added, "I volunteered to provide the TLC." Jack tucked the blanket around her, and he sobered. "If you'll let me, that is. I'd like to hang around. I want to be the one to give you the love and care you deserve. Not just now but…always."

Megan's heartbeat stuttered, and her breath backed up in her lungs. She searched for the words to tell him what he'd come to mean to her, how his love had given her strength and courage, direction and hope.

But a knock on her door interrupted her thoughts.

Abigail Harwood poked her head in the room, her expression hesitant. "May we come in?"

Megan glanced at Jack then nodded.

Burt followed his wife into the room, and after a brief guilty glance, looked everywhere but at Megan. He shoved his hands in his pockets and stared out the window, a bleak expression on his weathered face.

"I…We just wanted to check on you and…and tell you how sorry we are about all this," Abigail said. The redhead's eyes were bloodshot and rimmed with dark circles. Learning what Frank had done had to have been tough on their family.

Abigail pressed her lips in a thin line and dabbed at her eyes.

"We should have known…should have realized." Burt sighed and shifted his gaze to the floor. "Frank's always had issues. Problems with authority, trouble in his marriage, but…I never knew…never imagined…"

"Don't blame yourself, Burt," Jack said. "He fooled a lot of people."

"Not me," Abigail murmured then wiped a tear from her cheek. "I suspected…but didn't say anything."

Megan's stomach tightened. She remembered the night of Burt's birthday party, the odd looks that Abigail gave Frank when she found him with Megan in the kitchen.

Burt swung to face his wife, his expression dark, confused. "Abby?"

Abigail held Megan's gaze with a tearful gaze. "Frank… raped me, too. Just after Burt and I married."

Burt's face grew pasty. His jaw gaped. "What?"

"I know I should have said something, but…I was so young. I was a newlywed, and I didn't want to cause a problem in the family." Abigail swiped at her eyes, and her voice warbled. "I didn't want anything to hurt Burt, or start our marriage on the wrong track. That was a mistake, I know. But the longer I kept quiet, the harder I knew it would be to get anyone to believe me. I figured everything would be okay once Frank and Patrice got married."

She pressed a hand to her lips, and her face crumpled with anguish. "Forgive me, Megan. If I'd said something, all those years ago…"

Burt rushed to his wife and pulled her into his arms. "Ah, Abby. Oh, darling," he crooned. "Frank can't hurt you anymore." He lifted his head and spoke to Megan as well as his wife. "I've talked to the police. My brother's going to spend the rest of his life behind bars. That's a promise. They have all the evidence they need to convict him on a number of charges. And after this, no judge would dare grant him bail again."

Burt sighed and closed his eyes. "I just wish I'd recognized the signs sooner. I feel terrible." His jaw tensed. "My sorry brother even had the nerve to gloat to me that the scare of having a serial rapist on the loose made his home security systems sell like hotcakes. He was profiting from his dirty work." Burt swiped a hand down his face and sighed. "It just makes me sick."

Jack cleared his throat and stroked Megan's wrist with soothing strokes. "What about Patrice? How is she handling all this?"

"Remarkably well," Burt replied. "She seems…relieved. I think she's been living with the truth herself, not knowing what to do." Burt held his wife's shoulders at arms' length and studied her face. "If you'll excuse us, I'm going to take Abigail home now. You need rest," he told Abigail, "and then…we need to talk."

Abigail sent Megan another apologetic look then nodded to Burt. The couple repeated their apologies and wishes for Megan's rapid recovery then left quickly.

Megan made a mental note to speak to Abigail about seeking Ginny's counseling. Clearly the woman carried a heartload of guilt and grief.

Both Megan and Jack were silent for a long time after the Harwoods left. The legacy of pain Frank had caused staggered Megan, turned her stomach and left her soul feeling raw.

After a few moments, Jack scrubbed a hand over his face and shook his head. "How could Abigail have kept something like that a secret? How could she have kept silent if she suspected what Frank had done?"

Megan reached for Jack's hand. "Please don't judge her harshly. Telling someone you love that you've been raped is…so hard. Hard enough to deal with on your own. And talking about it is… Well, it changes things between people. Sometimes it's easier to repress the hurt and try to run from it." Her throat clogged with emotion. "That's part of why I couldn't tell you about what happened to me. I was afraid of how you'd react. My fiancé couldn't deal with the changes in me, with his own doubts. So he left. So did a lot of people I thought were my friends."

She saw pain flash in Jack's eyes.

"Jack, what—?"

"I did the same thing." Squeezing his eyes closed, he pressed her fingers to his lips. "I left you when you needed me. I let my own wounds cloud my perception, screw up my priorities."

He opened his eyes, and the piercing intensity of his gaze burrowed to her core. "Megan, if you'll give me another chance, I promise I will always be there for you. I was an idiot to walk out like I did." He swallowed hard and, clutching her hand over the steady thump of his heart, he leaned close. He nuzzled her cheek, kissed her temple. "I love you. And I will wait for you. As long as you need."

Megan threaded a hand through Jack's hair and kissed his head. "You may not have to wait so long."

He raised his gentle gaze to her and puckered his brow in question. "Really? What…?"

A smile ghosted across her lips as a tantalizing sense of fulfillment stirred in her like a cool breeze on a stifling summer day.

Her heart picked up an excited rhythm, her body's reaction getting ahead of her thought process. Frantically she tried to sort out her thoughts, the reason why her spirit seemed poised to take flight.

She reexamined her latest encounter with Frank Harwood, though this time she held the choking panic at bay.

His knife. Her defensive moves. The phone. Sam outside. Protecting Caitlyn. Survival strategy.

A flurry of information danced through her mind, but one clear message sorted itself from the rest and took center stage.

She'd done it.

She'd kept her wits about her and fought back. She'd not only defended herself, she'd protected an innocent child. She'd stopped her rapist. Brought him to justice.

The stunning realization took root and blossomed, warming her from the inside out. Maybe she'd finally found that *something* she'd been looking for.

Courage. Strength. Determination to not only survive but to win.

"I did it," she muttered. She blinked and turned her gaze to Jack, still trying to come to terms with the magnitude of her discovery. "I did it by myself. Well, mostly anyway. I—"

"What did you do?" Jack furrowed his brow, clearly trying to catch up with her racing thoughts.

"I held Frank off until help arrived. Without Sam. Without my gun." She sounded a bit dazed even to her own ears. But then, she felt a bit staggered by the implications, too.

"Hon, you did use the gun." Jack seemed reluctant to correct her, averse to spoiling her confidence. "And...I let Sam in with me. Remember?"

She heard the confusion behind Jack's statement and grinned. "I mean at first. Sam was in the yard and my gun was unloaded. The two main things I'd put my faith in for protection were no help to me."

She gripped his hand tighter, making certain he heard what she told him next. It was important to her that he understood the significance of her revelation. "I didn't have my crutches. I had to look inside myself. I used what I'd learned to protect myself, to save Caitlyn. *I* did it. Me. And we're okay. We're gonna be okay."

The corner of Jack's mouth tugged up, telling her he'd finally caught on. "Hell, yeah, you did it. I always knew you could."

"Still…if you hadn't come when you did…" She shivered, remembering the devastating fear that Frank would hurt Caitlyn or Jack, that he'd kill her and she'd lose the chance to spend her life with the man she loved. Pinning a hard look on Jack, she squeezed his hand. "I thought he was going to kill you and I—"

When her voice cracked, Jack caught her chin. He leaned close and seized her lips in a tender kiss. "You stopped him."

Megan swallowed hard and nodded. "I stopped him."

She took a deep breath and repeated the words, coming to grips with the reality, liking the way her triumph felt. "*I* stopped him." She smiled at Jack, the surge of renewed confidence and self-assurance energizing her. "I don't know where I found the strength, the will, the nerve, but when I needed it, it was there. I found what I needed to protect myself."

"Darlin', you didn't have to look far. I saw your strength, your moxie, the day you got me out of the shower to tell me Miss Adventure had escaped. I saw it when you bared your soul at the newspaper office then stood up to Burt when he tried to cast doubt on your story. I saw it when you made love to me so tenderly, despite the horrid memories and emotional scars you had." Jack brushed a soft kiss across her lips. "Your strength and courage are part of the reason I fell in love with you, Megan. They were always there."

Megan felt tears prickle her eyes. "Say that part again, about you falling in love with me."

Jack gave her a sexy, lopsided grin. "Forget falling. I love you, Megan Hoffman. And I promise that I will be there for you. Always."

"I love you, too, Jack. For so many reasons. But most of all, I love you for helping me find myself again." She laced her fingers with his and gifted him with a smile full of the hope that swelled in her heart. "I've put my life on hold far too long. Now that I've come to terms with the past, I want you and Caitlyn to be my future. If your offer is still good, I'd like very much to be your wife."

Jack sat straighter, myriad emotions crossing his face before he flashed her a megawatt smile. "Can I quote you on that?"

Megan reached for him, pulling him close for a kiss. "Absolutely."

* * * * *

Welcome to cowboy country...

Turn the page for a sneak preview of
TEXAS BABY
by
Kathleen O'Brien
An exciting new title from Harlequin Superromance
for everyone who loves stories about the West.

Harlequin Superromance—
Where life and love weave together in
emotional and unforgettable ways.

CHAPTER ONE

CHASE TRANSFERRED his gaze to the road and identified a foreign spot on the horizon. A car. Almost half a mile away, where the straight, tree-lined drive met the public road. He could tell it was coming too fast, but judging the speed of a vehicle moving straight toward you was tricky.

It wasn't until it was about two hundred yards away that he realized the driver must be drunk…or crazy. Or both.

The guy was going maybe sixty. On a private drive, out here in ranch country, where kids or horses or tractors or stupid chickens might come darting out any minute, that was criminal. Chase straightened from his comfortable slouch and waved his hands.

"Slow down, you fool," he called out. He took the porch steps quickly and began walking fast down the driveway.

The car veered oddly, from one lane to another, then up onto the slight rise of the thick green spring grass. It just barely missed the fence.

"Slow down, damn it!"

He couldn't see the driver, and he didn't recognize this automobile. It was small and old, and couldn't have cost much even when it was new. It was probably white, but now it needed either a wash or a new paint job or both.

"Damn it, what's wrong with you?"

At the last minute, he had to jump away, because the idiot

behind the wheel clearly wasn't going to turn to avoid a collision. He couldn't believe it. The car kept coming, finally slowing a little, but it was too late.

Still going about thirty miles an hour, it slammed into the large, white-brick pillar that marked the front boundaries of the house. The pillar wasn't going to give an inch, so the car had to. The front end folded up like a paper fan.

It seemed to take forever for the car to settle, as if the trauma happened in slow motion, reverberating from the front to the back of the car in ripples of destruction. The front windshield suddenly seemed to ice over with lethal bits of glassy frost. Then the side windows exploded.

The front driver's door wrenched open, as if the car wanted to expel its contents. Metal buckled hideously. Small pieces, like hubcaps and mirrors, skipped and ricocheted insanely across the oyster-shell driveway.

Finally, everything was still. Into the silence, a plume of steam shot up like a geyser, smelling of rust and heat. Its snake-like hiss almost smothered the low, agonized moan of the driver.

Chase's anger had disappeared. He didn't feel anything but a dull sense of disbelief. Things like this didn't happen in real life. Not in his life. Maybe the sun had actually put him to sleep....

But he was already kneeling beside the car. The driver was a woman. The frosty glass-ice of the windshield was dotted with small flecks of blood. She must have hit it with her head, because just below her hairline a red liquid was seeping out. He touched it. He tried to wipe it away before it reached her eyebrow, though, of course that made no sense at all. Her eyes were shut.

Was she conscious? Did he dare move her? Her dress was covered in glass, and the metal of the car was sticking out lethally in all the wrong places.

Then he remembered, with an intense relief, that every good medical man in the county was here, just behind the house, drinking his champagne. He found his phone and paged Trent.

The woman moaned again.

Alive, then. Thank God for that.

He saw Trent coming toward him, starting out at a lope, but quickly switching to a full run.

"Get Dr. Marchant," Chase called. "Don't bother with 911."

Trent didn't take long to assess the situation. A fraction of a second, and he began pulling out his cell phone and running toward the house.

The yelling seemed to have roused the woman. She opened her eyes. They were blue and clouded with pain and confusion.

"Chase," she said.

His breath stalled. His head pulled back. "What?"

Her only answer was another moan, and he wondered if he had imagined the word. He reached around her and put his arm behind her shoulders. She was tiny. Probably petite by nature, but surely way too thin. He could feel her shoulder blades pushing against her skin, as fragile as the wishbone in a turkey.

She seemed to have passed out, so he put his other arm under her knees and lifted her out. He tried to avoid the jagged metal, but her skirt caught on a piece and the tearing sound seemed to wake her again.

"No," she said. "Please."

"I'm just trying to help," he said. "It's going to be all right."

She seemed profoundly distressed. She wriggled in his arms, and she was so weak, like a broken bird. It made him feel too big and brutish. And intrusive. As if touching her this way, his bare hands against the warm skin behind her knees, were somehow a transgression.

He wished he could be more delicate. But he smelled gasoline, and he knew it wasn't safe to leave her here.

Finally he heard the sound of voices, as guests began to run around the side of the house, alerted by Trent. Dr. Marchant was at the front, racing toward them as if he were forty instead of seventy. Susannah was right behind him, her green dress floating around her trim legs.

"Please," the woman in his arms murmured again. She looked at him, the expression in her blue eyes lost and bewildered. He wondered if she might be on drugs. Hitting her head on the windshield might account for this unfocused, glazed look, but it couldn't explain the crazy driving.

"Please, put me down. Susannah… The wedding…"

Chase's arms tightened instinctively, and he froze in his tracks. She whimpered, and he realized he might be hurting her. "Say that again?"

"The wedding. I have to stop it."

* * * * *

Be sure to look for TEXAS BABY,
available September 11, 2007,
as well as other fantastic Superromance titles
available in September.

Welcome to Cowboy Country...

TEXAS BABY

by *Kathleen O'Brien*

#1441

Chase Clayton doesn't know what to think.
A beautiful stranger has just crashed his
engagement party, demanding that he not
marry because she's pregnant with his baby.
But the kicker is—he's never seen her before.

Look for TEXAS BABY and other fantastic
Superromance titles on sale September 2007.

Available wherever books are sold.

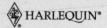

EVERLASTING LOVE™

Every great love has a story to tell™

Third time's a charm.

Texas summers. Charlie Morrison.
Jasmine Boudreaux has always connected
the two. Her relationship with Charlie
begins and ends in high school. Twenty
years later it begins again—and ends again.
Now fate has stepped in one more time—
will Jazzy and Charlie finally give in to
the love they've shared all this time?

Look for

Summer After Summer

by
Ann DeFee

**Available September
wherever books are sold.**

**Don't miss the first book in the
BILLIONAIRE HEIRS trilogy**

THE KYRIAKOS
VIRGIN BRIDE
#1822

BY TESSA RADLEY

Zac Kyriakos was in search of a woman pure both
in body and heart to marry, and he believed that Pandora
Armstrong was the answer to his prayers. When Pandora
discovered that Zac's true reason for marrying her was
because she was a virgin, she wanted an annulment. Little
did she know that Zac was beginning to fall in love with
her and would do anything not to let her go….

On sale September 2007 from Silhouette Desire.

BILLIONAIRE HEIRS:
They are worth a fortune…but can they be tamed?

Also look for
THE APOLLONIDIES MISTRESS SCANDAL
on sale October 2007
THE DESERT BRIDE OF AL SAYED
on sale November 2007

Available wherever books are sold.

REQUEST YOUR FREE BOOKS!

2 FREE NOVELS PLUS 2 FREE GIFTS!

Silhouette® Romantic

SUSPENSE

Sparked by Danger, Fueled by Passion!

YES! Please send me 2 FREE Silhouette® Romantic Suspense novels and my 2 FREE gifts. After receiving them, if I don't wish to receive any more books, I can return the shipping statement marked "cancel." If I don't cancel, I will receive 4 brand-new novels every month and be billed just $4.24 per book in the U.S., or $4.99 per book in Canada, plus 25¢ shipping and handling per book plus applicable taxes, if any*. That's a savings of at least 15% off the cover price! I understand that accepting the 2 free books and gifts places me under no obligation to buy anything. I can always return a shipment and cancel at any time. Even if I never buy another book from Silhouette, the two free books and gifts are mine to keep forever.

240 SDN EEX6 340 SDN EEYJ

Name _____ (PLEASE PRINT) _____

Address _____ Apt. # _____

City _____ State/Prov. _____ Zip/Postal Code _____

Signature (if under 18, a parent or guardian must sign)

Mail to the Silhouette Reader Service™:
IN U.S.A.: P.O. Box 1867, Buffalo, NY 14240-1867
IN CANADA: P.O. Box 609, Fort Erie, Ontario L2A 5X3

Not valid to current Silhouette Intimate Moments subscribers.

Want to try two free books from another line?
Call 1-800-873-8635 or visit www.morefreebooks.com.

* Terms and prices subject to change without notice. NY residents add applicable sales tax. Canadian residents will be charged applicable provincial taxes and GST. This offer is limited to one order per household. All orders subject to approval. Credit or debit balances in a customer's account(s) may be offset by any other outstanding balance owed by or to the customer. Please allow 4 to 6 weeks for delivery.

Your Privacy: Silhouette is committed to protecting your privacy. Our Privacy Policy is available online at www.eHarlequin.com or upon request from the Reader Service. From time to time we make our lists of customers available to reputable firms who may have a product or service of interest to you. If you would prefer we not share your name and address, please check here. ☐

SRS07

ATHENA FORCE

**Heart-pounding romance
and thrilling adventure.**

Professional negotiator Lindsey Novak
is faced with her biggest challenge—to
buy back Teal Arnett, a young woman with
unique powers. In the process Lindsey
uncovers a devastating plot that involves
scientists from around the globe, and all of
them lead to one woman who is bent on
destroying Athena Academy…at any cost.

LOOK FOR

THE GOOD THIEF

by Judith Leon

*Available September
wherever you buy books.*

AF38973

Romantic

SUSPENSE

COMING NEXT MONTH

#1479 MIRANDA'S REVENGE—Ruth Wind
Sisters of the Mountain
With the clock ticking and a murder trial on the horizon,
Miranda Rousseau has one last chance at clearing her sister's name.
But James Marquez, the tall, sexy private investigator she's hired to
solve the case, is fast becoming much more than just a colleague in
the face of danger.

#1480 TOP-SECRET BRIDE—Nina Bruhns
Mission: Impassioned
Two spies pose as husband and wife in order to uncover a potential mole
in their corporations. As they work together, each new piece of the puzzle
pulls them further into danger, and into each other's arms....

#1481 SHADOW WHISPERS—Linda Conrad
Night Guardians
She is determined to have her revenge on the Skinwalker cult. He's seeking
the truth about his family. Now they will join forces to uncover secrets long
buried...and discover a passion that could threaten their lives.

#1482 SINS OF THE STORM—Jenna Mills
Midnight Secrets
After years in hiding, Camille Fontenot returns home to solve the
mystery of her father's death. But someone doesn't want Camille
to succeed, and she must turn to an old flame for protection...while
fighting an all-consuming desire.